His Stubborn Sweet Bride

A Christian Western Romance Novel

by

Chloe Carley

Table of Contents

Be a part of the Chloe Carley family ...

Your opinion can impact my stories, but we have to connect first!

The core soul of the book you are about to read was influenced by passionate readers that took the step to be part of my "family"! The title, the cover, the essence of the book as a whole was affected by these wonderful people!

I personally want to thank them for their support on my journey! I devote this book to them!

If you are not a member yet, you are only one click away to influence my upcoming stories! After you sign-up I will send you as a BONUS My Full-Length Novella, "Boston Bride Salvation":

Free Exclusive Gift
(available only to my subscribers)

Click the button below to get the BONUS:
https://chloecarley.com/ccbbsa

PERSONAL WORD
FROM Chloe Carley

"Once upon a time..."

...my best childhood nights had started with this wonderful phrase!

Ever since I can remember, I loved a good story!

All started thanks to my beloved grandfather! He used to read to my sister and me, stories of mighty princes and horrifying dragons! Even now, sometimes I miss those cold winters in front of the fireplace in my hometown, Texas!

My best stories though were the ones from the Bible! Such is the spiritual connection that a sense of warmth pass through my body every time I hear a biblical story!

My childhood memories were not all roses, but I always knew that the strongest shelter would be always there for me! It was Him!

Years passed by, and little-Chloe grown up reading all kind of stories! It was no surprise that I had this urge to write my own stories, and share them with the word!

If I have a God's purpose on Earth, I think it is to spread His love and wisdom, through my stories!

Brightest Blessings,

Chapter
One

"Denver to Cheyenne and points north, boarding now on Platform One!"

Nate Trowbridge pulled a golden watch out of his vest pocket and checked the time. To his satisfaction, the Denver Pacific Railway kept a precise schedule, even with its minor runs. Since he was shortly going to be living in one of the smallest towns in Colorado, it was comforting to know that the DPR wasn't going to penalize him for it.

Unlike some others he could name. Nate smoothed his moustache in irritation.

His butler in London had been close to tears but had solemnly informed him that he couldn't possibly live in a place as uncivilized as the American frontier.

"There are natives there, sir," Jeffers had told him in a horrified voice. "They live outdoors, in the rain, and barely wear clothes. And the settlers, they say, are only slightly different."

Nate returned his watch carefully to his pocket and gestured for a porter. It had been a deuced inconvenience to lose his butler, but he had risen to the occasion. In Jeffers' absence, he'd packed his own bags, and he had filled several large trunks with what he considered the bare minimum for a young gentleman in transit—twenty changes of clothes, five pairs of shoes, five pairs of boots, a half dozen hats for various activities, a complete shaving and toilette kit, Bay Rum and aftershaves, a few sets of matching tie tacks and cufflinks, and some amusing books and magazines.

Besides which, he had also packed a few things as gifts for his little sister Leonie, who had come over from London before him and had been staying with their friends the Chiswicks in Denver. He had collected Leonie but was holding her gifts back until they arrived at their new home when he would present them. Leonie was inordinately fond of silly, frippery things.

Nate glanced down at her and smiled indulgently. Leonie had amassed quite a collection of fripperies. Her own line of trunks was almost long enough to qualify as a train in its own right.

"Well, was Denver amusing?" he inquired. "I suppose you and Francie kept yourselves busy."

Leonie glanced up at him, and her blonde curls bobbed. "We were very entertained," she agreed and twirled a frilly parasol from her gloved fingers. "There are so many young men in Denver! And all of them are so ... so different from the boys in London!"

Nate raised an eyebrow. "Here now," he objected, "is that any way for a young lady to talk? You don't want to give people the idea that you're a man hunter, my dear," he admonished her and pinched her nose. "Probably the fault of those ridiculous romances you're forever reading."

Leonie giggled and pulled her face away. "Oh, Nate! You're so old-fashioned," she complained. "You're even worse than Momma and Poppa were! Can't I even talk about boys? I'm sixteen now, you know," she reminded him significantly.

"Yes, you're ready for parliament, I daresay," he mumbled and flagged down a porter.

"Can you see to our bags?" he asked and pressed a crisp bill into the man's hand. The porter's face lit up.

"Certainly, sir! Where are they?"

Nate turned to point at a large cart, groaning under more than twenty trunks, and the man's face fell, but he swallowed and gave them a sickly smile. "Yes, sir."

"Good man."

Nate extended his arm; Leonie took it, and they strolled down the platform toward the first-class carriages.

"Have you seen Uncle Clayton's house yet?" Leonie asked him, and Nate shook his head.

"No. But they tell me the main house is damaged," he sighed. "There was an Indian attack," he told her and widened his eyes for dramatic effect. "Devilish business."

Leonie's eyes widened appreciatively. "Oh, Nate, how exciting! Do you think we'll meet any Indians?"

"I trust not," he replied faintly. "I'm told the ones in question were taken off to another state."

Leonie's pretty expression darkened. "That's just my luck, too," she complained. "Nothing exciting ever happens to me!"

"And that's the way we're going to keep it," he muttered and helped her climb the narrow steps into the train car.

***

The interior of the club car was as opulent and comfortable as Nate could wish, but he would never have dreamed of travelling in anything but private compartments. He presented their tickets to the smiling man just inside, and they were led immediately to a beautiful, and comparatively roomy, salon.

He sat down in a plush seat opposite his sister and sighed as an ornate menu was pressed into his hand.

"Would you like some time to decide, sir, or shall I take your lunch order now?"

Nate pulled off his kidskin gloves. "I'll have black coffee and a steak, medium rare, with new potatoes. And the lady will have café au lait and the chicken cordon bleu, with spring vegetables."

"Very good, sir."

The waiter took their menus, bowed, and retreated, but as soon as he was well out, Leonie frowned at him.

"You won't even let me order for myself!" she pouted. "I'm not a child anymore, Nate!"

He returned her glare with a mild look. "I know what you would've ordered. It saves time," he replied.

"I get so put out with you," Leonie complained, but Nate gave his little sister a fond glance. Leonie was sunny-tempered, and her pouts never lasted for long.

"Nate, you're simply going to have to get a house in Denver. How am I supposed to find a husband if I'm stuck way out in the wilderness, where there are no parties or dances? Francie tells me that there are no interesting people in Indian Rock whatsoever."

Nate's eyes were on the passing scenery. "You mean, there are no boys in Indian Rock, I expect," he murmured. "We'll see. I need to confirm that the house is in an acceptable condition where I can throw glittering parties to ensnare eligible young men."

"You make that sound like it's wrong."

There was a knock at the door, and soon the porter entered pushing a narrow cart covered with silver. He pulled hinged trays out from the wall to form tables and set them with linen and silver before pouring hot coffee into two china cups.

Nate raised one to his lips and murmured: "Will we have time to finish lunch, do you think before we arrive at Indian Rock?"

The porter nodded. "Yes, sir. It's still more than an hour away. I'll give you plenty of warning. It's such a small little place; you'll miss it if I don't."

He winked, grinned, and disappeared to bring their meal, but the cloud returned to Leonie's face, and Nate suppressed a sigh and watched wearily as the wild scenery rolled past.

Chapter
Two

A discreet knock on the door, a little under an hour later, alerted Nate that their stop was imminent. He folded the newspaper that he'd bought at the station and answered:

"Yes?"

A uniformed porter opened the door. "Indian Rock will be coming up in thirty minutes, Mr Trowbridge."

"Thank you. Can you have our trunks ready?"

"Certainly, sir."

The door closed, and Nate returned to his paper. The Denver news was full of glowing prophecies about the business opportunities that Colorado's new statehood was sure to bring. That was of interest; he had an ambition to build his uncle's ranch back up again and to continue its reputation as an influential concern.

Nate turned the page, and the society column caught his eye. Their friends the Chiswicks were leading lights in Denver society, and their recent charity ball had been written up in the paper. Nate twitched his moustache in distaste and suffered a flicker of mortification on the Chiswicks' behalf. No respectable family wanted its doings bandied about in the press for all to see.

He swallowed a sigh. Still, it was understood that parties and balls were necessary when a family had three daughters, as the Chiswicks did. Leonie's friend, Francie was the youngest, Rose was the middle child, and Emmaline was the oldest.

Nate stared at the paper momentarily without seeing it. Emmaline was a beautiful, elegant young woman, and very soft-spoken. He'd had the pleasure of her company two or three times since coming to Denver. Emmaline had dark hair, a creamy, perfect complexion, and a slender figure.

Nate folded the newspaper neatly in half and placed it on the seat beside him. After a few confirmation visits, he was satisfied that Emmaline Chiswick would make him an admirable wife.

The Chiswicks and the Trowbridges had often intermarried, over three generations and two continents, and he had decided to uphold the family tradition. Once he was settled into his new house and had established his business, he meant to write Emmaline and propose marriage.

And in spite of their slight acquaintance, the offer would not surprise her. It was the tradition of their families for the prospective groom to make one formal appeal, and for the prospective bride to accept through a proxy, usually her father.

There would be plenty of time for him and Emmaline to get to know one another after they were married.

Leonie pressed her bright ringlets against the glass of the window and cried: "Oh, there it is, Nate! And look—have you ever seen a tinier little station, in all your life?" she giggled. "I've seen doll's houses that were bigger!"

Nate glanced up and had to bite back a shocked exclamation. He'd been prepared for a small town, but no one had given him any warning just how small.

The whole of Indian Rock consisted of a single dirt road with a handful of clapboard buildings. The Indian Rock train station was hardly bigger than a guard shack, and Nate looked at the tiny platform and feared that it actually might be too small to hold their baggage.

There came another knock at the door. "Sir, this is your stop."

Nate sighed, pulled on his gloves, and extended an arm to his sister before they sallied forth to inspect what their uncle had left them.

***

To Nate's relief, their luggage was waiting for them on the platform when they debarked the train. He gave the hopeful porter two crisp bills, and the man's face brightened. "Thank you, sir!"

Nate walked to the rear of the platform. He had telegraphed the staff of the ranch two days before to warn them of his arrival. And when he looked, to his relief, there was a carriage waiting for them on the road below, and also a wagon for their things.

The man driving the carriage took off his hat and extended a hand. "Afternoon, Mr Trowbridge." He smiled. "Welcome to the Circle T!"

Nate shook his hand limply. "Thank you," he murmured. "My sister and I have travelled from Denver, and are tired. Are our rooms ready?"

"Yes, sir, as nice as we can make 'em. The house did get pretty busted up in the fight. You'll see what I mean."

"I daresay," Nate muttered and extended a hand to help Leonie into the carriage before following. "Well, drive on. I suppose we'll see for ourselves."

The man touched his hat and jumped up into the driver's seat, and soon they were rolling down a dusty dirt road.

As they crashed over the fourth pothole, Nate made a mental note that the road desperately needed to be repaired, and the springs on the carriage were severely lacking. He determined to buy a new rig just as soon as one could be delivered. They were jouncing over every pothole and rock on the road, and the dust was so bothersome that they were soon digging for their handkerchiefs.

But one thing almost made up for the wretched ride and the near-deserted town—the glorious landscape. Nate felt his mouth falling open more than once as he scanned the breathtaking sweep of the rolling green meadows, ringed by distant grey mountains. The countryside reminded him almost of the Alps, with its near vertical mountain slopes, its bright, chattering, ice-cold streams, and its vivid greenery.

Wildlife surprised them at every turn. A deer bounded out of the underbrush, vaulted across the road ahead of them, and disappeared into a stand of aspens. A hawk swooped down to perch on a tree limb on one side of the road and watched them with its fierce yellow eyes as they passed.

Leonie tugged at his sleeve, crying: "Look, Nate, there!"

He turned just in time to catch a glimpse of a huge creature with antlers as broad and high as a wagon.

The driver saw them staring and laughed at their expressions. "That's a moose," he told them, nodding toward the creature. "You have to be careful of them. They can be dangerous, and they're faster than they look. I've seen one clear a nine-foot fence!"

Leonie turned to him and giggled, and Nate allowed himself to smile.

When they turned into the ranch gates at last, Nate was favourably impressed with the scope of his new property. His Uncle Clayton's ranch was every bit as big, and a good deal more beautiful, even than their family's ancestral holdings in Devon. Of course, the land here was wild and untended, but there was a good fifteen-minute drive from the gates to the front door, which he considered the correct scale for a proper country house.

Leonie leaned out a bit to catch sight of the house as it crept into view. "Oh, Nate!" she gasped.

Chapter
Three

As they rounded the last bend in the drive, and the big house slowly crept into view, Nate felt his mouth drop open at the sight that met his unwilling eyes. The house had been an elegant white-columned mansion, but it was missing its front door. The whole entrance had been smashed in as if a locomotive had ploughed through it. All of the first-floor windows were shattered, and many more on the second-floor, and the whole façade was pockmarked with bullet holes.

"Good heavens!" Nate gasped and gripped the back of the driver's seat. "It's devastated!"

Their driver glanced at them apologetically over his shoulder. "There was a regular battle here, all right," he told them, "twixt the U.S. Cavalry and the Cheyenne Nation. No love lost there, I can tell you."

Nate shook his head in disbelief. "But—but I was told that the house was still liveable," he stammered. "It's standing open to the world!"

The man glanced back at him again. "Oh, it's still good," he assured them. "The first floor got the brunt of it, but the second floor is still almost just like it was, 'ceptin for a few bullet holes in the walls. You still have locking doors up there, anyway."

"Why—we can't possibly—turn the rig around, this instant," Nate commanded."We'll have to return to

Denver. I wouldn't think of spending the night in such a—"

Their driver frowned at them in puzzlement. "Go back, you say? Why, mister, the train don't stop here again until tomorrow night. You're going to have to bunk up here for at least that long unless you stay at the hotel in Indian Rock. I've been there before, Mr Trowbridge, and if you take my advice, you won't chance it. There's no tellin' who's been there before you, and last time, I came away scratchin'."

Nate stared at him in speechless outrage and turned away to keep from blurting the very ungentlemanly words that flashed across his mind. He was going to fire the lout who'd given him such a false report. What had his name been—Will, that was it. Will something-or-other.

But in the meantime, it seemed he had no choice but to make the best of a very unsatisfactory situation. With a mighty effort, Nate regained his composure, turned to Leonie, and put on his most reassuring expression.

"Well, my dear, since it can't be helped—it seems that something exciting is going to happen after all," he told her.

Leonie smiled at him weakly, but her eyes were uncertain, and he felt moved to pat her hand. "There, there," he soothed. "Buck up. We'll—we'll live like the wild Indians, out in the open. It will be an—an adventure."

To his annoyance, their driver seemed to find that funny, though he wouldn't explain why he was laughing. Just one more irritation to add to an outrageous afternoon.

When they pulled up to the entrance at last, to Nate's horror, the destruction was even worse than he'd feared. Shattered glass covered the front steps and foyer like a prickly carpet, and the smashed double doors lay twisted and splintered on the walkway. Spent shell casings and broken arrows littered the ground. The front steps and entryway were heavily stained with what looked like dried blood.

"We can't walk through this. There must be a side entrance," he told the driver.

"Yessir. The kitchen door, around the side of the building. It's not quite as bad. Watch your step, miss."

Nate reached for Leonie's hand and led her through the appalling debris of what must have been a massacre. Nate found himself mumbling: "Don't look, Leonie," and "keep your eyes on me."

Their driver picked his way through the debris littering the grounds and around the left side of the house. At the back, there was a small portico, but its door was hanging askew, and debris covered the ground.

Nate gingerly led his sister through a maze of smashed and broken furniture that had been piled up against the door as a barricade. He found himself in a large and well-appointed kitchen, but here, too, the signs of a savage conflict were everywhere.

"Take us upstairs by the nearest way," he commanded, and the man touched his hat and led the way through a small door to the left, and up a service stairway. To Nate's intense relief, as they climbed, the bullet holes and scorch marks lessened, and when they stepped out into the elegant upper corridor, they might almost have been in some grand house in London.

"It is better up here," he sighed.

Their guide leaned against one wall and pointed. "Here's the lady's chambers, through this door," he told them, indicating the elegantly carved door at the end of the hall, "and then two-three guest rooms, and then the late Mr Trowbridge's den, and his bedroom suite, at the other end."

Nate fixed the man with a disapproving frown. "Why hasn't this been cleaned up?" he demanded. "It looks as if it happened yesterday!"

"Yessir," the man replied in glum agreement. "It's just that we who lived on the place were thrown out of a job when Mr Trowbridge passed. Some left after the funeral, but the ones that stayed had their hands full with the animals. There's lots of cattle on this ranch still."

"Oh."

"And what with the doors smashed in, we figured it'd make more sense to worry about guarding the place than to clean it. The glass and the piles of furniture do discourage thieves."

Nate looked at the man's honest face and had the grace to go red. "I see. I'm grateful to the men who … who stayed. I suppose it's been a challenge to keep the place going."

"That it has, Mr Trowbridge. I won't lie to you."

Nate stripped off his gloves. "You may tell the men for me, that those who want to stay may begin work tomorrow morning, and that any back wages due will be added to their pay packets this Friday."

The man looked up at him sharply. "Yes, sir."

"And tomorrow morning, if anyone can be spared, have them ride into town and bring back any men who are willing to clean this debris away. I'll pay the going rate, plus a bonus."

"I'll do it."

Nate looked down the hall with a sigh. "Where's the cook?"

The man rubbed his stubbly chin with one hand. "Well—there ain't no cook here now, Mr Trowbridge. There used to be, but she left."

"Where is she now?"

"She lives a bit outside Indian Rock."

"Go and get her. Give her some money,"—he reached into his jacket and pulled out his wallet—"and tell her to buy what she needs in town, and then come and cook our dinner tonight, and our breakfast tomorrow. Tell her she's working here again." He handed the man a wad of cash.

The man looked up at him and grinned with tobacco-stained teeth. "That's good news to a lot of people, I can tell you," he replied; and he touched his hat again and disappeared down the stairs.

Nate watched him go with dark eyes and then returned ruefully to Leonie. "Shall we inspect the lady's chambers?" he asked gently and extended his arm. Leonie gave him a wan smile, but took it, and together, they began to explore their new home.

Chapter
Four

That evening, Nate sat shrouded in cigar smoke and gloom in his uncle's upstairs den. The leather chair was comfortable and deep, and the elegant room was mostly untouched by the murderous brawl that had ruined the rest of the house.

But Nate rolled his head back onto the chair and blew a smoke ring toward the ornate ceiling. For the first time, he wondered if Jeffers had been right. The American frontier was proving a very hard place indeed for a gentleman, to say nothing of a young lady like his sister Leonie.

The whole affair was strange.

His uncle's house was a shambles, and what was more, the circumstances of his death were suspicious. Why would a healthy man fall down the stairs of his own home? Nate wondered if the official explanation—death by misadventure—had been the right one.

Of course, it was a moot point now.

Personally, he had very little memory of his uncle. His mother had spoken of Clayton seldom during his childhood, and when she did, it was in a tone that suggested there might be something wrong with him. But since Clayton lived in Colorado, and they lived in London, the awkward subject seldom came up.

That is until he received a cable from a strange solicitor in New York, informing him that Clayton had died and that as Clayton's nearest relatives, he and Leonie had fallen heir to their uncle's considerable wealth.

Nate sighed and tapped cigar ash onto an enameled tray. Nothing had proceeded as he'd expected, but he had embarked on this adventure, and he refused to accept anything less than success. He planned to restore his uncle's estate and to marry Emmaline Chiswick, and he was going to carry them out no matter what outrageous hardships blocked the way.

But the outrageous hardships had so far been formidable, and they just kept coming. Nate rolled his eyes back to the ceiling and sighed. They had barely gotten their dinner that evening. The cook arrived from town—a strange, silent woman named Maria—and had made them some weird local dish that had set their mouths on fire.

He had sent her back to the kitchen with a command to make steaks, and she had returned with a much more palatable meal, but even so.

Leonie was safely tucked away in a large and elegant suite at the end of the hall, but she was shivering in her new bed because the windows had been shot out, and he had evicted an owl that had somehow gotten in and set up housekeeping in her closet.

The creature had flown right into his face, and he'd had the deuce of a time getting it out of the bedroom. Leonie had thought it was funny, and he was grateful for that, at least; that she hadn't been frightened.

Once the house was properly cleaned and repaired, and an orderly routine established, he'd be able to move forward. But it was going to take a long time, much longer than he'd imagined, to be in a position to host parties, or even to receive guests.

He would overcome the difficulty, of course.

Nate tilted his chin up to the ceiling and blew another contemplative smoke ring.

***

The next morning, Nate was awakened by a soft rapping at his bedroom door. It was their driver of the day before, informing him that the men had arrived from town to clean up the house.

"Excellent," Nate replied and reached for his robe. "They can start straight away. I'll be down after breakfast."

Nate walked into the big dressing room and began his morning toilette. He ran a doubtful hand over his chin, poured water out of a china pitcher into a matching bowl, and began to shave.

Morning light was streaming through the big bedroom windows, and he felt much better after a long sleep. The scent of coffee wafting up from below told him that breakfast was on the way.

Life was falling back into some semblance of order—however rough.

When he'd finished dressing, he walked down to the dining room, where a table from Leonie's boudoir had replaced the one that had been smashed. He found his sister in high spirits.

"Oh, Nate, I can't wait to tell Francie all about this," she told him and took a sip of coffee from a china cup. "It's such an adventure!"

Nate closed the door behind him because the sounds of heavy boots, and the sound of men's voices, and the heavy scrape of lumber was threatening to drown out her voice.

"Well, that's one way to look at it," he replied and sat down opposite her. "But I wish you wouldn't tell Francie about our difficulties just yet," he added and shook out a napkin. "Let us salvage something of our family's reputation!"

Leonie's eyes widened, and she leaned across the table to murmur: "So you've noticed, too! I think Uncle Clayton wasn't much liked," she confided.

Nate took a sip of coffee. "You may be right, my dear. All the more reason for us to maintain the proprieties. We're somewhat at a disadvantage, I think."

Leonie's brow clouded. "You mean people might dislike us because they disliked Uncle Clayton?"

"It is just possible."

She raised rueful eyes to his face. "That's hardly fair!"

"I won't argue. It is human nature, nevertheless."

The door opened suddenly to admit the cook—a short, round woman with dark hair and eyes. She carried in a steaming platter of scrambled eggs and bacon and set it down on the table. Then she turned without a word and walked out again.

Leonie followed the woman with her eyes. When the cook had disappeared, Leonie leaned across the table to whisper: "Is she going to be like that all the time?"

"Like what?"

"She never says a word. It's so odd!"

Nate took a sip of coffee. "Nonsense. Servants are supposed to be discreet. It's a sign of good training."

Leonie looked doubtful and filled Nate's plate with bacon and eggs. "Francie told me that they don't like the word servant, over here."

"What word do they like?"

"They call them employees."

Nate took a bite of scrambled eggs. "What's the difference?"

Leonie looked thoughtful. "I don't know. Francie didn't tell me that part."

The door opened again, and Maria walked up to the table, deposited a bread basket full of biscuits and corn cakes, and marched out in stony silence.

Leonie watched her go and then rolled her eyes to Nate's face. They looked at one another for a pregnant moment and then broke down in smothered laughter.

Chapter
Five

By lunchtime, the crew of men from town had removed all the debris from the first floor and had swept the shattered glass away. Nate congratulated them warmly and paid them their wages.

"Who was my uncle's ranch foreman?" he asked them.

"Jem McClary," one of the men replied, "and he's still here, but he got shot when Mr Trowbridge raided the Cheyenne, and he still ain't quite a hunnert percent."

"Is he well enough to work?"

"Well sir, it depends on what you mean by *work*. Jem took a few slugs, and he's still kinda puny, but for indoor work, he'd be all right, I guess."

"Call him," Nate replied and added in a harder tone: "And is there someone on this ranch named *Will*?"

"Why—yessir."

"Tell him I want to talk to him." Nate looked up and added: "And any of you who want to come back tomorrow, there's lots more work here to be done. I need more cleanup, fence repair, and I'm told the barn is a mess."

The men thanked him and dispersed, and Nate watched them go ruefully. His local cleanup crew could only do the rough repair work. He needed new windows, new doors, wall repair and wallpaper, new furniture ...

Which meant more trips to Denver for skilled carpenters and supplies.

He retreated to the first-floor library, and was pleased to see that the desk there had escaped destruction. He sat down at it and pulled a sheaf of papers out of the top drawer.

He was still in the middle of compiling his to-do list when there came a knock at the door.

"Come in."

The door opened slowly, and a young man about his own age stood in the opening. He was a cowboy and had sandy blond hair, bright blue eyes, and a pleasant expression, but he was leaning slightly to one side, and walked slowly.

"I'm Jem McClary. It's nice to meet you, Mr Trowbridge," the man said and extended his hand. Nate shook it and motioned toward a chair.

"Sit down."

The man lowered himself gingerly into the seat. "I was told you wanted to see me."

"You were my uncle's foreman, weren't you?"

"That's right."

"I'd like you to be my foreman as well. Do you think you're up to it?"

The man smiled and shook his head. "Maybe in a little while, but not now," he replied frankly. "An Army doctor had to dig lead out of me a few months ago."

"How long before you think you'll be back to normal?"

The man raised his brows. "I don't know. If I start out slow and easy and don't go too hard, maybe in a month or two."

Nate nodded. "That sounds reasonable to me. I need a man to report to me about how my herds are doing and to give my orders to my men. I'm not an expert on ranching, so I could use a man who has experience."

"I'll be proud to do it," Jem replied slowly. He rubbed his chin and added, "But the state of your herds is that you have half the number there was last year. The Cheyenne stole a lot of your beeves, and they shot all the animals they could see when they attacked this ranch. Some of the Circle T hands died, too, fightin' 'em. We've had a skeleton crew since. Only the hands who were willing to gamble, stayed."

Nate looked down at his desk. "Did ... any of those men who perished have families?"

"One or two, yes."

Nate opened his desk and pulled out an envelope. He filled it with money and handed it to his guest. "Since you know who they are, I'll leave it to you to get this to them. If—if improved burial arrangements need to be made, just let me know."

Jem looked up at him with respect. "I will, Mr Trowbridge. And I know they'll be grateful."

Nate folded his hands on the desk and looked at his new foreman. "I want you to make a list of the things and people we're going to need to get the herds and this property back up to speed. Are we in danger of new attacks?"

Jem rubbed his chin. "I'd never say never, Mr Trowbridge, in this part of the world—but I think it's mostly over now since the Cheyenne have gone to Oklahoma. There might be a raid here and there, but I think what we had here was the last big fight in these parts."

"From your lips to God's ears," Nate muttered. "Very well. Hire as many men as you need to run the place and defend it. Buy whatever animals and supplies you require. Can you get them locally?"

Jem cracked such a wide grin that Nate felt his ears going red.

"Oh, no sir. That'd be Denver, or Cheyenne. But don't worry; I know where to get the things we'll need."

"Good man. Oh—and if you need any medical attention, just let me know."

Jem smiled again and shook his head. "I don't expect I will, Mr Trowbridge. But thanks for making the offer."

He rose slowly, gripping the chair back. "I'll start tomorrow, and I'll let you know how it goes."

Nate nodded and was soon alone again, but five minutes had barely passed before there was another knock on the door.

"Come in."

To his surprise, a boy of about eight years old walked in. The boy was scruffy, defiant-looking, and not overly clean.

"Well, here I am," he said. "And if you're gonna fire me, you might as well say it right out and save us both some time."

Nate stared at him in astonishment. "Who are *you*?"

The boy scowled at him. "Didn't you ask for me, mister? Warn't my idea to come here."

Nate frowned at the child in dawning comprehension. "Are *you* ... *Will*?"

The boy's scowl deepened. "Who did you expect, a girl? Go ahead and say what you want with me, straight out. I can guess what it is!"

Nate's face gathered darkness. "*You* were the one? I should *beat* you for playing us such a trick—sending us the message that this house is *liveable*!" he barked. "I traveled hundreds of miles because of it, only to find that the place is *ruined*!"

The boy crossed his arms. "Mister, I don't know what you're talking about. This is the best house within a hundred miles. It might not have a front door, but it's got a feather bed upstairs that men would fight for, and plenty of room, and big windows, and nice furniture everywhere. If you call that *unliveable*, you ain't *ready* for this country."

Nate's eyes widened in outrage. "How do *you* know there's a feather bed upstairs?"

The boy bit his lip and shrugged. "Mr Trowbridge, he—he bragged about it sometimes."

Nate massaged the little throbbing spot between his eyes. "What's your job here?"

The boy answered defiantly: "I was the stable boy for your uncle. But he was a fool and a drunk and almost got me and an innocent woman kilt one night, and after that, I didn't care *what* I said to him. I told him to his teeth what I thought of him, and he would've kilt me for it, I guess, if it warn't for the Army bein' there at the time. They put him under house arrest, and he died soon after.

So I just stayed here like some others who'd worked the ranch.

"Now you can fire me if you want, but the world is better off without that polecat, and that's the God's truth about it."

Nate stared at the boy, and when he realized his mouth was open, he closed it with a *snap*.

"Where are your parents?" he demanded.

The boy looked down at the floor and shrugged. "Ain't got none. I lived with a preacher's family in Denver for awhile until the old man died and his wife remarried. Her new husband kicked me out, and that was when I came to the Circle T to work."

Nate looked down at his hands. "I see," he said softly.

"Well, go ahead and fire me," the boy grumbled. "I caint stand suspense!"

Nate glanced up at the boy's face. "Look here, boy," he said at last, "you're an impudent fellow and *very* ungrateful for the job my uncle gave you. But since I didn't know him, I can't form an opinion.

"Why don't you and I start fresh. You can go on working in the stable if you want to stay. I warn you though—*mind—your—mouth*. If you talk as disrespectfully to *me* as you did to my uncle, you'll be off this ranch before the sun goes down.

"Understood?"

The boy looked at him keenly but finally nodded. "Deal," he replied slowly and extended a grimy hand.

Nate sighed but took it and then nodded toward the door. "Go and get something to eat. Tell Maria I said it's all right."

And as the boy scampered out, Nate called after him: "And tell her to draw you a bath! If you work here, you *must* bathe!"

Chapter
Six

"Oh, Clarice," Reginald breathed, "your beauty is only surpassed by your good breeding and immense fortune. I ask nothing better of life that you should be my bride. Alas that your cruel brother frowns on my suit!"

The young Lady Pomeroy hid her burning cheeks behind a painted fan. "Oh, sir," she blushed, "you put me quite out of countenance! I am a simple girl, in spite of my family name. Do not make my poor heart your plaything!"

Leonie closed her eyes, pressed the book to her heart, and sighed rapturously. Francie had loaned her the latest romance by the legendary Mrs Willifred Smythe-Thompson, an inspired female author and recognized authority on courtly love. It was titled *Scandalous Flight* and was the sequel to the equally palpitating *Noble Obsession*.

"Come away with me, my darling," Reginald whispered and took her hand. "Since your brother has hardened his heart against our love, let us fly to Gretna Green tonight, and be married at once!"

"Oh, Reginald!"

A knock at her bedroom door rudely interrupted this flight of fancy. Leonie raised her head and pursed her lips in exasperation.

"Yes?"

Maria's flat voice called from the other side. "Miss Leonie, your trunks are here. I can unpack them if you'll show me where you want your things."

Leonie put the book down regretfully, rose from her bed, and went to open the door.

Maria's bland face met hers. A stack of heavy trunks were piled up in the hall outside her door.

Leonie brightened. "Oh, good, they're here. I've been lost without my curlers! Do you know how to style hair, Maria?"

"No, miss."

Leonie was only momentarily nonplussed. "Oh. Then I suppose I'll have to ask Nate to hire a ladies' maid."

"Yes, miss."

Leonie sighed. "You'll be wishing me at Jericho, I suppose," she thought aloud. "I'll get out of your way. Just put my clothes and hats and shoes and slippers in the closet, and my jewelry and gloves and handkerchiefs and scent bottles on the dressing table, and petticoats and unmentionables in the top drawers, and my dressing gowns in the lower drawer."

Maria stared but said nothing, and Leonie smiled at her. "You can see now why I need help, can't you, Maria? Well, I'm going down to tease Nate until he gets me a ladies' maid."

Maria watched her go without a word, but once her young mistress had disappeared, she walked to the bed, turned the novel over, and read a page curiously.

***

Leonie tripped downstairs to the library, where she knew her brother had been hiding all morning. The door was closed, and the sound of an unfamiliar voice told her that Nate was talking to one of the hired men.

Leonie looked this way and that, and then pressed an eager eye to the keyhole. She could only see a tiny sliver of the room inside; she got a glimpse of Nate's patient face and another man's back. The young fellow was an American, and his voice was pleasantly masculine.

But to her disappointment, they weren't talking about blood-soaked battles or earthshaking secrets, or the beautiful women they had loved and lost.

They were talking about *cattle*, and *ranching supplies*.

Leonie pulled her lips down in disappointment. Nate was *so* dull. She honestly couldn't imagine how he'd ever find a wife if it weren't for the family's medieval custom of arranging their marriages.

Leonie shuddered. She had resolved *never* to submit to such a barbaric tradition. According to Mrs Willifred Smythe-Thompson, arranged marriages were without exception disastrous and sometimes even the motivation for lurid crimes, such as the murder detailed in her thrilling *Driven to Despair*.

Leonie shuddered deliciously but was brought sharply back to the present by the sound of a chair scraping over the floor inside. She saw the man stand up, and she flounced off down the hall and around the corner, just in time to avoid being caught.

Leonie peeped around just as the man stepped out of the library. She'd learned that he was most likely going to Denver to buy cattle supplies, and since she had a letter all prepared to send Francie, Jem would make a perfect mailman.

Then, too, even though he was probably at least five years her senior, she thought Jem quite the best-looking young man she'd ever seen and pinched her cheeks before she launched out in front of him.

"Oh!" she stopped suddenly. "I'm sorry! I didn't see you there." She smiled and made play with her dimples.

Jem straightened up and took off his hat. "Afternoon, miss," he said. "If you're looking for your brother, he's in the library."

Leonie leaned forward. "Oh, I wasn't looking for *Nate*," she assured him. "But I heard you say you were going to Denver, and I have a letter for a friend there. Would you take it there for me, *please*?" She looked up into his eyes pleadingly.

Jem smiled and frowned simultaneously, and his voice held scepticism. "Well sure, missy, but—a nice girl like you hadn't ought to listen at keyholes. Sometimes folks say things they don't want other people to hear."

Leonie dimpled again and waved the objection away. "Oh, not Nate," she assured him. "He's the stuffiest old thing in the world! I've been spying on him for *years*, hoping he'll surprise me, but he never does," she added—and then put a hand over her mouth in dismay.

But Jem laughed at her. "Give me the letter, missy, and I'll mail it for you when I go. But don't let me catch you listening at *my* door," he teased. "I got *lots* of secrets I don't want told."

He took the letter, pulled one of her ringlets, and winked. Leonie giggled and went pink, and Jem smiled and shook his head as he walked off.

But by the time he disappeared around the corner, Leonie was already seeing the two of them as star-crossed lovers, *utterly* devoted to one another, yet meeting in secret for fear of her tyrannical and disapproving brother.

Except that Nate wasn't very tyrannical, usually.

Leonie put a pink finger to her lips. Everything else was made to order. Her uncle's mansion couldn't *possibly* be a more promising setting for a secret romance. It was the scene of a great battle and was probably *already* full of ghosts.

In fact, she wouldn't be at all surprised to discover a secret passage, dug in fear of Cheyenne raids, but perfect for a midnight tryst between persecuted lovers.

Like her. And Jem.

That Jem was ignorant of their fiery passion was only a minor objection. He would inevitably come to acknowledge his deep love for her, but only after fighting against himself for months, and suffering *agonies*.

She was prepared to be patient.

Chapter
Seven

Leonie found her brother still sitting in the library behind a large desk. He was scribbling something onto a paper and was frowning. She came and sat down on the edge of the desk and tickled his ear with the end of a pen.

"Stop it, Leonie," he mumbled, not looking up. "I'm busy now. Don't you have something else to do?"

"No," she pouted. "And I came down to beg you to hire me a lady's maid. I had to do my own hair this morning, and I'm sure I look like a hag."

Nate glanced up at her and then returned to his writing. "Your hair looks fine to me."

"Oh, that's the sort of thing you *would* say," Leonie complained, and crossed her arms.

"Would you like it better if I said your hair looked dreadful?"

Her mouth crumpled up. "*Does* it look dreadful?"

"Of course not. You know, Leonie, it's time we talked about how things have changed. We're in a different country now, and people have different ways here. Perhaps we should try to ... well, be open to new ideas."

"Like what?"

"Well, for example—I'm fairly certain the young ladies in Colorado style their own hair."

"Oh, that's not true! Francie and her sisters have a ladies' maid!"

Nate put his pen down on the desktop and folded his hands. "Well, but—you see what I'm saying, Leonie," he replied gently. "Yes, the Chiswicks have a ladies' maid, but they came over from London, just like we did. The people here do for themselves."

"But *surely* that's because they're too poor to have a ladies' maid," Leonie objected. "I'm sure that if they had enough money, they'd engage one at *once*."

"I'm not going to argue the point with you," Nate sighed. "We're going to have to make some sacrifices, at least at first, because the ranch here isn't doing as well as I'd hoped. We're going to have to give up a few things that we're used to, to make it profitable again."

Leonie's blue eyes widened, and Nate hastened to add: "It will be an *adventure*, Leonie. Think of it that way."

Leonie looked doubtful, and he opened the desk drawer and pulled out a package. "Which reminds me. I bought this in Denver for you," he smiled and handed her a little box.

At once Leonie's face brightened. "Oh, Nate, really? What is it?"

"Open it and see."

Leonie laughed, tore the floral wrapping paper, and opened the little box. Her eyes widened.

"Oh, Nate, it's beautiful! What is it?" She lifted up an ivory wristlet carved with fantastic flourishes.

"It's a carved bracelet made out of elk horn. Pretty thing, isn't it? And very romantic, I'm sure."

Leonie laughed and thrust out her arm. "Put it on for me, Nate," she commanded. "I want to see how it looks!"

Nate smiled and fastened the bracelet around her arm. To his amusement, Leonie was entranced with it.

"Oh, wait until I show it to Francie!" She laughed. "I'm like a real western woman now, aren't I, Nate?"

Nate raised his brows and laughed: "I daresay."

Leonie leaned over and gave him a peck on the cheek. "Thank you, Nate. You're sweet. I wish I'd thought to buy something for you in Denver. I'll get something when we go back. When *are* we going back?"

"I am going back in a few days," he told her.

"Oh, Nate, let me come with you!"

He shook his head. "I'm just going to order windows and doors and other things for the house," he replied. "You wouldn't like it at all."

"But I could visit Francie. I have a million things to tell her!"

"When the house is presentable again, you can invite Francie to stay here as long as you like."

"Oh, *Nate*."

"You should take your bracelet upstairs and put it in your jewelry box," Nate told her. "I was told that elk horn dries out if it's exposed to the air."

Leonie's face became serious at once, and she covered the bracelet with her hand and hurried out again with a rustle of frilly skirts.

When Leonie reached her own boudoir again, she was pleased to see that Maria had set out her clothing and other items. The big, airy suite felt more like home, with her own things in it.

Even if she *was* going to have to learn to style her own hair.

Leonie flopped down on the bed again and resumed her romance novel.

"Meet me at midnight," Reginald whispered into Lady Pomeroy's shell-like ear. "I'll wait for you in the garden, under the lover's arch."

"I'll count the hours!"

Leonie closed her eyes and put herself and Jem McClary into the pages of the story. She imagined Jem's handsome face, contorted with *agonies* of longing. She saw herself reaching out with a soft hand to smooth the frown from his brow.

Be patient, my darling, she told him.

Leonie put the book down and walked over to the big windows that overlooked the back yard of the house. There was a little garden down below, but it was peopled, not with hopeful lovers, but with grubby cowboys loading a wagon with smashed furniture.

Leonie sighed, but she was never downcast for very long. She had decided that her time would be best spent thinking of excuses to talk to Jem. She was confident that Jem would soon be struck with the same sense of destiny that she felt.

And if he didn't see the light immediately, she stood ready to do *this* little thing and *that* little thing to help their romance along.

Chapter
Eight

Nate pulled his watch out of his vest pocket and checked the time. It was 8 a.m. and the Denver Pacific Railway was right on time. He watched the train approach from his seat on Indian Rock's tiny depot platform and prayed he'd be long gone before Leonie found out.

She'd never forgive him for going to Denver without her, but he had serious business to conduct, and Leonie was forever distracting him with talk of shopping and parties and balls and other frippery nonsense that wasted time and left him feeling almost *dazed*.

The train pulled to a slow stop at the depot, and a railroad employee beckoned to him from the door of the first-class car. Nate rose, brushed his jacket, and gave the man his ticket.

"Right this way, Mr Trowbridge," the man said with a smile.

Nate allowed himself to be ushered into a plush private compartment, and just as before, he was seated in a wide, comfortable chair.

"Will you be having breakfast with us, sir?"

"No, thank you. But I will take something small. Perhaps a cup of coffee and a croissant."

"Yes, sir."

The man withdrew, and Nate watched as the locomotive picked up again and the landscape slowly began to glide past his window. He'd probably be staying in Denver for a few days at least. He had to order dozens of items for the house, and that would take some time.

Nate sighed and felt briefly unhappy. He *might've* asked Leonie to come with him, he supposed, but Leonie had been a handful for years, and now that she was approaching a marriageable age, it was more important than ever to restrain her vivacious nature.

She was only sixteen and *already* marriage-mad. Of course, most women were, but Leonie was particularly smitten. She absolutely could *not* be trusted to make a wise decision on her own.

So he thought it best to keep her strictly at home. Leonie had no judgment when it came to men, and his biggest fear was that she might run away with some *nouveau-riche* braggart with a bowler hat and a striped vest. And since he couldn't trust Leonie's discretion, the only way to prevent such a catastrophe was to make sure she *never had that opportunity*.

Maybe he could take Leonie back to London next year for the social season. The suggestion would thrill her, and it would give her the opportunity to meet a *suitable* fellow.

Maybe one of his old schoolmates from Harrow. Some dependable, established young man with conservative politics and prospects for advancement. He'd give it consideration later.

But at the moment, his task was to get the house repaired and to build up the ranch. Leonie's potential *affairs de coeur* were very low on his list of priorities.

Nate gazed out the window absently. That reminded him of the Chiswicks. Maybe he would visit them after he'd concluded his business in Denver. It would be pleasant to call on Emmaline again, and perhaps make some small overture that would prepare her for his later proposal.

Some expression of ardor. Most women expected that sort of thing, even if they weren't as bad as Leonie.

Nate brushed his moustache with the back of his hand. Thankfully, Emmaline was a sensible girl. She didn't expect a man to go down on one knee, or to babble a lot of ridiculous poetry or emotional nonsense.

He expected that the two of them would get along very comfortably, once they were married.

There was a knock at the door, and it opened to admit a uniformed porter carrying a tray. The man set a steaming cup of coffee and a small plate down in front of Nate.

"Enjoy your trip, Mr Trowbridge." He smiled.

Nate nodded and wondered absently why Americans always seemed to expect one to *enjoy* things. That was beside the point, surely.

One did what one *had* to do.

He lifted the coffee cup, took a sip, and opened the morning paper.

***

At a little past noon, Nate checked into the most elegant boarding house in Denver and sallied forth immediately after to find the carpenters, glaziers, smiths and wrights he required to repair his house. Within two hours, he had ordered ten thousand dollars' worth of custom doors, windows, frames, drapery, and furniture, and still wasn't done.

By three he was heartily sick of shopping, and determined to give himself the pleasure of afternoon tea with the Chiswicks before turning back to his rooms.

The Chiswicks' big mansion on Edwards Street was a comforting oasis of English respectability in the midst of the Colorado town. Nate climbed out of his cab and looked up at its imposing front doors in approval. When he entered the Chiswicks' home, he knew exactly what to expect. Everything in the Chiswick household was carried out according to established tradition.

Servant at the door; cane taken. Name given; short wait; servant returned; escorted to family.

When the parlour door opened, Edgar Chiswick looked up from his newspaper and rose, smiling. "Good heavens! Look who's in town," he remarked and extended his hand. Nate took it and gave it one firm shake before releasing his hold. "Nate Trowbridge! Come and join us, old man. We're just about to take tea."

"Thank you, I think I will."

"I'll make a cup for you. Milk, no sugar if I remember correctly," Clara Chiswick smiled and rustled off to the dining room of the house.

"Well, how's the move coming along?" Edgar asked. "Are you settled in now?"

Nate glanced at his prospective father-in-law. "Tolerably well, yes," he replied carefully. "Of course, we have to change the décor."

Edgar laughed heartily. "Ha! Your sister's doing, eh? There was never a woman born who could accept another woman's wallpaper and carpet." He laughed. "Is Leonie in town with you?"

Nate smiled but shook his head. "Not this time. I'm in town on business, and she would've been dreadfully bored."

The door opened, and instead of Clara, Emmaline entered. Nate straightened in his chair and allowed himself to admire a beautiful sight. Emmaline's dark hair was swept up in a beautiful loose bun on the top of her head, and her ephemeral white linen gown made her look like an angel. She was carrying a china cup.

"Well, Emmaline," her father greeted her, "come and say hello to Nate. He's in town on business and dropped by to see us."

Emmaline smiled and gave Nate the steaming cup of tea. "It's so good to see an Englishman again," she told him in a soft voice. "I miss talking to home folk."

Nate smiled back. "Thank you, Emmaline. And I know what you mean," he replied. "Leonie and I have only been here for a few days, and already we're homesick."

"How is your new home?" Emmaline asked.

Nate gave her a quick glance. "Unfinished. In need of everything," he admitted wryly. "That's why I'm here. I have to order a whole new set of furniture and endless furbelows."

Edgar laughed again. "Well, rest with us for awhile, Nate. You can take a break from interior décor."

Nate smiled at him but met Emmaline's eyes over his china cup and was gratified to see her go pink and lower her eyes.

Clara re-entered the room just then, and her quick eyes seemed to catch the exchange between them. She put a hand lightly on Emmaline's shoulder.

"We're not quite ready yet with tea," she announced. "Emmaline, why don't you show Nate our new garden while we get the table ready? I'm sure he'd enjoy it."

Clara's eyes turned to his, and Nate nodded and murmured: "Oh, yes, absolutely."

Emmaline smiled shyly, then stood and beckoned. "It's still not very grand," she apologized, and he hastened to assure her.

"If you had a hand in it, Emmaline, I'm sure it's *perfection*," he replied and presented his arm. Emmaline took it, glanced at her mother, and followed him outside.

Chapter
Nine

"There comes a time in a man's life when he begins to think about stability and order," Nate said carefully. Emmaline was seated on a garden bench next to him and was listening with earnest attention.

"He considers his time of life, and his station, and his duty to family," he went on. "He begins to think about *settling down.*"

Emmaline's eyes were glued to his face with an almost painful intensity. She nodded.

"And, he hopes that the girl of his intentions is not *wholly* unaware of his plans," he added, looking up at the sky.

Emmaline made a small noise that sounded like assent.

"When one's family traditions have laid out a very—*definite* order of events in such matters, one hopes that any—overtures one may make will be correctly received."

Emmaline's mouth formed a perfect O, but she recovered instantly. "Oh, yes," she murmured. "One *hopes.*"

Nate cleared his throat and gave her a small glance. He felt as if he was botching this deuced ardor thing, but thankfully, Emmaline seemed not to notice. Or perhaps seemed not to *care* that he was botching it.

He glanced at her in admiration. Emmaline was a beautiful, modest, and respectable girl. Forgiving, too, by the looks of it since she didn't seem to hold it against him that he was mangling his speech.

He cleared his throat. "Well! I'm glad to see that we're in agreement about that," he told her.

"Oh, *yes*—yes, we are," she assured him. "Perfect agreement!"

Emboldened by this encouragement, Nate reached over and patted her hand. "Then I shall know how to proceed," he told her warmly. "Thank you, Emmaline, for putting my mind at ease on the matter."

"Oh, *yes*, Nate."

They sat there for awhile longer, staring at the sky until Clara appeared at the garden gate and called them back in for tea.

When they all settled in for tea, Nate pointed out, when he could work it gracefully into the conversation, that his financial situation was excellent, his reputation good, and his prospects bright.

And more than once, he saw Edgar and Clara exchange hopeful glances, and his mood brightened. All the signals he was picking up from Emmaline and her parents encouraged him that they would welcome his proposal of marriage.

Of course, any other outcome was *unthinkable*, but even so.

***

That evening, in his own rooms at the boarding house, Nate allowed himself to feel satisfied about a good day's work. His plans to repair the house were well on their way, and he had laid a promising foundation for his eventual marriage to Emmaline. After their conversation, he felt emboldened to hope that his proposal of marriage would be met with the right answer.

He and Emmaline were upholding a family tradition that stretched back for two hundred years when the first Trowbridge parents had arranged the marriage of their son Timothy to Elizabeth Chiswick in 1672.

The custom had been loosely tied to the Bible. His memory of it was cloudy, but Nate had the vague sense that his ancestors had justified the idea of an arranged marriage by pointing to the story of Isaac and Rebekah. They reasoned that the match had turned out well, and so, such an arrangement must be a good plan.

And so it had proved: From their very first marriage, the Trowbridges and Chiswicks had routinely intermarried and had been to all appearances happy as larks. There had been only a handful of Trowbridge sons who married girls of their own choosing, and they had generally come to bad ends.

In his own case, Nate was certain that he'd be as happy with Emmaline as ever Isaac had been with Rebekah, and it inspired him to thankfulness.

He knelt down beside his bed and clasped his hands in prayer for the first time in months.

"O Lord," he prayed, "thank you for your manifold blessings. Please be with me, and with Leonie, as we build our lives in this new land. And as Abraham sent his servant to find a wife for Isaac among his people, so too, please prepare the way for me to marry my helpmate, and help me to be a satisfactory husband to her. Thank you. Amen."

Nate rose with the warm assurance that God had heard his prayer, that all was as it should be, and that he was well on the way to achieving his plans. He dressed for bed, blew out the bedside lamp, and drifted off to sleep more at peace with the world than he had been for many a day.

***

Nate spent the rest of the week in Denver, visiting shops and ordering mostly replicas—or as close to replicas as he could get in Denver—of the furnishings that had filled their family home in England. These items came very dear, but in spite of the ranch's reduced condition, Nate resisted the temptation to economize.

He couldn't bring Emmaline home to a shabby house, nor could he hope to encourage the right sort of friends for Leonie, without a home that was refined and elegant.

On his last day in town, Nate came away from the merchant district with a profound sense of relief. He had completed a dreaded task, and now that it was over, he was ready to return to his own home with the assurance that it would soon be a place of beauty.

He stood on the curb and scanned the street for a cab. He was so intent on this task that a quick rustling sound was his only warning before another pedestrian plowed right into him and knocked him face-first onto the pavement.

Nate suddenly found himself face down on the ground with dirt on his teeth, and he pushed back up to his feet indignantly. He pulled a handkerchief from his pocket and cleaned his mouth, swiped dust off of his jacket and trousers, and rounded on the offender to deliver his soul.

But to his astonishment, the person kneeling on the pavement was a woman. The angry words died on his tongue, and he held out a hand to help her up again. But some rebuke was certainly justified.

"Good heavens, woman—watch where you're going!" he gasped.

The woman looked up through her hair and allowed him to help her stand up again. She was pretty, in a coarse, sloppy kind of way, but obviously a menial worker of some sort. Her hair was a flaming red, and it had been knocked free of the hasty bun she had made on the top of her head. She was a bit too buxom for her cheap cotton gown, and Nate forced himself to look away as she raised herself up again.

"I'm sorry, mister," she apologized in an earthy voice with an Irish accent. "I didn't mean to knock you right side up! I wasn't looking where I was going," she explained breathily.

"That's evident!" Nate agreed and brushed a dirty scrape mark off his elbow.

"Sorry about that," she repeated and retrieved a small bag from the ground. "I'm running behind for work. I need to be there on time."

"At any price, I see!" Nate retorted, and bit his lip. The cab he had hailed finally pulled up to the curb, and he looked back over his shoulder to deliver one parting shot.

"Next time, pay attention!"

He got a glimpse of the woman's oddly poignant blue eyes staring up at him, and then the cab pulled away. Nate adjusted his defiled jacket and grumbled under his breath for a few blocks before returning to the rest of his day.

Chapter
Ten

Within a few days of Nate's return to the Circle T, the items he had ordered began arriving by train. It wasn't long before the afternoon freight was delivering things to their depot every day, and to his amusement, Leonie was beside herself with excitement.

She hovered nearby, as curious as a child to see what emerged from the packing crates. No matter what they proved to be, she declared herself delighted.

"Oh! Aren't they beautiful!" she exclaimed as Jem McClary opened a crate full of custom drapes.

Jem stood up carefully and rubbed the back of his neck. "They are that, miss." He put his hands on his hips and laughed as Leonie unfurled the drapes like the train of a ballgown and twirled around the room.

The next day, she peeked over Jem's shoulder as he prised open a box full of wallpaper rolls. "Open them up," she begged, and Jem cut through the wrapping and pulled up the box lid.

"*Ohhhh,*" Leonie gasped, "they're hand-painted! Have you ever *seen* more beautiful roses?"

Jem shook his head and smiled. "No missy, I can't say I have."

Leonie unfurled a roll and ran her hand over its silky surface. "It's divine," she sighed and looked up soulfully into Jem's eyes. "But I'd rather live with *the man I love,* than live in the prettiest mansion ever built."

Jem rubbed his neck again. "Yes'm. Well, I guess most girls would say the same."

Nate noticed that his sister was so interested in the repairs, in fact, that she planted herself in the rooms where they were going forward and refused to leave.

She tilted her head as Jem and another hand helped unpack chairs from a big wooden crate.

"Come and put a chair down here, Jem," she begged and dimpled: "Next to me?"

***

Soon the carpenters and skilled artisans Nate had hired in Denver began arriving, and he quickly became busy giving them instructions and overseeing their work.

For many weeks the house was full of the sound of hammers, saws, and mallets. The shattered windows were replaced with gleaming new ones; the front wall of the house was repaired and new doors hung, and the broken front steps were replaced.

Inside, the bloodstained flooring was sanded and stained fresh; the trim repaired and repainted, and the walls covered in custom wallpaper. The rooms filled up with beautifully upholstered chairs and sofas in light green satin, elegant grandfather clocks, cherry wood dining suites, billiard tables, pianos, and white Persian rugs with intricate green embellishments.

At about a month out from his buying trip, Nate stood in the middle of the front salon with his hands on his hips. The mansion was finally beginning to look like the house he'd envisioned when he left London. It was spotlessly clean, light, airy, and elegant. It still smelled strongly of new paint and sawdust, but there were few if any reminders of its shattered past in the bright, beautiful house before him.

And now that he'd restored the house to an acceptable level of elegance, he could apply himself to the business of *paying* for all the things he'd just purchased.

***

"How are things going?"

Nate settled down in the wooden chair opposite Jem McClary's desk in the bunkhouse office. Jem scratched his jaw.

"Well, the barns are back to what they were, and most of the fences are repaired. We haven't had any raids against our cattle. So stable. *Stable* is how things are. If we keep on like we're going, we should make enough this year to cover expenses and make a decent profit. Not a big one. So I'd be conservative if I were you, Mr Trowbridge," he added, with a straight look. "It's harder, and costs more than you may think, to build up a herd. A hard winter, or a big raid, could put us in the red real quick."

"I see. What are we doing to anticipate those things?"

"We have close to a full crew of hands now, almost a hundred men. That should be enough to beat off a raid if we need to. But I doubt we'll need to. Most of the Cheyenne are gone, and what few are left aren't fool enough to make a big raid on a place like the Circle T. We're good here.

"As for a hard winter, those things are in the hands of the Almighty. We do what we can to prepare. I'd say we're about as ready for that as we can be."

"Good. I'll rely on your judgment, then," Nate replied. "Thank you, Jem."

"Yes sir. Oh—and I'm feeling well enough, I think, to get back in a saddle again," Jem added with a smile. "Maybe if I take it slow, I can ease back to where I was. The only thing bothering me now is a sore tooth."

"Good man," Nate replied heartily. "I'm glad to hear it. If I can help in any way, just let me know. And if you feel well enough, take the weekend off," he added. "You've been working very hard for the last few weeks."

Jem's face brightened, and he grinned. "Thank you, Mr Trowbridge."

***

Nate left the bunkhouse feeling satisfied that the ranch was in reasonably good shape for a place that had only barely escaped destruction, and that his finances, while not as flush as they could be, were nevertheless steady and solid.

He began to think of writing to Emmaline and asking her to marry him.

He stuck his hands in his jacket pockets as he walked back to the house. There was really no reason to delay, now that the house had been put right. Barring some unforeseen disaster, the Circle T's future looked bright.

Leonie met him in the garden at the back of the house. She smiled and slid her arm through his.

"What makes you look so *grim* this morning?" she teased.

He raised his brows. "Do I look grim? I don't feel grim. In fact, I'm quite happy," he told her.

"Really? You were frowning something *terrible*." Leonie laughed and made a face. "But I'll take your word."

Nate looked down at her smiling face fondly. "Leonie, how would you feel if—if someone else came to live with us here?"

Leonie stopped dead and pulled him around to face her. "Oh *Nate*," she gasped, "are you going to propose to Emmaline at last? Oh please," she pleaded, "don't write a horrid *letter*. Go and ask her yourself! I can help you if you don't know what to say. I know a thousand *divine* proposals by heart! I'll write one out for you."

Nate felt an unreasonable flicker of irritation. "Leonie, it isn't becoming for you to speculate about my relationship with Emmaline," he told her. "If we ever decide to—to marry, I will tell you at the proper time."

"Oh, Nate, you're hopeless." Leonie giggled. "I suppose Emmaline knows what she's doing, but I wouldn't marry you for a million pounds! You're so serious, and so—*unromantic*!"

Nate pulled his arm out of his sister's and adjusted his lapels and his ruffled sensibilities. "When you grow up, Leonie—and stop expecting life to be like those ridiculous romance books of yours—you'll see that there's much more to marriage than mere sentiment. It's more important to find a mate who's respectable, agreeable, and of your own social status, than to expect rubbishing emotional thrills."

"If you say so." Leonie giggled. "But you can be easy in your mind, Nate. I adore Emmaline, and I would *love* to truly be sisters with my dear Francie."

Nate's expression softened. "Of course you would." He reached out and pulled her arm through his again, and they resumed walking. "And, if there's anything to tell, you will of course be the first to know."

"*Promise?*"

Nate smiled as Leonie leaned over and gave him an impulsive peck on the cheek.

"Yes, I suppose."

Chapter
Eleven

Nate walked slowly to his den and shut the door behind him. He sat down at the writing desk, pulled out a sheet of paper, and sat staring at it.

He was keenly aware of the solemnity of the moment. A proposal of marriage was irrevocable for a man of honour. Once offered, it could never be withdrawn.

He reviewed all that he knew about Emmaline and her family, replayed every word Emmaline had ever said to him. He had every reason to believe that she was the sweet, agreeable young woman that she seemed.

And she was undeniably beautiful. Nate conjured her up in his mind, with her dark hair swept up in a perfect bun, her flawless complexion, and her modest, downcast eyes.

He dipped the pen into the inkwell and wrote:

My dear girl,

I am keenly aware that the two of us have known each other very briefly, and your maidenly sensibilities must shrink from joining yourself to a man you have only just met. But I hope that you will not allow our imperfect acquaintance to prejudice your answer to the question I am about to ask.

Our last meeting led me to hope that you would look favourably on my request for your hand in marriage. You are a sweet and beautiful young woman, and I would count it an honour beyond my deserving if you would agree to be my wife.

I do not have the gift of a glib tongue, and it is difficult for me to express my feelings. But be assured that should you agree to be my wife, I will do my utmost to make you happy and to make your life as comfortable as is within my power.

I await your answer with a hopeful heart.

Sincerely,

Nate Trowbridge.

Nate sighed and read the letter over again. There was really nothing else to say, and so he waited for the ink to dry, and then folded the letter up, placed it in an envelope, and addressed it to Emmaline Chiswick, 501 Edwards Street, Denver, Colorado.

Nate affixed a stamp, and sat staring at the envelope for what seemed a long time. He looked up at the ceiling and murmured:

Oh, Lord, please grant me success. Allow me to marry the girl you have chosen.

Then he stood up, put the envelope in his jacket pocket, and walked back downstairs again.

To his surprise, Jem McClary was in the foyer when he arrived. The young man met his eyes and hailed him.

"Mr Trowbridge, I just came by to ask if you needed anything in Denver. I'm taking the train this morning."

Nate stared at the young man's face, wondering if he could trust him with such an important mission, but he finally reached into his jacket and gave him the envelope.

"If you don't mind, I'd appreciate it if you could mail this letter for me," he asked quietly. "It's an important message, so if you don't think you can, please tell me now."

The young man grinned. "It'd be no trouble at all," Jem assured him and opened his hand. Nate stared at Jem's big brown palm momentarily before entrusting the letter to him.

"I'll be back on Monday morning," Jem told him and smiled again.

"Have a good time in Denver," Nate told him. "But not *too* good."

"I make no promises." Jem laughed and waved briefly before disappearing through the front doors.

Nate watched him go from the foyer and sighed, but he looked up when a small hand slid around his arm.

"Important message, *hmmm*?" Leonie smiled and leaned her head on his shoulder. Nate put his arm around her, and together they watched as Jem climbed up on his horse, waved, and turned it away.

"Very important," he replied softly.

Chapter
Twelve

Molly Clanahan looked up into the angry face of the young stranger she'd just knocked to the ground. He was a young swell, almost a dandy, with his suit and his hat and his gloves just *so*, and he wasn't happy that she'd sent him sky-west and crooked. He jumped up off the ground and turned as if he was going to give her the thrashing of her life.

But the anger in his eyes died when they made eye contact, almost as if it had been wiped away, and he extended his hand like a proper gentleman.

Molly reached for it and allowed the stranger to help her to her feet.

"I'm sorry," she told him and was uncomfortably aware of what he must be thinking of her shabby dress and messy hair. They were even messier now and covered with street dust and grime, and she swiped them uneasily.

"I'm running behind for work. I need to be there on time."

He had a few tart words for her, as she might've expected, having put him bottoms-up, but then he climbed into a cab, and it rolled away.

Molly watched him go and then caught herself up because she needed to be gone, too. Mrs Tarrant at the dressmaker's wouldn't be as forgiving as that young man if she blew in to work five minutes late. There were any number of young women in Denver looking for work, and she could easily be replaced, and the old harpy held it over her head like a mallet.

She snatched up her bag and her skirts and went down the sidewalk at a run. Some lads on the corner whistled at her as she ran by, and her cheeks went as red as her hair, but if she stopped to tell them to go to the Devil, she'd be late.

She arrived at Tarrant's Dressmakers just on the stroke of twelve, and to her irritation, Mrs Tarrant was standing at the door with a watch, which she stopped with a *click* as Molly ran in.

"Not a second to spare, Molly Clanahan!" she cried, as Molly hurried in. "You're coming to work later and later every day! You barely made it in time today, but I warn you—get here *one second* past noon tomorrow, and you're out on your ear, my girl!"

"Yes, Mrs Tarrant," Molly grumbled and quickly took her place at a table in the shop workroom. She pulled her packet of embroidery needles out of her bag and began to prepare for work. Her job was to embroider the beautiful gowns of wealthy ladies, with beautiful roses, or singing birds, or swirls and flourishes. The work was very tedious and delicate, but Molly enjoyed it and took pride in her skill. She had the best hand in Mrs Tarrant's shop and did the most delicate work. *She* knew that, even if no one *else* there acknowledged it.

Molly pressed her lips into a straight line. She didn't get paid enough for her skill, and it chapped her that the old woman was holding out on her, but she was in no position to haggle, and she knew it. Denver was becoming fashionable with the rich, and wealthy young ladies needed beautiful gowns.

Denver was also full of young women like her, who had only one skill that they could decently market.

Seamstresses and even detail workers were a dime a dozen.

Mrs Tarrant walked up and dumped a stack of fabric strips onto her table. "I want these figures finished by the end of your shift," she barked, and Molly nodded wordlessly.

She picked up the top one. The outline of a beautiful peacock was traced in pencil on a strip of silk fabric, and she threaded a needle and began to work.

***

By the end of her shift, Molly's eyes were burning, but her stack of work was complete. It was now almost eight o' clock, and the sun was setting.

"All right, girls, you can go," Mrs Tarrant called out, and the young women sitting at a half-dozen work tables rose and stretched.

Molly gathered up her stack of figures and deposited them in the basket Mrs Tarrant had placed on a table in front of her. The older woman held up a finger, and Molly quelled the temptation to roll her eyes as her employer counted through the stack.

"All right, you can go," she mumbled, and Molly fled before her employer thought of some *new* hoop for her to jump through.

***

She stepped out onto the pavement outside the shop and took a deep breath of the cool evening air. It was a lovely night, with a lavender sky and the North Star shining like a diamond over the tops of the mountains.

Molly started walking home and enlivened the stroll by imagining herself on the arm of a swell like the fellow she'd knocked down. Instead of chewing her out, she saw him sweep off his hat and make a gallant bow.

"A fine good afternoon to you, young miss," he was saying, and she curtsied.

"And to you, sir," she replied.

He'd been a handsome fellow, the swell: his hair was black and shiny and cut so precisely along the back of his neck that it looked as if his barber had marked the line with a pencil. He had a fetching moustache, a strong chin, and a fine, tall physique.

She saw him offer his arm and saw herself take it, and they walked to a glittering ballroom, where her cheap cotton dress magically transformed into an embroidered silk gown, and together they danced the night away.

Molly was so wrapped up in this pleasant fantasy that she almost walked past her own lodgings. Mrs O'Malley's boarding house was a ramshackle, two-storey clapboard house dating from Denver's earliest days. It advertised three meals a day, and room and board, for 50 cents a week.

It was *not* in the fashionable quarter of the city, and its residents were what Mrs O'Malley called 'up and comers.' Which was, Molly thought wryly, her way of saying, they had nowhere to *go*, but up.

She climbed the steps wearily. She was too late for dinner, but Mrs O'Malley always saved a plate for her.

Molly walked into the kitchen, and there on the table was a plate of chicken and dumplings and a little boiled cabbage. She took it with her upstairs and closeted herself in her own one-room apartment.

She had only just settled down at her table and taken a bite when there came a soft knock at her door. She put down her fork and went to answer.

Mrs O'Malley's broad red face filled the opening. "I'm sorry to disturb you," she said, "but I wanted to tell you before I forgot. There was a man here asking for you earlier. I told him you were off working, and he said he'd be back again. I asked his name, but he didn't give me no name. Do you know who he might be?"

Molly felt the blood draining from her face but shrugged as nonchalantly as she could and replied with a sturdy lie.

"No."

"Well, then, that's odd," Mrs O'Malley murmured. "He was a tall fellow, red hair, and a bit rough around the edges—meaning no disrespect," she added quickly, "many men around these parts are—but you *do* notice."

Molly licked her lips. "Sounds like a beggar to me," she scoffed, "trying to get in your good graces by pretending to know a lodger. If he comes again, you can tell him he's got the wrong place. I don't know any such man."

"Well, then ..." Mrs O'Malley smiled, "I'll tell him if he comes again, but he's probably seen his mistake by now and gone away.—Good night to you!"

"Good night, Mrs O'Malley," Molly echoed and closed the door softly behind her.

But as soon as her landlady was gone, Molly hurried to turn out her lamp and to pull the shades. She cautiously lifted one edge to look down into the street below. She searched the street anxiously, but there was no sign of Jack.

She leaned back against the wall and closed her eyes. How had he *found* her? She'd been so careful not to leave a trail.

But plainly, not careful *enough*.

Panic surged up in her. Jack had run her to ground, and if she made a dash for it, he'd be waiting.

She hugged herself, and a shudder of revulsion crawled up her spine. Once again, she was in the Golden Nugget, wearing a skimpy silk dress, hearing Jack's voice growl: "One more word from you, Molly, and I'll break your neck!"

She rubbed her jaw. Jack had knocked her down once, and if she hadn't broken a bottle over his head, she was sure he would've killed her.

"May God's curse find you, Jack McGee," she growled and shivered. "Unless a lead ball finds you first!"

Chapter
Thirteen

The next morning, Molly crept down the stairs fully dressed. It was still dark outside, and the old house was cold because even the landlady was still in her bed.

Molly glided across the front parlour as silently as a ghost and approached the front window. She was careful not to show herself but peered out into the street.

The narrow dirt road was empty, and the ramshackle clapboard houses that lined it were dark and sleepy. There were only one or two windows glowing at four in the morning.

Molly scanned the yard outside, the sidewalk beyond, and all the other houses. They were innocent of all but a grey alley cat, padding back home from a night of adventure, but Molly refused to be satisfied. She kept her silent vigil for close to half an hour, waiting and watching.

Jack was out there somewhere, watching the house, she knew it.

She bit her lip. It was pure spite and revenge that made him dog her. The money she'd taken was nothing to him and had only lasted her a week.

She had needed it so *desperately*, and Jack—he would've thrown it away on gin in a single night.

She was only sorry that she hadn't had the time to plunder his *strongbox*, as well as his pockets.

Molly resumed her vigil. She swept the yard with her eyes and straightened suddenly. There—behind the big fir tree bordering the sidewalk—a small red light glowed brightly and then died.

Jack's cigarette.

He was hiding in the yard, waiting for her to come out.

Fury and terror fought each other in Molly's chest for a long moment, and fury won. She pressed her lips together and pulled a small revolver out of her bag. She held it at the ready as she debated with herself.

She could drop Jack McGee where he stood. The world would instantly become a better place, and she'd be rid of him for good and all.

But she'd be caught, *sure*, and be sent first to the jail, and then to the gallows.

No one would believe her story. Once they found out where she'd been, and what she'd done, they'd write her off as a criminal.

But if she didn't kill Jack *now* when she had the chance—the chance might not come again. He'd ambush her in some dark, lonely place. He'd kill her outright or drag her back with him, which would be worse than dying.

The little red light in the yard flared and died again.

Molly cursed under her breath. As satisfying as it would be to pull the trigger and watch the red light sputter and fall, it wouldn't solve her problem.

She had to find some other way.

She returned the revolver to her bag and faded back from the corner of the window. A moment later, the back door of the house opened silently on its hinges and was replaced carefully.

A solitary figure moved soundlessly through the dark garden behind the house and out into the street beyond.

***

"You want me to do *what*?"

Molly felt her face going red but faced her employer grimly. "I'm asking for an advance on my salary, Mrs Tarrant. Payday is only two days away, anyhow, and I *have* to have the money."

Mrs Tarrant's eyes narrowed. "And why do you *have* to have the money, may I ask?"

Molly met her stare grimly. *It isn't any of your business, you old battle axe*, she fumed but forced herself to reply: "My mother's very sick. I need to take her to the doctor tomorrow, or she'll die, sure."

The old woman turned away and made a scornful sound. "*Huh!* If people were more careful about their habits, they wouldn't get sick."

Molly bit her lip and pressed: "Mrs Tarrant, *please*."

The older woman searched her eyes keenly. What she saw there inspired her to say, grudgingly: "Oh, very well! I'll give you an advance. But not on the whole amount. *Half*."

Molly restrained an angry reply by sheer willpower. It was embarrassing to have to beg for what was rightfully hers and humiliating to have to do it in front of all her co-workers, because the old bag had refused to speak to her privately.

The other girls were staring at her with open curiosity. Some were snickering behind their hands.

"I don't think half will be enough, Mrs Tarrant," she pressed, but the older woman snorted and turned away.

"Half is all you're getting, and you may be thankful you're getting that. I've never had *any* of my girls ask such a bold thing. If you press me too hard, Molly Clanahan, you may become more trouble than you're worth."

Mrs Tarrant opened a little lock box on the table and reluctantly counted five coins into Molly's waiting palm.

Molly bit her lip and stored them away in her bag, and she walked out of the shop with a burning heart.

But she walked out with her head held high because the old bag had shortchanged her for the last time.

"Here! Come back here at once, you impudent girl!" the older woman called after her, "I didn't give you permission to go!"

But Molly tossed her head, laughed into the woman's outraged face, and gave her the cheeky salute that she'd seen employed many times, in less reputable places.

Chapter
Fourteen

Jem arrived at the office of Fenton J. Maxwell, Dentist, just at the stroke of noon. It had been more than an hour's trip to Denver, and he was thirsty. He was longing for a cold drink and a soft chair, but he wasn't going to get them—or at least, not right away.

Because the nerves in his sore tooth had gotten more irritated with every mile of his train ride, and now they were a thunderous drumbeat in his jaw. He was beginning to think he was going to have to get his tooth pulled because the pain was getting bad.

But when he looked up, the dentist was locking his doors to go out for lunch.

"Hold on, Doc," he interrupted, "don't lock up just yet! I've got a tooth that's throbbing like a wasp stung it. Can you give me something for the pain?"

The dentist was a tall, portly man wearing a striped vest and large trousers, and he looked like he was thinking of a sandwich, but to Jem's relief, the man sighed, unlocked his door, and waved him in.

"Thanks, Doc," Jem mumbled gratefully. "You can't know how this thing is griping me!"

The man led him to a little room, and he sat down in the examination chair. The dentist leaned over him and shone a light onto his mouth.

"Open up."

Jem opened his mouth, and the man frowned. "Which one is it?"

Jem pointed to a tooth in his lower jaw, and the dentist grunted. "Looks like you have a cavity. You have an exposed nerve, and that's why your tooth hurts."

He turned toward a cabinet full of little bottles and retrieved a dark blue vial. "You need to have that tooth filled. It isn't going to feel good, so I'm going to give you some laudanum to dull the pain."

Jem rolled his eyes up and resigned himself to an unpleasant hour, but soon all his pain, and every problem he ever had, vanished into the sky without a trace.

***

A little more than an hour later, Jem walked out of the dentist's office with a smile on his face. He turned and waved as the dentist locked the door behind them.

"Thanks, Doc! You did a bang-up job, that's for sure," he nodded owlishly. "I don't feel a *thing*."

The man glanced at him. "I gave you a pretty strong dose. You should probably go home now and sleep it off."

Jem waved and set off down the street. He suddenly remembered that Mr Trowbridge had given him an errand, and one that his tooth had made him completely forget. He slapped his brow with one hand.

"How about that?" he mumbled. "Here I was supposed to *mail a letter*."

Jem reached into his vest pocket, pulled out the neat envelope, and squinted. He could just make out the address as 501 Edward Street.

He tilted his head back to look up at the sky. *Oh Lord*, he prayed impulsively, *I know you ain't heard from me very recent, and thank you for all you've done in the meantime; but now I've got a request. I'm a little bit drunk from the stuff the doc gave me, and I don't know where in thunder to look for this house, and it's the boss that sent me. Please point me in the right direction? Well, um—thank you. Amen.*

When he opened his eyes, there was an elderly man walking down the street toward him, and he called out: "Hey, friend—where's Edward Street?"

The man stopped to rub his jaw. "Why, that's just down the way, not two blocks over," he replied. "You go down this street, and turn left, and go two blocks, and you're there."

Jem touched his hat. "Thanks." He followed the stranger's directions as well as he'd heard: a leisurely stroll down the street, and then *turnnnn* left, and go two blocks.

Annnnd—you're there.

Jem squinted at the house numbers on Edward. The envelope read 501, and 501 was the house number right in front of him.

Jem raised his brows. It surprised him that as rich a man as Mr Trowbridge would have business with whoever lived in the shabby little white house—but then again, sometimes important men had friends they couldn't afford to talk about.

He took a deep breath and sauntered up the walkway. It was a little hard for him to stay on an even keel, but he righted himself a time or two, pulled his vest straight, and forged ahead.

He climbed the steps to the porch and knocked on the door until it opened.

A woman's face swam up in front of him, and he stopped to tip his hat. "Good afternoon, ma'am," he drawled. "Is this 501 Edward?"

The old lady smiled at him. "Yes, indeed. How can I help you? If you're looking for lodging tonight, you've come to the right place. A dime a night, or 50 cents for the week."

Jem considered. He *was* looking for a place to spend the night, so that had worked out lucky. He nodded.

"I think I will, ma'am, thank you. At least for tonight."

Her red face lit up. "Well then, why are you standing outside? Come in!"

He took off his hat and entered, looking around. "What I meant to ask you, ma'am, was, do you have any young ladies staying with you? My employer sent me to deliver a letter to this address."

"Oh?" The old woman's brows went up. "Well, I'm afraid I couldn't help you there," she admitted sheepishly, "I never learnt my letters, but we do have a young lady here. I'll call her, and you can deliver the letter yourself."

"Thank you, ma'am."

Jem closed his eyes. The room had suddenly turned over, and he sank down onto the couch.

When he opened his eyes again, a little while later, a young woman was standing in front of him. He stood up instinctively and pulled off his hat.

"Evening, miss."

The woman was a beautiful redhead with soulful blue eyes. He allowed his eyes to drift down. She was also a *very* curvy girl. He straightened up to his full height, squared his shoulders, and smiled.

"Mrs O'Malley says you have a letter for me," she said doubtfully. She had a soft and earthy voice, the kind that put a man at ease. He smiled at her again.

"That's right. My name is Jem McClary. I was sent to deliver this to you, personal." He handed it to her.

She frowned at the envelope. She looked as if she was about to say something, but then she glanced at something over his shoulder and seemed to think better of it.

"Thank you very much, Jem."

"Oh, it's no trouble, miss."

She looked over his shoulder again. "Will you be staying in Denver long?"

"No ma'am. Just the weekend. I have to get back to work on Monday. I was just delivering this letter for my boss."

At the words *for my boss,* the girl's brows went up. To his surprise, she tore the envelope open, unfolded the letter, and read its contents silently, right there in front of him.

Then she looked up at him and smiled winsomely.

"Have you had anything to eat, Jem?"

"Well, no ma'am, not much."

"Why don't I make you a plate. You're too late for lunch, but they always keep some over for stragglers." She smiled at him again.

"We have a little buttermilk, too—if you're dry."

Jem grinned: "Why, ma'am, you just read my mind."

Chapter
Fifteen

Jem groaned, opened his eyes, and looked up through his hair. His head felt like it was made of cement, and his mouth was dry. There was a bitter taste on his tongue.

The lamp in the compartment hurt his eyes, and he had a splitting headache, but he wasn't dreaming it—it had gone from noon to nighttime, instantly, and somehow, he was in a *train compartment*, and there was a *woman* with him. She was a busty redhead in a cheap dress, and he blurted out the first horrified thought that crossed his mind.

"Oh, lady, we—we ain't *married*, are we?"

The girl gave him a dry look but replied: "You needn't look so scared. Is it such an awful idea, being married to me?"

Jem licked his lips. "Oh, no, no ma'am—it's just—lady, you and me, we're *strangers*. I don't *know* you."

She gave him another shrewd glance. "Well, you can relax. We're not married. You brought me Mr Trowbridge's letter today, remember?"

Jem put his head in his hands. "Oh—oh yeah. I went to the dentist's, and then—came to you." He groaned. "Whatever that doc gave me, it musta put me on the moon. I've never been so drunk in all my life. Mr Trowbridge is going to have my—"

He caught himself in time, looked up at the woman again, and said no more. But the woman shook her table napkin out with a *snap*.

"You really don't remember what happened?" she enquired as calmly if she was asking about the weather. He shook his head miserably.

"How did I even *get* here?" he marvelled. "You must've rolled me here in a wheelbarrow. I don't remember a thing after eating lunch with you."

The woman took a sip of coffee, smiled, and said nothing. A resentful suspicion sparked in his mind, but no—no, it couldn't be true, *surely*.

The sign on the door had read *Boarding House*. Though come to think of it—it *had* been an older woman who'd opened the door.

He tried to gather his scattered thoughts. "Where is this train going, and why are you here with me?"

The girl put the coffee cup down. "Why, you really *don't* remember?" She seemed surprised. "You came and gave me Mr Trowbridge's letter, and now we're going back to his house in Indian Rock."

Jem's mouth fell open. He frowned at her because a terrible possibility had dawned on him. He licked his lips.

"*Why*?"

She tilted her head and stared at him as if he were a dimwitted child. "Why, so Mr Trowbridge and I can be married, of course," she replied. "He wrote to *propose* to me."

Jem stared at her in horror and then shook his head. There was no *way* that could be true, and Mr Trowbridge was going to fire him for *sure* for making such a mistake.

He'd delivered the letter to the *wrong address*, that was as plain as print, and there was no excuse that would make it right, not even that he'd been drunk. He'd been entrusted with the most important letter of his boss's *life*, and he'd given it to the *wrong girl*.

And now Mr Trowbridge was going to have to sort out the mess with *this* girl, and with the girl he'd *really* meant the letter to reach.

What he'd done was as close to the kiss of death as it got.

"Oh, Lord help me," he moaned, and the girl stared at him in irritation.

"If you don't stop moaning and groaning, I'm going to send you to second class," she told him tartly. "You ought to be saying, 'Congratulations, Miss Clanahan, on your upcoming nuptials,' or something like that. Not, 'Lord help me.' What's wrong with you?"

Jem refused to answer her and put his head in his hands. He was too groggy and stunned to talk. He was out of a job, that much was guaranteed. He tried to think of other places he could apply as a ranch hand—if they'd even have him, after the news of this got out.

After awhile there came a discreet knock on the door of the compartment. "Miss Clanahan, your stop is coming up."

"Thank you, porter," she called and took another sip of coffee.

Jem glanced at her suspiciously. Something had *happened* back at that house. He didn't know what, but it had all the makings of a setup. He'd eaten lunch with this girl, and that was the last thing he remembered for more than seven hours. Somehow she'd gotten him from that house to this train while he was passed out, 185 pounds of dead weight, and that was impossible without her having *some* kind of help.

What he feared, and what was likeliest to be true, was that she was a gold digger who'd taken advantage of his mistake to blackmail Mr Trowbridge.

Maybe she didn't expect to marry his boss—but to judge by what she was wearing, and where she'd been living, she'd figured out that a man like Mr Trowbridge would probably pay out a *lot* of money to keep her from embarrassing him.

Most of all—to keep his *real* intended bride, and her family, from getting hurt and embarrassed.

Jem pulled a hand over his mouth. She could keep Mr Trowbridge paying for her silence for *months*. Maybe even *years*.

And that was *his* fault, not Mr Trowbridge's, so it fell to him to make it right. He calculated that there was one chance in a million that the girl was telling the truth, and so he wasn't really gambling to put all his cards on the table.

He clasped his hands together and leaned forward. "Miss—"

"My name is Molly Clanahan," the girl replied calmly and without looking at him.

"Miss Clanahan. Now, I don't know how I got here, nor yet what happened back at the lodging house this afternoon, but I *do* know that you ain't the girl Mr Trowbridge proposed marriage to. No, you needn't deny it," he went on as she objected, "I know you *ain't*."

"If it's money you're after, I can give you money," he said grimly. "I'm the foreman of the Circle T, and I make a good wage. I'll send you half of it, to any address you give me, for as long as you like if you just stay on this train, and *keep going*."

To his astonishment, the girl looked genuinely hurt. She looked out the window and quick tears glimmered in her eyes.

"That is the most *hateful* thing anybody has ever said to me." She sniffed and dug in her purse for a handkerchief. "Money? How *dare* you," she mumbled, and blew her nose into a grubby hanky. "I'm a respectable woman, and I have been made a legitimate *proposal of marriage*. I have accepted it, and now I am going to meet my husband."

Jem stared at her, thunderstruck. "*Meet* him? Why, you brazen hussy—you mean to tell me you ain't even *seen* him before?"

The girl glared at him, and for an instant, he thought she might actually go for his jaw, but instead, she dug into her purse and produced the letter. "There!" she cried, and held the paper up, "*You tell me* that isn't a right and proper marriage proposal!"

Jem looked down at the letter she was holding.

My dear girl,

I am keenly aware that the two of us have known each other very briefly, and your maidenly sensibilities must shrink from joining yourself to a man you have only just met. But I hope that you will not allow our imperfect acquaintance to prejudice your answer to the question I am about to ask.

Our last meeting led me to hope that you would look favourably on my request for your hand in marriage. You are a sweet and beautiful young woman, and I would

*count it an honour beyond my deserving if you would
agree to be my wife.*

*I do not have the gift of a glib tongue, and it is difficult
for me to express my feelings. But be assured that
should you agree to be my wife, I will do my utmost to
make you happy and to make your life as comfortable as
is within my power.*

I await your answer with a hopeful heart.

Sincerely,

Nate Trowbridge.

"It says that you met him already," he answered, in a
hard voice, and for an instant she looked nonplussed,
but she recovered instantly.

"Of course we've *met*," she replied scornfully. "I meant,
I'm going to meet him *at his house*."

"Where's the envelope I gave you?" he demanded. "That'll
tell the story, quick enough! It was addressed to a woman
named Emma-something, I'll testify—not any Molly
Clanahan!"

She tossed her head and looked out the window. "I don't
know what became of it," she mumbled. "Why would I
keep it?"

"I know why," he replied angrily. "Because it proves
you're lying! If you've got any sense, you'll take my offer
while it still stands. Because if you follow me to the Circle
T, and Mr Trowbridge says he ain't never met you, I'll
kick you to the moon, bustle-first—female or *no* female!"

Another rap at the door made them both look up. "It's
your station, Miss Clanahan," the porter called.

Jem turned grim eyes to her face, but she smiled primly and stood up.

"Coming," she purred, and to his fury, swept out into the corridor as calmly as if she was already Mrs Nate Trowbridge.

Chapter
Sixteen

Molly arrived at the boarding house quietly and by the back door. She hated the thought of leaving, just as she was getting to make friends there, but she had no choice.

She slipped up the stairs and into her own apartment and packed the few things she had without lighting the lamp. Jack was still watching the place, and since it was a public boarding house, there was nothing to stop him from walking right in if he had a mind.

She wanted to be *long* gone when that happened.

She had the few paltry coins the old bag at the shop had paid her, and it wasn't enough, but it was going to have to do until she could find a new place and a new job.

She might pawn the gun if she got desperate enough.

A knock at the door made her jump. She didn't answer until Mrs O'Malley's voice called: "Molly, there's a fellow downstairs for you. Says he has a message to give you."

Molly's heart jumped, and the hairs on her neck prickled.

"Molly?"

"Is it—is it the same fellow you told me about before?" she croaked.

"No, it's another fellow this time. What I wouldn't give to have so many young men asking after me!" She giggled, and withdrew.

Molly bit her lip and then pulled the pistol out of her bag, hiked up her skirts, and strapped it to her leg with a garter. Then she shook out her skirts again, took a deep breath, and went down to the living room.

When she got there, to her intense relief, it wasn't Jack. It was a handsome sandy-haired cowboy. The fellow was roaring drunk and was half-lying on the sofa when she first came in, but as soon as he saw her, he jumped up and took off his hat.

Her eyes went to the doorway. There was nobody in it, and she moved to close and lock it behind the man before she greeted him.

"My name is Jem McClary. I was sent to deliver this to you, personal." He handed her a letter.

She glanced down at it. It was addressed to somebody else, but the possibility that it might contain cash made her open it.

To her disappointment, there was no money in the envelope. But when she read the letter, another, *better* possibility suddenly dawned on her. It was dishonest, and it was risky, but a golden opportunity had just fallen into her lap.

Some man named Nate Trowbridge was proposing marriage to a woman he hardly knew. He'd sent Jem to deliver this proposal, and Jem plainly didn't know the woman, either.

What if—what if *she* claimed the man's proposal and answered his letter?

The return address on the envelope told her that a little play-acting would be worth the effort. Nate Trowbridge was apparently the owner of the *Circle T Ranch, Indian Rock*. That meant he had lots of money.

The envelope also gave the woman's name—Emmaline—but she could throw that away and produce the letter as proof of her claim because it was only addressed to *My dear girl.*

If she could get alone with the man who wrote the letter, just for a few minutes, maybe she could persuade him to buy her silence. Just enough to get her a train ticket out of Colorado and to some place where Jack McGee would never find her.

Molly's conscience reared up unexpectedly and cuffed her hard for the idea; but she glanced out the window and into the yard and silenced it. She might feel bad for playing this Trowbridge fellow such a shabby trick, but she was penniless, she was desperate, and now she was being hunted.

She couldn't *afford* a conscience.

So she had smiled at the young cowboy, led him into the kitchen, and made him up a plate, and while he was busy eating, she poured out a glass of buttermilk and sprinkled the last of the Jack McGee Special into it.

He'd already been drunk, and it put him on the floor within minutes.

She'd sent a little neighbor boy up to Pine Street to hail a cab and gotten two of the men in the house to carry him out to it when it arrived, and while they were still there, she'd jumped into the cab with Jem and told the driver to hurry off.

He'd whipped up the horse, and they'd gone clattering down the street and away, but when she looked back over her shoulder, to her terror, Jack had risen from cover. He was standing in the middle of the road, watching her go with a pistol clenched in his hand.

She crouched down in the seat and prayed, but no shots came. After a few minutes, she dared to rise up again, and when she looked, this time the street was clear.

"Get us to the train station," she commanded the driver, "and hurry!"

They'd arrived there about seven o'clock, just in time for the last train out, and by that time, she'd found Jem's wallet and combed through it. He had about fifty dollars in cash, and she used it to pay the cabman, buy two first-class tickets to Indian Rock, and to bribe the porter to carry Jem out to their compartment.

The cowboy would wake up with a head like a bag of rocks and probably be pretty mad once he figured things out, but he looked like a decent sort, not the kind to raise his hand to a woman.

At least, that was what she was gambling.

And as for the man she was going to meet—she pulled the letter out and read it again—if he was as proper and stuffy in person as he was in his letters, it should be no problem at all to get a nice round sum in cash, and be on her way.

Probably within 24 hours, and that suited her down to the ground.

Because the sooner she got clean out of Colorado—the better.

***

By the time the train pulled into Indian Rock, it was completely dark, and the little train depot was shuttered and empty. Molly hung back and let the cowboy lead the way because she had no idea where the Circle T was. The little town was rolled up tight, except for one lonely light burning in the window of a little hotel.

The cowboy turned to her. "This is your last chance," he growled. "I'll pay you to stay at the hotel tonight, and if you leave an address, I'll mail you money from here on. But if you try to brazen this out, I'll see you in jail if it's the last thing I do!"

Molly bit her lip. It really *was* a good offer, but if she took it, *one*, Jem would go for his wallet to pay her hotel room and find out that she'd stolen his money. And *two*, she didn't have any address yet, and *three*, she didn't trust *maybe money*.

Cash on the barrel head was what she needed, and that was what she was going to demand.

So she shook her head. Jem cussed her and stomped off into the dark, and she followed.

But to her dismay, there was a little stable at the side of the train depot, just big enough for a horse or two. Jem pulled that one horse out, saddled it as she watched, and glared at her as she stood on the depot platform.

"All right, then. Have it your way!" he barked. "Sleep out here, with the bobcats and coyotes. It's good enough for you!"

Molly watched in dismay as he spurred the horse and bounded off in the dark, but now that she'd arrived, she had to play her hand out as best she could. She didn't dare to wait in town for fear that Jack might follow her. So she picked her way down the steps of the platform by the light of one lamp, peered forlornly into the empty stall, and started walking.

The sound of Jem's pony galloping away soon faded into the distance, and everything got quiet except the sound of owls hooting in the deep stillness. Molly became uncomfortably aware that she was in the deep wilderness, now, but luckily, the moon was out, and she could see just well enough to keep to the little dirt road; so she trudged doggedly on.

Her skirts were dragging in the dirt, and she hiked them up; then shrieked out as she slipped on an unseen rock and almost fell face down on the road. Molly threw her arms out and regained her balance, then pulled her mouth down and blinked back unexpected tears.

Nobody at the Circle T was expecting her, and nobody at the Circle T wanted her, but she was going to the Circle T anyway.

It felt *horrible*, what she was doing, and she supposed it *was* horrible. Just a year ago, she wouldn't have dreamed of it. But this was what her life had come to. She was a criminal now, or near enough, and she had no one and nothing except her own hands and her own wits.

It was almost like that story in the Bible that her mother had once read to her, about the outcast Ishmael. *His hand was against every man, and every man's hand was against him.*

It wasn't a very comforting thought, as she walked alone in the dark, but it was better than going back to the Golden Nugget with Jack McGee, and so she walked on.

Chapter
Seventeen

"What?"

Nate looked up from his desk into Jem McClary's apologetic blue eyes, closed his own, and shook his head as if to recalibrate it.

"I'm sorry, Mr Trowbridge," Jem said in quiet shame. "I delivered your letter to the wrong address. I was drunk off that stuff the dentist gave me for my tooth, and *I gave your letter to the wrong girl.*"

Nate stared at him in horror. The implications of this incredible news began to hit him like snow cascading off a roof. His proposal letter, the private letter that had bared his deepest feelings, and his offer of marriage, was in the hands of a stranger. It was *unthinkable.*

And now, he had to apologize. He had to explain, to a stranger, how a mistake that big had even *happened.*

Nate pulled a hand over his mouth. There was even the hideous possibility that the story might become generally known, or God forbid, even find its way into the *papers.* It could become a *scandal.*

There was even the possibility that the Chiswicks might find out. That Emmaline ...

He looked up at Jem in wordless appeal.

"I'm as sorry as I can be, Mr Trowbridge," Jem replied in a guilty voice. "I know I'm as good as gone, but if there's something I can still do to make it right, I will."

Nate wiped his chin with the palm of one hand and stared blankly at the wall. "No, you're not off the ranch, Jem," he replied softly. "You're a good man, and it was an honest mistake, even if it was a" —he took a deep breath—"a *big* one. I'll go to Denver tomorrow, find the girl, and explain."

Jem set his jaw. "That's not all there is to it, Mr Trowbridge," he mumbled tightly. "The girl that got your letter, is a—well, I may as well just say it—she's a low kind of woman, Mr Trowbridge, a real gold digger. She saw her chance, and she took it. You won't have to go to Denver to see her. I woke up this evening on the train with her sitting beside me—most likely she gave me something to knock me out, and I don't need to tell you what kind of woman knows those tricks—and she said that she was coming here to accept your offer of marriage.

"I tried everything I could think of to get her to flare off. I even offered her money, but she's dead set to come here and see *you*. I dumped her at the station in town, but she'll be here in a little while."

Nate stared at him in horror, but he set his mouth and began to set his thoughts in order.

"It's all right," he began after another deep breath. "Stay here with me. I'll talk to her when she comes."

He reached for the bell pull, and after a few minutes, Maria arrived at the door of the library. She stood in stolid silence as he commanded, "Maria, we're expecting a guest tonight. Will you go downstairs, please, and wait for her? Bring her up to me when she arrives."

Maria nodded and disappeared, and he placed both hands over his mouth. The woman would want money, of course, and he should be prepared to pay. Cash in exchange for the letter, that would be the bargain; though he wasn't in much of a position to haggle unless he employed tactics that no gentleman could contemplate.

"She claims that the two of you have met before," Jem told him as he unlocked a drawer in his desk and pulled out a small strongbox. "She's playing like she believes the letter was meant for her, even though I told her it was addressed to another woman. She threw the envelope away because it proves she's lying, but I saw it, Mr Trowbridge, and I'll testify that it wasn't addressed to her!"

"Do you know her name?"

"Molly Clanahan," Jem replied in a disgusted voice, and Nate closed his eyes and felt that his cup was full.

She was Irish.

They waited in tense silence, and ten minutes later, the sound of a woman's voice in the hall outside alerted them that she'd arrived. A moment later, Maria opened the door to admit Molly Clanahan.

Her dress was cheap, stained, and bedraggled with the long walk from the depot, but Molly Clanahan swept into the room as boldly as if she owned it, and she held her head as high as a queen. Nate stood up in outraged amazement.

"Why—you're the woman who knocked me down on the sidewalk!" he exclaimed. Jem's eyes questioned him with an expression of disbelief, and even the woman looked momentarily startled.

"You don't mean to say that you *know* her?" Jem blurted, and he shook his head.

"I was standing on the sidewalk in Denver, waiting for a cab, and she plowed right into me and knocked me down." He frowned. "Well, out with it, woman!" he told her sternly. "My man here tells me you wanted to see me. What's your price for the letter?"

But to his amazement, the woman reacted as if he'd slapped her. She dug in her bag for a handkerchief and began to cry.

"Oh, I never dreamed a man could be so cruel!" she sobbed. "To propose marriage, to get my poor hopes up, and then to spurn me so shameful! I came here in good faith," she wept. "A man of the world like you, with all the advantages of money and society, should be ashamed to mock a poor girl like me, with nothing to cherish but her dreams of love!"

"You lying bobcat!" Jem cried, but Nate held up his hand.

"You cannot expect me to believe your story," he replied in a soft, grim tone. "Jem says that you drugged him and threw away the envelope that proves I wrote the letter to another woman. Come now, give it up. Name your price, and let's have done with this tawdry charade."

"It's not tawdry!" she cried, and to his amazement, there were tears in her eyes. "Why shouldn't I have dreams, just like any other girl? And why shouldn't I believe it when your own man delivered your marriage proposal right to my door and asked for me, special? I didn't chase after you. You came to me!"

Nate frowned. "Bah, woman, you can't believe that I'd propose to someone I'd never met!"

Her crushed expression changed to one of confusion. "But—your letter *says*, we didn't know one another all that well," she objected. "It said, you hoped that our slight acquaintance wouldn't prejudice me against your proposal."

"Well, but—that's different," he sputtered. "I meant it for a *completely* different girl, and you had to know that!"

"Why?" she whimpered. "Men and women marry each other every day without knowing much about the other. Haven't you ever heard of a mail order bride?"

Nate stared at her in horror. "I would *never—*"

Molly tilted her head to one side and explained in a wounded voice: "That's what I thought this *was*, Mr Trowbridge. I took it for a proposal of marriage like those mail order brides. Of course you don't know your intended, but the man writes the woman, and makes an offer of marriage, and she accepts, and then comes out to where he lives, and they get married. They got all their married life to get to know one another."

Nate's mouth dropped open, and he shook his head wordlessly. Jem, seeing that his employer had been robbed of the power of speech, broke in: "You knew nothing of the kind, you gold digging wench! Get back where you came from or so *help* me—"

"I'm going to say it one last time," Nate broke in sternly. "*Name your price.* It's late, and I have neither the time nor the patience for bad acting."

Molly Clanahan's mouth crumpled up, and to Nate's dismay, she burst out into loud wailing.

But what happened next surprised them all. The door flew open, and Leonie stood there, with tears sparkling in her eyes, and her mouth crumpled up.

"It's too cruel!" she cried, and to Nate's outrage, ran over and took Molly into her arms. "Nate, if you send poor Molly away, I'll never *speak* to you again! She only wants someone to *love,* just like every other woman in the world!"

Nate stared at her in wounded dismay. "Leonie, go back to bed this instant! This conversation is not meant for your ears!"

"I heard every word!" Leonie shot back. "I'm sorry for poor Emmaline, but don't you *see,* Nate? The odds of this happening are a million to one. It was *meant* to be. It's your *fate!*"

"Oh, for—Jem, take her out of here," he commanded, and Jem moved to hustle Leonie out, but she pulled her arm out of his hand and cried defiantly: "Nate, I mean it, if you send her away, you're cruel and heartless, just like she said. All she did was believe what you wrote! Nate!"

Jem dragged her out, pulled the door shut after them, and Nate returned grimly to Molly Clanahan.

"Well, which is it? Are you going to come to terms now, or are you going to be thrown out of my house? Those are your choices."

Molly drew herself up and shook her head proudly. "I'm not a beggar, come here to plead for your mercy. If you don't want me, I won't push myself on you. But you're no gentleman, to raise my poor hopes only to dash them, and so I'll tell the world!"

Nate stared at her and ground his teeth in helpless rage. "*Name your terms,*" he growled.

And Molly Clanahan wiped her eyes, smiled primly, and settled herself comfortably in a chair.

Chapter
Eighteen

Nate crawled into bed, sighed, and closed his eyes. He was exhausted, and his feather bed was as soft as a cloud. But he would get no sleep that night.

He pulled his hands over his face. Molly Clanahan was a shrewd one; he had to give her that. She'd been quick to seize her opportunity, and relentless in exploiting it.

Although he could still hardly believe it, she hadn't asked him for a penny. Instead, she had clearly decided to play the part of a jilted fiancée, at least for now. His guess was that she'd taken one look at his house, and his furniture, and his land, and decided that she could do far better than a few hundred dollars and a train ticket.

And Leonie, in her innocent enthusiasm for romance, had supported her.

Nate sighed deeply. Leonie didn't yet understand that there were bad, ruthless people in the world, people who would take advantage of them for their wealth. Now, he would have to explain it to her, and hope that she would understand.

He turned over restlessly and jammed the pillow up under his jaw.

Under the façade of her 'wounded feelings,' Molly had threatened to publish her maltreatment to the world. And the price of her silence had stunned him.

She wanted him to marry her.

It was an outrageous demand, and he refused it at once, but she had promised—if such a woman's promises held any weight—to be discreet and conformable.

"There's lots of people who marry for convenience," she urged him. "I'll make no demands on you if you're afraid of *that*. But I'm as good a choice as another if you're of a mind to marry someone you don't know."

He'd sputtered in helpless fury, but she only stared at him. "Well, why *not* me? I've been told that I'm easy on the eyes, and I wouldn't make trouble. You should listen to your little sister."

At that, he'd roared: "If you think I'd let a woman like you anywhere *near* my sister—"

She had given him such a look then, from those lovely blue eyes that it made him glad he had a pistol in his desk, but she replied: "I won't say a word to your sister. Marry me, and let me live here for a year. Just one year! Then I'll move on, my hand on the Bible, and you can say that I abandoned you, and divorce me, and complain that you were hoodwinked by a crafty woman. Everyone will feel sorry for you. They *always* feel sorry for the man. They'll take you back into society. You won't lose."

He had stared at her in speechless rage and wondered for an instant if she was an escapee. He barked:

"You've come here to *hide*, haven't you? Are you running from the law?"

"No, I swear it! But you're going to have to take your chances with me, just like I'm taking my chances with you, that you mean what you say. Marry me, and the letter is yours, and I'll never speak of it again. I'll be the one taking all the risk."

He had scoffed at her and had come within a hair of throwing her out, letter or no letter. But he could hardly turn her out into the middle of the wilderness at night; that was basic decency, regardless of what she'd done.

So he had told her: "I'll tell Maria to give you a room tonight. But that does *not* mean that I believe you for an instant. Now go—get out."

She had risen up then, with that odd look of pride, and had swept out of the room. He had instructed Maria to put her in the servant's quarters, below the kitchen, and to give her only the basic necessities, but anger boiled in his brain.

His first impulse was to call the law down on her because he was quite sure that she was wanted for *something*. Or, alternatively, to take Jem's advice and demand his letter at gunpoint.

But the former would only ensure that she'd go public. And the latter, of course, would be barbaric and absurd, and give her a *genuine* excuse to accuse him of wrongdoing.

But he wasn't going to marry that redheaded strumpet, no matter what she threatened to do to him. He would make a clean breast to Emmaline and pray that she'd understand.

Emmaline. Nate pulled his hands over his face. What would she think of all this? He was very sure that she would shrink from the whole sordid affair. Emmaline was a refined young lady, and anything that smacked of intrigue, or blackmail, or low women like Molly Clanahan, was sure to be repulsive to her.

But Emmaline seemed a pliable enough sort of girl, and if he carefully explained how things had gone wrong, he might defuse the situation that way. He was hopeful that if he explained in just the right way, she would understand.

Of course, her parents were another matter. The Chiswicks were justifiably anxious that their eldest daughter should marry the right sort of man. Up until now, he *had* been the right sort, but a scandal might make the Chiswicks withdraw their support of his suit.

And even if both Emmaline and her parents forgave him all, there was still the threat of a tawdry article in the scandal sheets, linking his name to Molly Clanahan's. It would ruin their social prospects in Denver—and not just his and Emmaline's, but poor Leonie's, as well.

It was even possible that the news of this ridiculous misadventure might get back to *London*.

Nate stared at the ceiling grimly. It was one thing for him to risk his own future, but he had no right to gamble with Leonie's.

Of course he could denounce the woman as an adventuress and deny her claims, but the story would make both of them the talk of the town.

His family's unusual marriage customs would be put on display for the world to see and discuss. And it wouldn't be easy to explain to Emmaline how his proposal letter had ended up in Molly Clanahan's hands, instead of hers. At best, the story made him look like a fool, and at worst, it made him look like a cad who frequented brothels. People would think that he wrote an offer of marriage to one of the hussies during a drunken debauch and then reneged on the offer when he sobered up.

He groaned and placed his hands over his face. He had to find a way out of this mess that didn't result in social ruin for himself and his sister—but as the hours ticked away, Nate was finding that it was going to be much harder than he thought to get rid of Molly Clanahan.

Chapter
Nineteen

The maid led the way down the dark, narrow staircase, her lamp held high. She spoke only three words.

"Watch your step."

As Molly descended, she thought wryly that it was good advice because she'd just done the worst and most brazen deed of her life, and she wouldn't have blamed Nate Trowbridge if he'd thrown her out of his house with the garbage.

The cowboy had been mad enough to *slap* her, but the swell had been too much of a gentleman to allow it.

She had put on a brave face upstairs, but Molly felt heartily ashamed of herself, now that the deed was done, and it was forever too late to take it back, but she consoled herself with the thought that Jack McGee would never think to look for her *here*. He'd never stop in such a forsaken place as Indian Rock, first off, and even if he did, he wouldn't dare to come out to a place like the Circle T. There were too many men and too many guns waiting.

Jack didn't like to fight other men. He only fought *women*.

The maid unlocked a door at the foot of the stairs, and it opened onto a narrow corridor. They walked down to the third door. The woman unlocked it and let it swing open.

"You can stay here tonight," she murmured. "I'll bring you some food."

She turned to go but paused and added over her shoulder: "Mr Trowbridge told me to lock the door behind me, but I'll come down and unlock it tomorrow morning before breakfast."

Molly gave her a frightened glance but made no reply, and the woman vanished.

Molly walked inside the little room. The walls were made of whitewashed brick, and the furniture was as simple here as it was ornate upstairs. There was one single bed with a sheet and blanket, a side table with a water pitcher and a lamp, a chest of drawers, and a closet.

She sank down onto the mattress wearily. She'd had a very tiring day, what with wrangling the cowboy onto the train and walking all the way to the house from the depot, but she had no pleasure in her accomplishments. She reached down into the bosom of her dress, pulled out the neatly-folded letter, and read it again sadly.

It was clear that it had been written by an honourable man.

Only a year ago, she would've given *anything* to have had a letter like this from an honourable man.

She had been desperate then, too. She had lost her father and her brother to influenza during a terrible winter. They had been deep in debt and living on the hope of a good crop the next year. She had nothing with which to repay the bank, and it had finally repossessed their family farm. She had been forced out of her home.

She had no other family, and no one to turn to. She was just a farm girl who knew how to sew, but there were no jobs for seamstresses in Bolingbroke, Kansas.

She'd been penniless and desperate enough to answer an advertisement for a *mail order bride*.

Molly squeezed back tears and pressed her lips into a thin line. Oh, if *only* she had waited, if *only* she'd tried something else!

Anything else.

But she had replied to the ad, and she'd gotten a hopeful letter in return from a man named Jack McGee.

Dear Molly,

I was real glad to get your letter today. I was afraid maybe you had decided it was too big a chance to take, to come out and marry a man you ain't met.

I was glad to see you still got an open mind.

This is my picture. I took it this year, so it's a true likeness. I'd be pleased if you sent me one of you so I could put it on my mantelpiece. You sound like a real pretty girl, and I bet you are one.

In answer to your question, my dear wife departed last spring. I miss her something terrible. I know that a new wife wouldn't make me miss her less, but a man does need companionship in life.

I run a business in Cheyenne, and it's real successful too. It keeps me busy; but it ain't the same without a family to come home to.

I hope you understand.

Sincerely,

Jack.

Molly's mouth twisted. Jack *had* been good-looking, in a rough, grizzled kind of way. He was more than six feet tall and very muscular. He had dark red hair, and eyes that were so light they almost looked as if they were clear. He had a full moustache, but no beard.

But there were signs even in his photograph that gave him away if she'd only known what to look for. His nose looked as if it'd been broken once, and there was a white scar on his jaw that had been visible even in the photo.

But she had been a naïve farm girl who'd never even had a fellow of her own. What did she know about men?

She had sent a picture of herself, the only one she possessed, and Jack had written back quickly with a marriage proposal. He sent her the money to take the train to Wyoming from Kansas. At the time, she had thought it was the luckiest thing that ever happened to her.

But it hadn't taken long for her to find out that she'd fallen into a trap.

Molly stared at the wall blankly.

As soon as she'd arrived at the train station, Jack had dragged her back to his "business"—the Golden Nugget, a filthy saloon and brothel on the seamy side of Cheyenne. He'd thrown her into a back room with ten other girls and had ordered her to put on a dress and come out and "entertain the customers."

She had burst into tears, and one of the women there had taken pity on her. She walked over and put an arm around her shoulders.

"There now, dearie, don't cry," she had murmured. "Long as you do what Jack says to do, you'll be all right. Here, put on this dress, like he told you, and come out with us. All you have to do is put a little of the Jack McGee

Special into your gentleman's drink, smile, and be *friendly*."

The other women laughed, and her comforter slid a little vial of powder into her hand. "Just sprinkle it into his drink when he ain't lookin', dearie," the woman whispered and put a finger to her smiling lips.

She'd pushed away and dashed for the nearest door like a wild animal, only to find it locked from the outside. She had been in the act of opening a window when Jack had come in, jerked her around by one shoulder, and knocked her to the floor with one blow to her jaw.

"Put on that dress and get out on the floor, or next time I'll break your arm!" he'd roared, and then he turned on the rest of the silent women.

"Make sure she's with you," he growled, "or the rest of you will get it, too!"

She had huddled on the floor with a bruised and throbbing jaw, and the others had made her put on the dress. They pressed the vial back in her hand and yanked her to her feet.

"If you don't do as you're told, we'll *all* get thrashed," one hissed. "So *do what he says*!"

She had walked out into the saloon feeling terrified and ashamed because she was only wearing a red satin slip of a dress. The air was so smoky that the lights looked blurred, and the shouts and songs of drunken men filled the air.

***

The sound of the door opening made Molly open her eyes again. The maid was standing in the doorway with a plate and a cup.

She walked across the room and set them down on the table, then walked out again without another word.

Molly looked over at the plate. There was a piece of bread, what looked like fried chicken, mashed potatoes, and a slice of tomato.

She took the plate in her hand, picked up a fork, and then bowed her head and dissolved into tears.

Chapter
Twenty

After a few hours, Molly woke with swollen eyes and a red nose, and for an instant, she didn't remember where she was. She sat bolt upright and rolled terrified eyes to the door, and then her memory came flooding back.

There was no clock in the little room, and no window, and she had no idea whether it was morning or night. Molly got out of bed and threw a little shawl around her nightgown. The maid had promised to come back and unlock the door, but when she padded out into the little hall, it was still bolted shut.

A flutter of panic beat against her ribs. What if the maid had lied? What if she *never* came back?' What if Nate Trowbridge had solved his problem by locking her away forever?

It was an unlikely, but terrible enough prospect to drive Molly out into the little hallway to have a look around. Hers was the third door down on the little passageway. The other two doors were locked but seemed likely to be servants' bedrooms, just like the one she had spent the night in.

There was another door at the end of the hall, and Molly walked down to it and turned the handle. To her surprise, the big door creaked open. There was a cool breath of air, and a damp, musty smell, and she got the sense of a cavernous space, but it was too dark inside to see anything; so she walked back to her own room and brought back the kerosene lamp.

As she had suspected, the big room was a root cellar and was filled and lined with shelf after shelf of canned goods and preserved fruits and vegetables in glass jars. Molly shook her head and smiled. It took her back to her childhood when her mother had put up corn, squash, beans, and tomatoes for the winter. And it helped to banish the lurid fear that she might be trapped below ground forever because the cellar had enough food to last a year or more.

Molly wandered from row to row, shining the light on dusty jars full of peaches, apples, pears, and watermelon; green beans, tomatoes, cucumbers, and beets.

There was a wooden case full of empty canning jars, and beyond, a head-high wine rack full of dusty bottles. Molly lifted one up to the light. The label was written in some language she couldn't read, but it looked very old and very fancy.

Champagne, it said. She knew what *that* was, anyway, even if she didn't like the taste. She returned the bottle carefully to its place on the rack and lifted the lamp.

The wine rack was the last case unless you counted an empty case of shelves on the far wall. Molly tilted her head, wondering if the woman who had put up all this food had fallen ill, or moved away, and had to leave her preparations unfinished.

The empty shelves were dusty, and Molly reached out to write her name there, but when she leaned against the case, to her startled surprise, it swung back like a door to reveal another yawning passage.

Molly danced backwards and lifted the lantern high. Its light revealed a rough dirt tunnel crisscrossed with spider webs. A mouse at the edge of the lantern light squeaked and scurried away, and Molly put one hand on her hip and raised her eyebrows.

Well, well, well! she thought to herself in surprise. *Maybe Mr Nate Trowbridge isn't as squeaky clean as he pretends! What kind of a man has a secret tunnel running to his basement?*

A man with something to hide—that's who!

She picked up a stick lying on the dirt floor of the tunnel, swept the cobwebs away from the entrance, and slowly entered. The tunnel ran straight ahead and on into darkness, and she bit her lip and looked back over her shoulder. Light streamed in through the cellar door, and so far there was no sign of the maid.

She swept the air in front of her with the stick and advanced step by step. The tunnel ran straight for a hundred feet and then tilted slightly to the left. It ran on for another hundred feet without branching or turning.

Molly peered around as she walked. The end of old roots stuck out of the earthen tunnel walls and mysterious insects scuttled away at her approach. Once a bat flapped past just above her head, and she almost dropped the lamp, but she kept walking as the tunnel seemed to rise, and she came to its end at last, about four hundred feet from the cellar door.

It looked like a dead end; the tunnel just stopped, without any exit that she could see until she lifted the lamp up. There, on the ceiling of the tunnel, was another door that looked like a trapdoor.

And when she swept the area with her lamp, she found what was also sure to be there: a rough ladder. When she walked closer, to her surprise, it was free of dust and spider webs and showed the signs of recent use. She set the lamp down on the ground and propped the ladder up against the back wall of the tunnel. It provided a neat and sturdy stairway to the door overhead.

Molly stopped at the bottom of the ladder and looked up. If she was caught snooping in the house, the swell would throw her out *sure*, but on the other hand, it might prove useful—or even important—to know how to get out of this basement.

She had learned the hard way that a side door could come in *very* handy.

She gripped the sides of the ladder and tested its strength. It felt sturdy, and she set her foot cautiously on the lowest rung, then the second rung, and then the third. Step by careful step, she climbed the ladder until her head almost touched the door.

Molly braced her feet against the ladder, pressed the palms of her hands against the door, and pushed up.

To her surprise, the door, though heavy, opened easily. She lifted it just an inch or two and was surprised to see that the tunnel had brought her across the wide back lawn and beyond to the barn. The tunnel door had been covered in hay—some of it sifted down on her, as she lifted it—and she calculated that it was located within an unused stall or storage area, at the end of the building opposite the entrance.

Morning light was streaming across the floor of the barn, and a child's voice was mumbling what sounded like irritated obscenities not very far away. She lowered the door a bit but saw the child unlatch a stall and lead a horse outside.

Well now, what do you make of that, she mumbled to herself; and let the door fall gently back into place.

She climbed back down the ladder, set it back where she had found it, took the lamp in her hand and returned the way she had come.

Why in thunder would a man dig a tunnel from his barn to his house?

She couldn't think of any sensible answer unless the man was receiving deliveries that he didn't want to advertise.

Maybe of *goods*—or maybe of *people*.

Molly shuddered and hurried back through the tunnel to the root cellar. She pushed the empty case back against the wall. It fell into place with a soft *snap*.

She lifted the lantern and moved back to the cellar door, but as she stood there, to her dismay, there was the sound of a loud jingling from the opposite end of the hall.

The *maid* had come back.

Molly ran down the hall and dived into her own room, shut the door behind her, set the lantern on the table, and jumped into bed.

And not a moment too soon: she had hardly pulled the covers up before there came a rap at her door.

"Ma'am? Are you awake?"

Molly yawned loudly and mumbled a bit for effect before she called: "I am now. Is it morning already?"

"Yes, ma'am. If you come upstairs, I have some breakfast for you."

"Thank you. I'll be there directly."

Molly threw the covers back, but as she washed and dressed, she was thinking that maybe she'd bitten off more than she could chew. Her scheme had been based on the assumption that Nate Trowbridge was an honest man.

Things might go badly for her if she'd misjudged him. If Nate Trowbridge was a man with secrets, she was taking a bigger risk than she'd thought.

Molly's mouth twisted. *It just goes to show you*, she thought bitterly. If life had taught her anything, it was that there *were* no good men. Even the most seemingly upright man was doing *something* he couldn't admit in public.

It made no sense, but the thought that Nate Trowbridge was just another scoundrel disappointed her.

But the knowledge that the basement had a secret tunnel was a piece of information that might prove useful, and Molly tucked it away in her mind, to be called for later, if needed.

The world was a dangerous place for a woman alone. A girl needed all the insurance she could get.

And so, Molly hiked her skirts up and tucked her pistol into her garter before going forth to meet the new day.

Chapter
Twenty-One

Leonie opened her bedroom door, crept to the top of the staircase, and pressed her ear to the lintel. She could just hear Nate talking to Jem in the downstairs hall.

"I'm going to Denver this morning to get this nonsense straightened out," he barked. "I may spend a few days there. When that woman comes out, I want you to march her to the train depot and put her on the first car going *anywhere*."

"Yes, *sir*. It'll be my pleasure."

"Give her one last opportunity to sell the letter. Maybe if she sees that I mean business, she'll give in."

Jem uttered a grunt expressive of doubt but said no more, and Nate's quick footsteps faded off down the hall.

Leonie hurried downstairs, peeked around the corner, and saw Jem drift outside and sit down in a chair on the front porch. She scuttled off into the front salon and down the hallway leading to the kitchen.

When she peeked through the little window in the swinging door, she saw Molly seated at the kitchen table drinking coffee, and she swept in.

Leonie draped herself across the doorway for dramatic effect. When no one looked at her, she cried: "Oh, you *poor* creature! My heart simply *breaks* for you!"

Molly's hand froze in the act of lifting the cup to her lips. She rolled doubtful blue eyes to Leonie's face.

"I won't let them send you away," Leonie declared with a quick glance over her shoulder. "It isn't right to *cast you on the world*, and Nate will come to see it by and by. He isn't as cruel as he seems. Don't take last night to heart, dear Molly!"

Maria received this outburst stoically, but her face darkened as she turned back to washing dishes. She mumbled: "*Chica estupida! Mojar la cabeza en agua fría.*"

When Molly offered no commentary, Leonie came to herself, hurried over to the table, and pulled up a chair beside hers.

"Don't despair," she pled. "I won't let Nate spurn you! Your coming here was *so* romantic—and you're *just* what Nate needs! Oh, when I *think* of the two of you meeting *by accident* in Denver—it was just a *miracle*! And then, Jem bringing Nate's proposal right to your door! It's *obvious* that your love is just *fated* to be, but Nate is just too stubborn to admit it!"

Molly listened to her breathless speech in silence, set her coffee cup down on the table, and folded her hands in her lap.

"You're Mr Trowbridge's little sister?" she ventured.

"Oh, yes, I'm sorry." Leonie giggled. "I was so excited, I forgot to introduce myself! *Leonie Trowbridge.*" She smiled and gave a quick curtsy.

Molly smiled back. "Glad to know you, Leonie," she returned. "I'm Molly Clanahan."

Leonie practically bounced in her chair. "Now that you're here, we'll have to mount a *campaign* to help Nate see how wrongheaded and stubborn it is for him to propose to Emmaline Chiswick when it's clear that *you* are his soul mate! And as much as I would've loved to have Emmaline and my dear Francie as *real* sisters, I must make the sacrifice for true love, and Nate's happiness!"

Molly smiled a bit. "You're very generous," she demurred.

"Well, but don't you agree, dear Molly?" Leonie asked anxiously. "You and my brother Nate were *meant* to be wed! Surely you must feel it?"

"Oh, yes, *yes* I feel it," Molly was quick to agree, "and the sooner, the better, as far as I'm concerned."

Leonie beamed at her. "There, I *knew* it must be so! And to think, of *all* people, Nate has been blessed with a fate-ordained romance! I might almost say he doesn't *deserve* it, being so unromantic usually, but one mustn't give in to envy."

Molly laughed a little and took another sip of coffee. "You're a pretty girl. I expect you'll find a young man someday." She smiled. "Just be sure he's after you, though—and not your money."

A plate shattered abruptly on the kitchen floor, and Maria bent over to retrieve the pieces, mumbling angrily in Spanish.

Molly shot her a respectful look and cleared her throat. "Well, ah—have we got any word what your brother is doing this morning, Leonie?"

Leonie's blonde curls bobbed. "Oh, yes. He's gone to Denver. He said he's going to straighten things out there with the Chiswicks. And I'm afraid he asked Jem to—to escort you to the train depot."

Maria muttered devoutly in Spanish, and the plates in the sink rattled.

Molly bit her lip. "I *see*."

"Oh, but don't be downcast, Molly!" Leonie said brightly. "*I'll* protect you! We'll go up to my rooms, and you can stay with me. Jem won't *dare* come in on us. And I'll lock the doors."

Molly glanced at the kitchen door. "Where is Jem?" she enquired.

"I saw him sitting in a chair on the front porch," Leonie replied. "But don't worry. We'll go up the back stairs, and he won't see us."

Molly glanced warily at Maria as she washed the dishes, but she said nothing, and Leonie grasped her hand and led her out by the service stairway.

"This is going to be so exciting!" Leonie told her thrillingly. "It's the first real adventure I've ever had!"

Molly looked down at her with a sympathetic expression and went a little pink. "Well, but—just remember, girl, there's such a thing as too much excitement. You're a young lady, and young ladies can't be too careful. You'd do better to be like your brother. *Cautious*."

Leonie's earnest blue eyes met hers in dismay. "Oh, *never!*" she vowed. "Nate is so deadly boring!"

"There's worse things than being *bored*," Molly mumbled and followed Leonie up the narrow staircase.

Chapter
Twenty-Two

"You have *such* pretty hair," Leonie marvelled, as she brushed Molly's long red hair with a silver brush. "It's so long and shiny." She giggled suddenly and picked something out of it. "But how in the world did you get a piece of *hay* in it?"

Molly looked up at her quickly and bit her lip. "Oh—maybe a piece blew into my hair, in town last night," she mumbled, and rubbed her nose.

Leonie giggled and brushed the long, red strands flat. "You know, you really should put your hair up on top of your head," she went on. "That style is all the rage in Paris this year."

"You don't say."

"*Mmm.* And I wager you'd be *perfection* in a green dress. *I know*, Molly," she said suddenly, "why don't you let me dress you up, just the way I see you in my mind, and Nate will come back from Denver and simply be *slain* by your beauty and will fight against his passion for *weeks* but finally have to surrender to your charms and profess his undying love!"

Molly blinked at her. "All that, huh?"

"Oh *yes*. It happens all the time in Mrs Willifred Smythe-Thompson's romances," Leonie replied earnestly. "She's an acknowledged authority on courtly love."

Molly stared at her own reflection in Leonie's gilded mirror. "If you say so."

Leonie pulled Molly's hair up on top of her head. "I'm learning to style my own hair," she confided, "and I'm going to practice on you. Is that all right?"

"If you want to," Molly murmured, and Leonie smiled in triumph.

"I'm going to ask Maria to make you some dresses," Leonie nattered on, "a green one and a yellow one and—I think, a white one. Redheads look especially elegant in white, don't you think?"

Molly gave her a quick look. "I don't know. I haven't had many dresses that colour."

"Then we'll have to experiment."

Leonie stepped back and surveyed the result of her work with pleasure. "You look *very* elegant with your hair swept up," was her assessment. "You should wear it that way more often."

Molly gave her a quick glance. "I'm grateful for your help, Leonie," she said tentatively, "but what I'd love more than anything right now is a nice long soak. Any hope I could get one?"

"Oh, of *course*!" Leonie cried and set the brush down at once. "I'll ring for Maria and have her draw up a hot bath. I should have thought of it before!"

"Oh, I'm not complaining," Molly replied quickly, "you've been more than kind, but I've been away from home for awhile now."

"Say no more," Leonie reassured her.

***

Thirty minutes later, Leonie saw Molly off to the big marble bathroom and returned to her own chambers feeling the warm glow of a good morning's work. Molly was a beautiful young woman, and with a little help, she couldn't fail to win Nate's heart, even if he *was* unpromising material for a romance.

Love—and *fate*—would conquer all.

After a few minutes, there came a brisk rapping on her chamber doors.

"Who is it?"

Jem's voice came from the other side. "Miss Leonie, Maria told me that woman is in there with you. Your brother told me to take her out of this house, and I'm going to. Open the door now. You've played long enough."

"I'm not playing," she replied serenely. "Molly is a wronged woman, and I support her. It's my apartment, and I can entertain whatever guests I like."

"She ain't a guest, Miss Leonie, she's a gold digger and a—well, all *you* need to know is that she's trying to take advantage of your brother. She ain't your friend, or his."

Leonie twined a shining curl around her finger and picked up a romance. "I'll be the judge of who my friends are, and who they're not," she replied, then threw the book down and went to open the door.

Jem was standing on the other side, frowning. He glanced over her shoulder, and seeing no one in the apartment, turned his eyes to her face.

"Where have you got her hid, Miss Leonie? Come on now, don't make this hard."

She looked up into his eyes and dimpled, "You don't have to call me *miss*." She smiled. "My friends call me Leonie."

"All right then, Mi—Leonie," he replied in a level voice. "But if you really want to be my friend, then tell me where you got that woman hid. The sooner she's out of this house, the better for all concerned."

"Can't I be friends with *everybody*?" Leonie asked in a mischievous tone.

Jem frowned at her. "No, not this time you can't," he replied flatly. "You have to choose between your brother and a low-down, sneaking bobcat who's come here to take advantage of him. I would think it'd be *easy* to choose," he told her.

"But what if it's not that simple?" Leonie smiled and leaned toward him. "What if she's his *soul mate*?"

Jem sputtered and put his hands on his hips. "Your brother is right, Mi—*Leonie*. You got a head full of birds and flowers and pretty words, but life ain't always like that. In fact, life *usually* ain't like that, and the sooner you get that straight in your head—"

"Oh, I can't help it if I'm a *romantic*," she teased and pushed his hat back from his brow with a pink finger. Jem took his hat away from her and asked, sternly:

"Where's that woman, Leonie?"

Leonie pouted. "Oh, since you *will* be a grouch about it—she's in the bathtub."

"*In the—*"

"Well, it's customary to let your guests freshen up if they want to."

"For the last time, *she ain't a guest.*"

Leonie lifted her chin. "She is to *me*. And leave her alone, Jem McClary, or I'll tell Nate that you tried to kiss me."

Jem's mouth fell open. "*Tried to*—but that's a *lie*, and you know it!"

Leonie nodded. "But Nate doesn't know it," she added significantly. "You just leave Molly alone, and I won't tell Nate any such thing. Though—" she leaned toward him and dimpled— "you *could* kiss me if you *wanted* to."

"I ain't never laid a finger on you, and I ain't never going to!" Jem gasped and took a step backward.

Leonie frowned. "Well, that's a nice thing to say!" she replied crossly. "Don't you think I'm pretty?"

"Well—"

"I must say, if you're going to come here and boss me around, and insult me, I'm not sure I want to be your friend after all," she pouted. "Saying you don't *want* to kiss me is just the same as calling me ugly."

"Now listen here, Leonie," Jem began, but Leonie waved him away.

"You go on about your business, Jem McClary," she told him airily, "and I'll go about mine." She went to close the door, but Jem put his hand on the edge.

"Your brother gave me an order, Leonie," he told her quietly. "Molly Clanahan has to go."

"Oh, you look so worried! But everything will be all right," she told him sunnily. "You can just *ignore* Nate like I do."

Jem looked down at the floor and then up into Leonie's serene face. "Leonie, you don't have the authority to ignore your brother, and neither do I!"

"Oh, yes I do," she countered sweetly. "Because I own *half* this ranch. Didn't Nate tell you *that*?"

Jem's mouth fell open, and Leonie closed the door with a *snap*.

Chapter
Twenty-Three

The compartment door closed behind the porter with a *snap*, and Nate glared at it for a second or two before he turned back to his newspaper. That made the second time he'd been unnecessarily short with the porter, though the man had done nothing to warrant a rebuke.

The prospect of baring his soul to Emmaline and her parents had set him on edge. No one had been able to do anything right for him all day, and it was nothing but rubbishing *nerves.*

The sound of a soft knock on the door made him jump, and he barked: "Yes, what is it now?"

The porter opened the door and approached him warily. "Your breakfast, sir." The man set a steaming plate of buttered eggs, bacon and biscuits before him, and withdrew as quickly as was seemly.

Nate gave the plate his tepid consideration. His appetite had vanished, and he pushed the bacon and eggs away. Instead, he bit at his fingernails.

Just a week ago, his future had seemed bright and promising, but now all was dark and dreary. How was it possible that one silly mistake could have such disastrous consequences?

That redheaded adventuress had knocked him down in every sense of the word, and now he found himself having to swipe dirt off his reputation, just as he'd had to swipe it off his clothes.

For the thousandth time, he wished he'd never met Molly Clanahan, but it was useless to indulge in fantasy. He would have to confide in Emmaline, and in her parents, and trust that their long family friendship would withstand this sordid scandal.

Nate closed his eyes and prayed fervently:

Oh, Lord, help me. Please help me preserve our family's good name, and please show me mercy when I explain to the Chiswicks.

And Lord, please smite that redheaded gold digger!

Amen.

***

All during the train ride to Denver, and his stroll back to the luxurious boarding house, Nate rehearsed the speech he had composed in his head. It was critical that he get it committed to memory because he didn't trust himself to explain things on the spot.

Emmaline, sometimes even the most scrupulous and upright person can —through no fault of his own—occasionally find his reputation dragged through the mud.

I have dedicated my life to upholding my family's name, and my own reputation; but I am mortified to tell you that I have been the victim of a—a shameless adventuress, who hopes to bend me to her will.

He stopped in the middle of the sidewalk and started over again.

Mr Chiswick—Edgar—I could not come to this house or speak to your daughter with a clean conscience if I did not disclose the heavy stroke of misfortune I have suffered in the last week.

I can only hope that you will hear me with an open mind, and—

"We're glad to see you back again, Mr Trowbridge."

To his own surprise, Nate looked up into the mild face of the boarding house manager. He had walked from the train station to the boarding house without any memory of having done it.

"Oh … yes. I'll be staying here a few days."

"Will you require your usual room, Mr Trowbridge?"

"Yes, thank you."

The manager carried his bags up to the second storey of the elegant brick mansion and unlocked the doors of his suite. "If you need anything at all, just ring, Mr Trowbridge."

The manager deposited his bags on the Persian carpet, and Nate handed the man a crisp bill. The manager smiled and closed the door behind him.

Nate settled into his elegant suite of rooms and put his own things away into drawers and closets. He had been obliged to soldier along without a valet for months and was feeling only *half* an Englishman.

If he didn't have such a cloud hanging over him, he would relish his visit to the Chiswicks' proper English household, but now his joy in it was quite taken away.

He settled into a chaise lounge near the big picture window and unfolded the morning paper lying on a nearby table. Perhaps he could chat with the Chiswicks about the day's news before moving on to the subject of his visit.

When he unfolded the paper, a blaring headline jumped out at him.

SCANDAL. DENVER BUSINESS LEADER IMPLICATED IN BLACKMAIL SCHEME. BAWDY HOUSE MADAME CLAIMS JOHN WITHERS WAS THE REAL OWNER OF HER HOUSE OF PROSTITUTION.

DENVER--John Withers, chairman of the Denver Chamber of Commerce, is the subject of a scandal. A Mrs Beulah Barricks has come forward to the Denver Bugle with information that Withers was the real owner of her house of prostitution, known as Mrs Barricks' Boarding House. She has given the Bugle items of interest connected to the charge, such as accounting books, patron lists, and personal letters from Withers revealing his ownership and interest in the enterprise.

Mrs Barricks tells the Bugle she came forward when Withers threatened to close the house down. She says he claimed that he was being bled by an unknown blackmailer and could no longer afford to run the establishment.

"*Oh!*"

Nate uttered a strangled gasp and fell back against the cushions in horror.

How could he approach the Chiswicks with news of his *own* scandal, now that the whole town was abuzz with talk of corruption, and blackmail, and—*boarding houses that were really bawdy houses*?

Oh Lord, he prayed, *I was prepared to tell them all — but how can I do that now?*

Nate let the paper fall from his fingers and sat staring at the wall for some time. When he finally came to himself, he reached the conclusion that he had only one honourable course of action. He would have to—to *confess* that his reputation was forever compromised, apologize to Emmaline and the Chiswicks, and retreat from their social circle in disgrace, never to return.

He would have to sell the Circle T, take Leonie back to London, and pray that the news of this ridiculous affair would never follow them.

For the first time, Leonie's madness presented itself to him in a favourable light. She was quite prepared to fall in love with the first attractive man she met, and so getting her married off to a suitable fellow should be short work, once they returned to England. If news of the scandal did eventually reach London, then *her* prospects at least would be unaffected.

Nate closed his eyes. It was like a waking nightmare—but he was going to the Chiswicks', and do what had to be done.

Once he had made his determination, Nate rose, straightened his jacket, put on his hat, and sallied forth as briskly as if he had a good day ahead of him.

Chapter
Twenty-Four

The house at 501 Edwards—an address he would never forget—loomed up in front of him. Nate closed his eyes, took a deep breath, and knocked on the black door.

When it opened, the Chiswicks' man Bagwell stood in the opening, stolid and unsmiling as a statue. And just like clockwork, the familiar ritual was carried out: servant at the door; cane taken. Name given; short wait; servant returned; escorted to family.

To Nate's chagrin, Edgar Chiswick was in the salon reading the morning newspaper as he arrived. He looked up from the lurid headline, and his face broke into a smile. Nate returned it weakly.

"Well, hello Nate!" he said jovially, "Sit down! I'll have the man bring you something. Have you dined?"

"Oh—thank you, but I'm not very hungry this morning."

"You do look a little pale, old man. Not feeling ill, are you?" Mr Chiswick replied.

"No, I feel quite well. That is to say …"

"Well, you've come to find things in an uproar here," the older man grunted and pointed to the newspaper with his glasses. "The Chamber of Commerce chairman's gotten himself ruined. Running a fancy house, they say! I actually had dealings with him. Just goes to show you can never be sure about people!"

Nate swallowed. "I daresay."

"Blasted fool," Edgar rumbled. "Some men just can't stay away from the chippies! Never ends well." He shook his head and then added:

"Well, Nate! It's good to see you again. Business in Denver, eh?"

"Actually, I—"

Before he could commence his speech, the door opened, and Mrs Chiswick came in. She broke out into a delighted smile at the sight of him.

"Hello, Nate!" she said and beamed. "We're glad to see you. Did you bring Leonie with you this trip? Francie has been teasing me to ask her to come down and stay the week."

Nate glanced up at her weakly. "No, Leonie isn't with me this time," he replied softly. "She sends her love."

Edgar shook the paper toward her. "I was just telling him about Withers, my dear," he explained. "Shocking thing!"

"Oh, yes," Mrs Chiswick replied, settling down comfortably on the settee. "I met his wife once at a party. She seemed like such a nice woman, too. I feel so sorry for her. She'll never be able to hold her head up again."

Nate licked his lips. "I daresay it wasn't her fault," he ventured. "Sometimes things *do* happen that are beyond one's control."

"Oh, you're right," Mrs Chiswick agreed. "She's blameless, of course! It's always the innocent who suffer."

"What does Mr Withers say about the accusations?" Nate pressed. "Surely *his* side of the story should be heard?"

Edgar grunted. "He says what you'd expect such a man to say. All a mistake, not his fault. *Blackguard*."

"Oh, but surely." Nate laughed tunelessly, "He's only been *accused*. A man isn't guilty until he's *proved* to be so."

"Proved to *my* satisfaction," Edgar grunted, and Nate felt his face going red. "Papers are full of it. Anyway, his reputation is rubbished. Once that happens, it almost doesn't *matter* if he was guilty or not. He won't be received anywhere in town, now. Probably have to move. His kind always does!"

Nate closed his eyes, and for an instant, the room went grey.

"Why, Nate—are you all right?" Mrs Chiswick cried anxiously. "You look positively ill!"

Nate opened his eyes at once. "I'll be all right," he murmured dully.

"Here, now, you do look pale!" Edgar rumbled and reached for the bell pull. When his servant arrived, he ordered, "Bring Mr Trowbridge a brandy, Bagwell."

"It's all right," Nate replied faintly, "I'm all right."

"You're as white as a sheet," Edgar countered. "A brandy will fix you up. Get your blood flowing again."

"Really, it's—it's all right," Nate replied, "And as much as I'd like to, I can't stay. I just meant to—to drop in and say hello, while I was in town."

"Oh, but you're going to stay to lunch, surely?" Mrs Chiswick cried. "Emmaline will be so disappointed!"

Nate glanced at her apologetically. "I'm afraid that won't be possible," he demurred. "Please—give Emmaline my apologies," he murmured. "Must dash." He stood up, and the room swayed momentarily.

"Let us call you a cab," Mrs Chiswick suggested to Nate's relief. He pulled a handkerchief out of his jacket pocket and pressed it to his brow.

"Thank you; that *is* a good idea."

"Bagwell, go out and hail a cab for Mr Trowbridge," Edgar commanded, and the man obeyed.

Nate turned to them, straightened, and said, stiffly: "I just want to thank you both for all that you've done for Leonie, and me, since we came over."

Mr Chiswick stared at Nate over the rim of his glasses. "Not at all." He frowned.

"Do come back again when you can, Nate," Mrs Chiswick called after him. "Bring Leonie with you!"

Nate paused in the doorway but didn't reply. He looked down at the floor; then drew himself up, squared his shoulders, and walked out.

Chapter
Twenty-Five

"Mr Trowbridge, there's something I need to tell you."

Jem waited on the Indian Rock platform, hat in hand, as his employer stepped off the train. His worried eyes searched Mr Trowbridge's face. It was plain that something wasn't right.

"Mr Trowbridge?"

His employer was staring off into the distance and acted as if he hadn't heard a word.

"Mr Trowbridge, I need to have a word with you."

At last Mr Trowbridge turned to him. "What?"

"I said, I need to have a word with you, sir."

A porter appeared carrying three large suitcases, and he set them down on the platform beside them. Mr Trowbridge automatically reached into his pocket and gave him a bill. The man tipped his hat and smiled. "Thank you, sir!"

Jem waited until the man had disappeared into the car again, and until the train began to move, to urge: "Mr Trowbridge, you look like you might not be feeling well. Are you all right?"

Mr Trowbridge's eyes were still on the horizon. "I'll be all right directly," he mumbled. "What was it that you wanted to say to me?"

Jem pulled him away from the depot window and said, in an undertone: "It's about that woman, Mr Trowbridge. I went to march her right off the Circle T, and you know how glad I was to do it. But your sister's taken a shine to that bobcat, being too innocent to know what she is. Miss Leonie's got her locked up in her apartments and says the woman's her *guest*. She's taken up for that bobcat, and nothin' I told her made any difference."

Mr Trowbridge seemed to revive. "What's that you say?" he cried. "You mean that woman is still in my house?"

Jem nodded grimly. "Yessir, she is. Your sister won't let me take her away."

His employer drew himself up to his full height. "Bring my bags. I'm going to straighten this out with Leonie *right now*, and then I want you to get rid of that viper. Let her sleep in the forest, with all the other snakes!"

"Yes, *sir*."

"Now that we're ruined, I'll at *least* have the pleasure of seeing that fatal woman evicted from my home!"

"*Now* you're talking," Jem replied briskly.

He loaded the suitcases in the front seat of the buggy and climbed up carefully. "You just get your sister to hand that hussy over, and I'll be glad to show her the gate."

He settled into the seat, whipped up the horse, and the buggy went rattling briskly down the long dirt road.

When they pulled up to the house at last, his employer jumped down from the buggy and stormed into the house. Jem grinned and left the suitcases in the rig because something was about to happen that he wanted to *see*.

He had to step lively because Nate Trowbridge was moving fast, but to Jem's surprise, when he got inside the house, he saw his employer stop dead at the foot of the main stairs as if something had struck him speechless.

Jem looked up. There, at the top of the stairs, stood Molly Clanahan, resplendent in an elegant white satin gown trimmed with black velvet. Her glowing red hair was swept into an elegant updo, and a pearl necklace circled her white throat.

Jem's mouth fell open. If he hadn't seen her before he would've *sworn* it was a different woman. He didn't have any use for Molly Clanahan, but he had to give the woman her due: she *was* beautiful. And she filled out that white gown better than any woman he'd seen in his life.

Mr Trowbridge recovered before he did. "I suppose I have Leonie to thank for this!" he barked. "But after what you've done to me and my family, nothing could move me. Out—out of my house, this *instant!*"

This awful command flushed Leonie from cover. She popped out from her hiding place near the top of the stairs and cried: "You don't have the right to order my guests out of this house, Nate Trowbridge! I own half this ranch and half this *house* if it comes to that, and I can have whatever guests I like!"

"Leonie, go back to your apartments, *right now*, or I'll drag you there myself!"

Leonie took one look at his tight mouth, and his grim face and burst into tears. "Oh, Nate, you're impossible!" she wailed, but her brother climbed the stairs, and Leonie, reading defeat in his face, fled before him.

Jem watched as Mr Trowbridge gained the top landing and stood toe to toe with Molly Clanahan. He said nothing but pointed wordlessly—to *him*.

Jem took his cue and walked to the foot of the stairs. "Well, are you coming down, or do I climb up to get you?" he asked.

The woman was as pale as her gown. Her eyes moved uncertainly from Mr Trowbridge's grim face to his disgusted one, and she raised an eyebrow and lifted her chin proudly.

Jem shook his head. "All right, then," he replied in irritation. "I'll march you out since you won't go on your own!"

He climbed the stairs, and Mr Trowbridge stepped aside. He took the woman's arm, but she pulled back, so that he had to take her arm again.

"Come on, now," he growled, "don't make this hard!"

He pulled her arm harder, and she was compelled to take a step or two, but she pulled back again, and this time, to his surprise, Mr Trowbridge intervened.

"Step back," he commanded, "you're an injured man. You don't need to pull your wounds." He stepped up, grabbed the woman's arm, and yanked her harshly down the stairs with him.

But to Jem's horror, instead of taking the first step, Molly Clanahan tripped on her gown, fell out of Nate's grip, and plunged headlong down the stairs. She rolled violently to the floor far below, and Leonie shrieked from the top of the landing.

"Oh, Nate, how could you!" she sobbed and flew down the stairs to sink down at Molly's side.

Jem rolled startled eyes to his employer's face, and if it had been white before, it was marble now. Nate Trowbridge was staring at the crumpled heap at the foot of the stairs as if he couldn't believe his eyes.

"Molly, Molly, speak to me!" Leonie was sobbing. "Oh, Nate, she's unconscious!"

Jem came to himself and hurried down the stairs. He pushed Leonie out of the way and put his hand to Molly Clanahan's throat.

"She's got a pulse," he told his employer, and scanned her white arms. "It doesn't look like she's got any broken bones."

Nate's voice croaked from the top of the stairs. "Is ... is her neck broken?"

Jem bit his lip. Molly's head was tucked under, and he reached down gingerly to pull it up.

"I don't think so," he said at last. "But she's got a big knot on her head already. I think she hit it on the stairs as she came down."

Nate leaned heavily against the banister and closed his eyes. "Call some men in here to carry her upstairs. Then call the doctor."

Jem nodded and hurried off to comply, but as he went, he was thinking that Molly Clanahan was the worst case of bad news he'd ever seen, and he sent up a heartfelt prayer—not for her, but for Nate Trowbridge, who looked even worse than she did.

Chapter
Twenty-Six

Jem returned an hour later with Hezekiah Odom, who was the closest thing to a doctor that Indian Rock could boast. Hezekiah had been a scout for the Army once, and he had experience tending bullet and stab wounds, childbirth, and blunt force injuries, so they were in luck.

Hezekiah had been in Indian Rock's only eating establishment, Ma Laney's, having a beer and a plate of liver and onions. He had looked put out with the interruption but had agreed to come to the Circle T. He took one last gulp of beer, wiped his grizzled mouth, and said, "My rate is two dollars for a home visit, cash up front."

Jem frowned at him and forked over two dollars, and Hezekiah's mood improved. "Fell down the stairs, you say?" He cackled. "That's the third time that's happened, over to the Circle T. Them must be *mighty* slick steps."

Jem's frown deepened. He hadn't considered that Mr Trowbridge might have *charges* brought against him, but the old man was right.

If Molly Clanahan recovered, she could claim that Nate pushed her. Of course, he and Leonie could testify that it wasn't any such thing.

But Mr Trowbridge might still get a name as a violent woman-beater in town, even if he wasn't charged with a crime. And that was a shame because to a man like Mr

Trowbridge, a bad name was worse than getting thrashed.

***

By the time they got back to the Circle T, Molly had been carried upstairs to one of the guest bedrooms. She had been laid on the bed, and as they entered the room, Leonie and Nate Trowbridge rose to greet them.

Hezekiah motioned toward Molly with his cigar and turned to Mr Trowbridge jovially. "Well, well, you like the fancy ones, eh?" He cackled, and winked. "Is she conscious?"

Nate looked offended, and Leonie shook her head tearfully. "We haven't been able to rouse her in all this time," she wept.

"Huh," Hezekiah grunted and reached into his vest pocket. He unstoppered a small vial.

"Gah!" Nate cried, and Leonie grabbed frantically for her handkerchief. Jem put his hand over his nose because whatever it was, was the most inhuman stench he'd ever suffered in his life.

Hezekiah stuck it right under Molly's nose, and to the gratification of everyone there, she coughed, and gagged, and opened her eyes with a gasp.

"Oh, Molly!" Leonie sobbed, and would have thrown her arms around the invalid, but Hezekiah stopped her.

"Don't touch the patient," he warned in a gravelly voice and withdrew the vial. "Now let me take a look at that knot."

He leaned over and inspected the bump on her brow. There was an angry purplish bruise, and the swollen place was as big as a hen's egg.

"Well, you've got quite a shiner," was his assessment. "How bad does your head hurt?"

"It's burning," Molly replied in a faint voice.

"Well, that's about right since you smashed it agin the floor," Hezekiah mumbled. "Here's what you folks should do: put cold water on that knot to take the swelling down, and make her some willow bark tea. Keep giving it to her as long as she has pain."

He turned back to Molly. "Do you hurt anywhere else besides that knot on your head?"

Molly closed her eyes and moaned: "My right leg."

Hezekiah grunted: "Try to move your arms and legs."

Molly moved her arms feebly, but when she tried to move her legs, she cried out in pain. "It's my right leg," she cried. "It hurts when I move it!"

Nate closed his eyes and fell back in his chair.

Hezekiah swiped his mouth with a grimy hand. "I'm going to have to pull up your gown, miss, to look at your leg," he told her, and said, over his shoulder: "If you gentleman will step out of the room for a minute, I'll take a look."

Jem stepped out into the hall and was soon joined by Mr Trowbridge. He rolled his eyes to his employer's in sympathy.

"It looks like she may have a broken leg," he murmured.

Mr Trowbridge massaged the spot between his eyes and nodded. "If that's the way of it, Leonie will get her wish," he replied grimly. "Molly Clanahan will be staying here *indefinitely*."

"You don't think she might bring charges against us, Mr Trowbridge?" he murmured. "Old Hezekiah was hinting at it, on the way over."

Nate shook his head. "I put nothing past her," he growled. "But why should she bring charges when all she has to do is *threaten* to get anything she wants?"

Jem looked at his boss sorrowfully. "I wish there was something I could do, Mr Trowbridge," he mumbled. "I feel responsible for all this."

To his surprise, Mr Trowbridge patted his shoulder. "You're not to blame for this, Jem," he replied. "There's only one person to blame for this."

The door opened, and Hezekiah Odom came out. He closed the door behind him and took Mr Trowbridge's arm.

"It looks to me as if she's got a cracked bone," he told him quietly. "There's no sign of a break, but when there's pain, that's usually what it is. What she needs is to stay in bed and rest that leg. Put cool cloths on the leg and the bump, and give her willow tea, and she should get better in time."

"How long will it take for her to recover and walk again?" Nate asked.

Hezekiah shrugged. "She probably won't be able to walk normal for about seven, eight weeks."

"Eight *weeks!*"

Hezekiah raised his bushy eyebrows. "That's about what it takes," he replied. "Just let her rest and put cool cloths on the break and the bump, and call me if anything changes."

"Thank you," Nate replied mechanically, and Jem motioned to Hezekiah. "I'll drive you back to town."

"Thankee," Hezekiah replied, and they turned to go downstairs, but as they paused at the head of the stairs, Jem noticed uneasily that Hezekiah was looking at the stair steps as they descended, and he scanned the floor at the bottom of the stairs as they passed.

Chapter
Twenty-Seven

Jem returned to his office in the bunkhouse as soon as he could after the accident. If Molly Clanahan was going to be living in the main house, he wanted to be as far away from it as he could.

But it was hard to carry out his plan because Leonie kept calling on him to do little errands. It was a nuisance, and he hinted as much to her, but the message just went right over her head.

"I need you to carry some boxes up to my apartment," she dimpled, and pushed his hat back from his brow.

Or:

"Jem, is that you? Come over here, please, and put your finger on this bow, so I can tie it."

And, finally:

"Jem, I need your help."

Leonie looked up at him with big blue eyes and smiled prettily. "Nate needs to apologize to Molly for the shocking way he treated her, and for the accident. I know Nate didn't *mean* to make Molly fall, and he won't have a minute's peace until he makes it right."

He stared at her in disbelief and put his hands on his hips. The suggestion that anybody needed to *apologize* to that gold digger made his ears burn, but he couldn't tell Leonie anything—he'd learned that already.

"Well, I don't know what I can do about that, Mi—Leonie," he replied uneasily. "Seems to me that would be between Mr Trowbridge and that tr—I mean, Molly Clanahan."

Leonie's frown was like a cloud passing over the sun. "Nate is too proud. He doesn't want to apologize, but he'll be miserable until he does," she insisted. "He has a *very* strict conscience. He *hates* to be in the wrong," she sighed.

"Well, but—"

Leonie put her hands lightly on his arm. "Please, Jem," she pleaded, "you're the closest to Nate, of all the people here. Can't you just—casually *suggest* that he should apologize to Molly?"

He couldn't keep from scowling and shook free of her hands. "No, I couldn't," he replied tartly. "If anybody needs to apologize, it's that catamount, for sinking her fangs into your brother's neck! She's a blood sucking leech, and everybody can see it, but you!"

"*Oh!*" Leonie gasped and stepped back quickly as if she'd been stung. "That's a—that's a hateful thing to say, Jem McClary!"

"No it ain't. It's the truth all day long, and I ain't going to tell your brother a thing except to get rid of her the fastest way he *can*."

But Leonie's face crumpled up. She fanned her face.

"I thought you were a nice man!" she sobbed and shook her head so that her blonde curls bounced. "I thought you had *feelings*!"

He stared at her in dismay and pulled a hand through his hair. "What—well, of course I have *feelings*," he sputtered. "But that don't mean—"

"Molly could have been killed, and all you can think about is getting rid of her!" Leonie cried. "And she's not all those hateful things you said; she's just a woman in love!"

Jem shook his head and looked down at the ground. "We ain't *ever* going to agree about that, Leonie," he told her flatly.

Leonie nodded tearfully. "You just wait, Jem McClary," she replied. "You'll see! Molly and Nate are destined to be together, and it isn't her fault that she knows it!"

"You know what, you need to round up all them books you been reading and toss them on a pile of kindling and light a match to it," he told her with asperity. He tapped her pretty forehead with his finger.

"Them romance books ain't a thing in the world but *moonshine*, and they're *addling your brain*."

Leonie fixed her big, tear-stained eyes on his.

"You mean you don't believe in *love*, Jem?" she quavered.

And to his horror, there was something about her broken little voice and the way she was looking at him—like she thought he was the best and bravest man in the world—that made him want to grab her and *kiss* her.

But that was the very last thing on earth he should do, or was going to do, so he stepped back.

"I think the less we talk about *love*, the better for your brain, and my job," he blurted frankly, and turned to leave, but Leonie put a hand on his arm.

And when he looked back, she leaned forward and planted a kiss on his cheek.

"I'm sorry I was cross with you," she confessed adorably. "Forgive me, Jem?"

But Jem tore his eyes from her face, sent a guilty glance down the hall, and thanked God that his boss was nowhere to be seen.

The rest of his thought processes were so scrambled up that he could only mumble something that didn't make sense even to him; then he got gone as fast as he could.

And the overriding lesson that he took away from his encounter with Leonie was that he had a second and much more important reason now, to stick to the bunkhouse and mind his own business.

But he shook his head, and felt a pang of deep sympathy for his boss, and a spurt of equal gratitude, that it wasn't *his* job to deal with two such crazy and troublous women.

Chapter
Twenty-Eight

Leonie watched Jem stalk off down the upstairs hall, dimpled, and closed the door to her apartments.

Jem had looked so *cute* when she kissed him. So adorably *embarrassed*.

Which meant that their romance was progressing exactly as it should. The man was *always* supposed to resist when confronted with his love for the woman; and Jem had responded beautifully.

Leonie nibbled her fingertip and dimpled. Jem had been all at sixes and sevens when she kissed him because he wanted to kiss her *back* and didn't want to admit it.

He had entered the *fighting his passion* phase of their romance, and so things were right on schedule. Mrs Willifred Smythe-Thompson's classic *Virtuous Torment* made it clear that this resisting phase could last for months—even *years*—if the man's sense of propriety was very strict.

Fortunately, Jem's sense of propriety didn't seem to be *that* demanding.

Leonie, cheered by these reflections, abandoned her boudoir and made for Nate's private den. She walked right in and found her brother sitting in a leather chair, smoking.

She coughed and waved her hand in front of her face. "Why must you smoke those vile cigars, Nate?" she complained. "Smoking is a vulgar habit. It will make a poor impression on Molly, I warn you."

Nate frowned. "Leonie, we must talk. Since that—since Miss Clanahan has come here, our social situation is very much changed."

Leonie brightened instantly. "I think so, too! We'll have *much* more interesting guests going forward." She settled down in a chair and smiled at her scowling brother.

"Nate, I know why you're in a funk. You're feeling guilty and miserable about what happened to poor Molly. But you can set it right in a trice! If you only open your heart to her, I'm sure she'll forgive you."

Nate stared at her. "I have no intention of offering Miss Clanahan anything except an invitation to *leave*, as soon as that becomes possible," he replied evenly.

Leonie listened tolerantly. Nate was clearly also in the *fighting his passion* phase of his romance with Molly. It was unlucky for Molly that Nate's sense of propriety was so dreadfully severe because they might have *years* of denial to work through.

"Why are you so set against Molly?" she asked gently. "She's plainly head over ears in love with you. Is it right to *punish* her for her feelings?"

"Leonie, I'm sorry if it distresses you, but Miss Clanahan is not in love with anything except money. She is not a respectable woman. I will not go into detail. You must trust me on that point."

"What has Molly done that's so terrible?" she enquired mildly.

Nate rolled dark eyes to her face. "She's threatening to ruin us with a sordid scandal if I don't marry her," he drawled.

Leonie's mouth fell open. "*Oh Nate*," she gasped, "how *exciting!*"

Nate looked at her sadly. "You only think so, Leonie, because you don't understand what that *means*. It means that my hopes of marrying Emmaline are dashed. It means that we are forever sundered from our friends—even the Chiswicks, I fear," he added softly. "It means that we will not be received in any decent home in Denver. It means we're ruined, Leonie. *Cut off.*"

Leonie blinked at him. "Only if you don't marry her, Nate," she replied.

Nate's temper flared briefly. "Oh, for the love of—do you really expect me to marry a woman who's blackmailing me?" he demanded.

"Oh, but surely she's only doing it because she's *desperate*," she objected, and her brother laughed bitterly.

"Yes, I can believe that she's *desperate*," he retorted. "A sane woman would never take such wild chances!"

"Love can make a woman desperate."

"So can the prospect of going to jail. I'm certain that she must be wanted by the law for something, and she thinks that if she marries a wealthy and influential man, she'll escape punishment."

Leonie blinked at him. This new information compelled her to readjust her ideas, but only slightly. Nate's life was finally becoming *interesting*. His romance with Molly promised to atone for more than twenty wretched years of boredom.

And Molly's love for Nate was wilder and bolder than she had ever *dreamed*.

Leonie gave her brother a twinkling glance. "Speaking of Molly, Nate—she asked me to beg you for a private talk."

Nate glowered in his chair. "Why would I do that? I don't *trust* myself alone with her."

Leonie brightened. "You're beginning to come around, Nate! But you *must* speak to her, of course."

Nate frowned at the wall. "Maybe you're right," he murmured. "Maybe there *are* a few things I'd like to say to her that are best said in private."

Leonie folded her hands. "I will say no more about your *secret tryst*," she replied primly. "My lips are sealed."

Nate massaged the space between his eyes. "Leave me, Leonie," he grumbled. "I won't be proper company for much longer."

Leonie gave him a knowing smile and spirited herself out of the room, and in spite of having told a deliberate lie, considered that she'd done a good morning's work, advanced her own romance, and helped to promote her brother's happiness.

Chapter
Twenty-Nine

Nate abandoned his den and walked down the hall to the guest room where Molly was staying. His words to Leonie about not trusting himself alone with Molly had been meant as a bitter joke, but now he wondered if he really *should* call for someone else to go in with him.

He was so angry that his hands might really go for the hussy's throat.

He took a deep breath and rapped loudly on the door.

"Come in."

He turned the knob and walked inside. He found Molly Clanahan wrapped in a frilly white dressing gown and her hair swept up in a loose bun on the top of her head. There was a breakfast tray on the bedside table, and she was sipping tea from a china cup.

She had made herself *completely* at home.

He bit back the rage that was choking him and closed the door behind him. "Well, you look as if you're feeling better," he noted in a brittle voice. "The doctor says that you should be ready to walk again in a few weeks."

Her eyes moved to his. "Thank you for calling him," she murmured. "I know that can't have been easy, after what I did to you."

Nate frowned at her. "As soon as you're well enough to walk, I want you out of this house," he told her grimly. "I'd rather be ruined than married to you!"

Her face went red, and she had the grace to look ashamed, but he didn't trust her downcast eyes or her trembling mouth. She was a playacting adventuress and had no doubt *practiced* every expression he was seeing now.

"Come now—out with it! What have you done, and who are you hiding from?" he demanded. "You're wanted for some crime and hope that my name and my money will save you from the consequences. You might as well admit it!"

The china cup froze in midair, and he nodded grimly. "Yes, I see *that* hit close to home! But if you're more than just a *blackmailer*, you needn't think that I'll harbour you from the authorities. It would give me the greatest pleasure to hand you over to the law!"

Nate smiled angrily, but if he was expecting her to respond in kind, he was disappointed. She put down the china cup and dabbed her eyes, which had pooled with tears.

"Isn't it enough that you've insulted me in every possible way?" she asked plaintively. "Must you also call me a criminal? Aren't you satisfied, even when you almost *broke my neck*?"

Nate bit his lip, flushed, and looked down at the floor. "You must—you must *know* that I never meant to—"

She gave him a look of gentle reproach. "Oh, I forgive you," she sniffed, "in the spirit of Christian charity! But when you call me a common *criminal*—"

The chastened look on Nate's face vanished. "Forgive!" he exploded, "What have *you* got to forgive? *Christian charity*? You shameless hussy, you don't even know what those words mean!"

She sat bolt upright in bed, her eyes blazing. "I *do* know what those words mean!" she cried, "My mother was a Christian woman, and she took us to church every Sunday! I was raised in an upright family!"

"Then they have my deepest sympathy!" Nate shot back, "They must be too mortified to claim you!"

She fell back against the pillows, and her angry look melted into tears. "My folks are dead," she replied in a small voice. "If they were alive, why—I'd have no *need* to be part of an arranged marriage."

Nate's anger cooled only slightly. "Well, you can pursue whatever *arrangement* is acceptable to a woman like you," he retorted, "as soon as you leave this house. And as far as I'm concerned, that day can't come too soon!"

"Why do you hate me?" she wailed and buried her face into her handkerchief. "I only want you to do as you *promised*!"

Nate stared at her in dumbstruck amazement. "*Why*? You've all but ruined me and my family, that's why! You came here in a brazen attempt to blackmail me!"

"I was desperate!" she sobbed. "I didn't mean to hurt you!"

"Didn't *mean—*"

She looked up from the handkerchief hopefully. "You needn't be ruined," she pled. "What if we married in secret? What if *nobody* knew except the two of us? And after a year, I'd be gone. Then you could divorce me quietly, and go and marry whoever you please, and no one would be the wiser. You wouldn't be ruined at *all*. Just one year. That's not too bad, is it?"

Nate stared at her, and a cold thrill slithered down his spine. "You must be mad!" he gasped. "You *are* mad if you think that I'll yield to your threats. And if you've committed some crime, my home will be no protection to you, so put that out of your mind at once!"

Nate stared down at her face in irritation, but seeing her tears, he decided to try a softer approach. He pulled up a chair and sat down beside the bed.

"Look here," he said quietly, "if you'll do the honourable thing and give back my letter, as you should have at the first, we'll forget this ever happened. You can go on your way with a clear conscience, and I won't utter a word to anyone that you tried to blackmail me. How's that, *mmm*?"

He leaned forward a bit and did his best to plead with his eyes, but he must have botched the pleading thing because Molly Clanahan's mouth crumpled up like Leonie's.

"I'm a good person," she wept, "and not a blackmailer! If I've done things in my life that I'm not proud of, God is my witness that I did them because I was desperate, not because I was wicked, or wished anyone harm!"

Nate pushed back from the bed in frustration. "Bah!" he cried. "It's useless to talk to you! But I warn you—if you insist on playing this game, then be prepared to play it out to the end. Because if you persist in this ridiculous charade, I won't relent until I see you behind bars!"

The sound of Molly's sobs was his only reply, and Nate surged to his feet and stalked out of the room in righteous indignation.

But the memory of Molly's tears followed him long after the sound of her sobs had faded, and Nate wondered, with irritation, how it was possible that he could be so completely *right*—and yet feel so unaccountably *guilty*.

Chapter
Thirty

The next morning, Nate rose early and left the house for Denver. He had decided that he wasn't going to passively accept Molly's presence in his house for the next eight weeks. Instead, he was going to hire a detective to find out about her.

He was confident that the man would find plenty of scandals and possibly even crimes in Molly's past that might be traded for his letter. If the venture was successful, he and Leonie might not be ruined after all.

Just the thought of such deliverance made him weak with relief—and he hurried off to the station to implement his plan.

***

The next day, Nate found the Burlington offices in a small side-street off one of the most fashionable boulevards in Denver. They were located in a discreet brick building, with one small brass plaque opposite the front door.

When Nate entered the building, a neatly-dressed young man seated at a desk stood and greeted him.

"Good afternoon, sir. How can I help you?"

"My name is Nate Trowbridge," he replied briskly. "I have an appointment to see Detective Jameson."

"Yes, he's expecting you. If you'll follow me."

Nate followed him as he led the way up a narrow staircase to an office on the second floor that overlooked the street. The secretary opened the door and then returned downstairs.

Detective Lucius Jameson looked up as Nate entered. He was a tall, broad-shouldered man with dark brown hair, long sideburns, and a ferocious handlebar moustache. He rose from behind his desk and extended a broad hand. Nate stripped off his gloves and shook it, and the detective waved toward a chair.

"Please sit down, Mr Trowbridge. I understand you're having a problem with a blackmailer, is that right?"

Nate set his hat on the desk, sat down in the chair, and crossed his long legs. He hated to share his most private affairs with a stranger, but the prospect of getting rid of Molly made it worth the pain.

"Yes, a woman. I sent my man to deliver a letter proposing marriage to a young lady here in Denver. But the man mistakenly delivered it to the wrong address. He gave it to a woman named Molly Clanahan, who instantly saw her opportunity to blackmail a wealthy man, and seized it. She arrived at my home the same day and demanded that I marry her at once. When I refused, she threatened to denounce me as a cad. She said she would use my letter to prove her claim."

"Let her," Jameson replied stoutly. "You can't prevent her from denouncing you in any case."

"True," Nate replied carefully, "but I still have hope that the young lady of my heart, and her family, may be prevented from hearing of this sordid affair. In my social circles, Mr Jameson, even the faintest breath of scandal can be fatal. And Miss Clanahan is—how shall I put this? —redheaded, very well-endowed, and of uncertain occupation."

"I see."

"I have begged her to give up her charade, but she refuses to abandon the pretense that my letter is a legitimate offer of marriage."

"Take the letter by force, then," Jameson barked. "She has to have it on her somewhere."

Nate glanced at him in distaste. "As convenient as that might be, Mr Jameson, I would not contemplate laying hands on her. Not least because it would be worse than what she now accuses me of doing."

"Have one of your servants steal it, then. If you recover the letter, she has no claim," Jameson countered. "Nine chances out of ten, it's on her somewhere."

Nate replied: "Again, Mr Jameson, I'm desirous to *avoid* scandal if at all possible. I came here in the hope that you can find out who this woman is, and if she has anything in her past that might be used to silence her. Something that she would not want to become generally known. I'm hoping you can discover a crime since I doubt she would be moved by a scandal."

"I'll certainly try."

"She was living at a boarding house in town, a Mrs O'Malley's, on 501 Edward Street."

Jameson scribbled on a pad. "I'll check it out."

"That's really all I know of her," he added, "except that she claims to have been raised by Christian parents, and that they went to church when she was a child. Oh, and she seems to know all about mail-order marriage."

"Has she shown any signs of being crazy?"

Nate glanced at him. "Yes. She proposed that we should marry in secret, and that the marriage need not last for more than a year. Why just a year, I have no idea. She promises to disappear after that time and leave me in peace. I think she may be fleeing the law and hopes to escape punishment by marrying me, or at least, by hiding in my house."

"That might be useful. I'll check if there are any outstanding warrants against a woman of her description. How old is she?"

"I'd say in her early twenties. She's about five feet six inches, long red hair, pale skin, blue eyes. I estimate her weight at roughly 135 pounds. She has a distinctive voice. Soft and a bit raspy."

"Any accent?"

"An American accent," Nate replied dryly, and Jameson smiled and shook his head.

"I'll see what I can find out. If I turn something up, I'll be in touch." He leaned over the desk, extended his hand, and Nate shook it.

"Thank you very much indeed, Mr Jameson," Nate told him in a relieved tone.

"And—*good hunting to you.*"

Chapter
Thirty-One

Molly dried her eyes with the frilly handkerchief that Leonie had given her and blew her nose. She was still trembling from the encounter she'd had with Nate Trowbridge.

She had come dangerously close to telling him the truth. She *had* told him a good deal of it: about her family, anyway. She didn't know why. Maybe it was because Nate Trowbridge looked and sounded like an honest man. When he'd pulled up a chair and asked her plainly to stop the charade, she had almost confessed to him.

It *had* been good of him to promise to let bygones be bygones, after the rotten trick she'd pulled.

Molly shook her head and blinked back a new wave of tears. The longer her playacting lasted, the more lies she had to tell to keep it going, and the lower and guiltier she felt. But she didn't *have* another plan. She couldn't change her tune now.

Molly dried her eyes, sniffed, and pulled herself upright in bed. She tilted her head and listened intently, but there was silence in the hall outside.

She threw the covers back, rose silently out of bed, and crept to the bedroom door. She opened it just a tiny bit and peeped out into the hall. She had to make sure no one was coming. She couldn't let anyone see her up and walking.

Once she saw that the coast was clear, she pushed the door softly closed and went to wash her face at the pitcher on the bedside table.

It had been a funny kind of luck, to fall down a full flight of stairs, and the throbbing knot on her head was real enough. But it had occurred to her, as they carried her upstairs, that if she faked a leg injury, she could hide out at the Circle T indefinitely.

That fat old buzzard who'd looked at her leg didn't have any more idea of being a doctor than she had of being president. So when she told him she had leg pain, he just guessed at what it was.

And that guess had been *just* the right kind of *wrong*.

Molly's conscience reared up and slapped her. The sly smile faded from her lips, and her cheeks went a guilty red.

She hardly *recognized* herself anymore, what with all the lies she was telling, and the rotten things she was doing.

It was true that she'd been raised in church, and little Molly Clanahan, choir member of the Gospel Church of Bolingbroke, Kansas was a world away from Molly Clanahan, blackmailing hussy of Indian Rock, Colorado.

Molly stared at her reflection in the mirror. That sweet little blonde girl had made up her hair, given her fancy clothes to wear, and had treated her like family from the first day she arrived.

And because of the effort Leonie had devoted to her, she looked like a *real* lady now, with her hair fixed up pretty, scented soap to wash with, and even a little cologne to dab behind her ears.

Molly let her eyes fall and felt heartily ashamed of the way she'd treated Leonie and her brother. Although—now that she was here, it was hard not to dream about living in such a place all the time. Wouldn't it be the life, to wake up and have your breakfast already there on a tray, and to have a closet full of satin gowns and lacy underthings, and pretty little shoes? And to really and truly have a sweet little sister like Leonie?

Wouldn't it be fine to be married to Nate Trowbridge--to be married to an upright and honourable man?

Molly's mouth twisted. *That* was a laugh, though. Nate Trowbridge hated her, and he had a right to. She was keeping him from the girl he *really* wanted to marry. Emmaline something-or-other.

Molly raised her chin and gave herself a speculative look. She wondered if Emmaline was prettier than her, and what colour her hair was. Was Emmaline tall and slender, or curvy, like she was herself?

Not that it mattered. Molly let her glance fall with a sigh. The important thing was that Nate Trowbridge wanted to marry the woman, and Molly Clanahan was standing in the way.

The best and most unselfish thing she could do would be to just pack her things, leave Nate's letter on the bedside table, and disappear. No one but Leonie would be sorry to see her go, and they'd all be better off without her.

The sound of approaching footsteps shook Molly out of her daydreams. She leaped into bed, pulled the covers up around her, and leaned back against the pillows.

An instant later, there came a soft knock on the door.

"Molly, it's me," Leonie called. "Can I come in?"

"Of course." Molly tried to still her galloping heartbeat. She hadn't heard Leonie coming, in her soft little slippers, and had almost been caught out of bed.

The door opened, and Leonie's mischievous face peeped out from behind it. "Are you feeling up to company?"

"Oh, I'm always well enough to talk to you," Molly assured her, and Leonie smiled and came in. She closed the door behind her and settled into the chair beside her bed.

"I've been *dying* of curiosity," she confided breathlessly, "so please don't be cross with me if I ask what Nate said to you the other day. I know he came to talk to you. *I sent him.*" She giggled.

Molly smiled uncertainly. Most of what Nate had said to her couldn't be *repeated* to his sister.

"Well—*um*—he halfway told me that he didn't *mean* for me to fall down the stairs," she said, after a long pause.

"I knew it!" Leonie laughed and clapped her hands in glee. "I *knew* Nate would relent, and do the right thing! He cannot bear to be in the wrong, you know. Even if it hurts him, he *will* be true to his standards."

Molly looked down in shamefaced chagrin. "That's—that's real good of him," she mumbled.

Leonie beamed at her. "Yes, I know that once you get to know him, you'll love Nate even *more*," she said confidently. "Nate can be a little trying sometimes, but he's the *soul* of decency."

Molly turned her head and scratched behind her neck. "I won't argue," she replied uncomfortably. "That's—that's what I've found."

"Yes, *I know* your love for Nate," Leonie gushed and reached over to hug her.

"I've never heard of a—a woman who fought for her love more *fiercely!*"

Molly received the embrace ruefully and rolled her eyes to Leonie's face. "You haven't, eh?"

"No!" Leonie replied thrillingly, leaning back into her chair. "It's just like one of Mrs Smythe-Thompson's books!" she exclaimed. "The lovers must do all *sorts* of extraordinary things to protect their love, but if they only persevere, they are always united in the end."

Molly looked down at her hands thoughtfully. "You don't say."

"Oh yes! Mrs Smythe-Thompson is an *authority* on courtly love, and she has declared it over and over again."

"Did she have anything to say about love that—that *ain't* courtly?"

Leonie looked puzzled by the question. "Not in so many words," she said at last, "but I'm sure she would say just the same!"

Chapter
Thirty-Two

That night, Molly turned down the bedside lamp and snuggled into her goose down pillow. Moonlight slanted through her big picture window and painted the floor white.

The big house was so sleepy and serene, that now and then she could hear the distant yip of a coyote or the hoot of an owl from outside, but she'd never felt safer in her life.

This remote ranch was the last place on earth Jack McGee would ever think to look for her, and he wouldn't dare to come here if he did think of it.

And anyway, Jack had only come after her because she'd hurt his pride. The money she'd stolen was just change to him; what he'd spend on liquor in an hour or two. No, what had chapped *him* was that a *woman* had put him on the floor of The Golden Nugget and made him look like a fool to his customers, and even to the other women. She'd set an example that might encourage *them* to fight back sometime.

Jack wanted to take her back because he wanted to make an example of her to everybody who'd seen him lying on the floor of his own saloon. He wanted to show them that he was still the boss.

She didn't like to think of what Jack might do to her if he ever caught her. Kill her, sure—but not right away. Molly shuddered.

But if there was one thing that gave her hope, it was that it had been a long enough time now that Jack had probably given up looking for her and gone back to Cheyenne. It didn't make sense that he'd stay in Denver. Travel was expensive, and staying away from The Golden Nugget was risky for him. If he stayed gone too long, some of the other girls might take a notion to do like *she* had, and bolt.

Molly pictured how Jack must've looked when he pulled himself up off the floor, and saw everybody there laughing at him. She smiled to herself and pulled the coverlet up around her ears.

Yep, I showed you a thing or two, you rattlesnake, she thought and slowly drifted off to sleep.

Molly slept sound and dreamlessly for a long time. But sometime in the night, she turned over and moaned in her sleep.

She was back inside the Golden Nugget.

A layer of tobacco smoke hung under the ceiling like fog, and the feeble yellow lamp lights were blurred. The din of drunken men laughing, singing, and shouting drowned out all other sounds, and the reek of cheap alcohol and unwashed bodies was so thick that it almost choked her.

Jack had practically thrown her into the lap of a drunken miner, and when she tried to pull away, the man had laughed and wrestled her back against his chest. He reeked of gin and cheap snuff, and he slobbered brown tobacco juice all over her neck.

When she looked up, Jack was glaring at the man's beer. She had palmed the little vial, and when the miner buried his face in her neck, she passed her hand over his cup. A little sprinkle of white powder fell into the drink, and her job was done.

173

She wrestled herself out of the old man's arms in disgust, but no sooner than she had, another drunken miner reached for her.

"Come on over here, missy!" He cackled. "Ain't seen *you* here before! My, my, my, ain't *you* a healthy gal!"

She'd been groped and pawed like a piece of meat, and after thirty horrible minutes she broke free, sobbing, and pushed for the door.

Jack had barred her way with a scowl. "Where do you think you're going?" he barked. "I *told* you what'll happen if you don't do like you're told!"

"I have to pee," she told him angrily. "You *do* let us pee, I guess?"

"You mind your mouth," he growled. "I could *kill* you, and nobody in Cheyenne would know or care. Just one less whore at The Golden Nugget, that's all. The lawmen here are some of my best customers. You *remember* that. And get one of the girls to go into the crapper with you because I don't trust you.

"I'm watching you."

He grabbed her shoulder and pushed her so hard that she almost fell headlong. She saved herself, regained her balance, and shot him a murderous look over her shoulder.

One of the other women came and took her by the arm. "Come on," she hissed. "You do your business and get back out on the floor, or Jack will make us all pay for it."

The woman pushed her into a dark little room, hardly big enough to turn around in. There was a chair with a hole cut out of the seat, and a big porcelain pot underneath.

She had stood there in the dark with her head in her hands. She burst out crying, but those tears hadn't been tears of despair. They had been tears of *rage*.

Naïve she might be, but she knew what *whore* meant, and she had a fair idea of what she could expect if she let the sun go down on her in that den. And she decided, then and there, that she'd rather be *dead*.

Having made up her mind, she opened the door, walked out past the woman, picked up a wine bottle from a table in passing, came up behind Jack McGee, and smashed it across his head as hard and as fast as she could.

The bottle shattered into smithereens, and Jack crashed to the floor like a tree. She knelt down quickly beside him, reached into his shirt pocket, yanked out a wad of cash, and streaked out the front door like a wild animal. She kept running until she couldn't hear anyone shouting anymore, and huddled down in a back alley, pulled herself into a ball, and cried for a long time.

When she'd cried herself out, she counted up her money, and decided that she needed to make it last. So she crept into the back of a dry goods store, and when the clerk went outside to relieve himself, she ran in and snatched a display dress off the rack, and a pair of shoes, and was out again before he came back.

An hour later, she was sitting in a third-class train car bound for Denver, in an ill-fitting dress, shoes a size too big for her, and with just enough money to rent a room for a week.

Molly moaned, turned restlessly, and woke up. It was still deep night; the setting moon sent white light slanting across her bedroom floor, and an owl murmured softly from somewhere outside her window.

Molly's eyes darted across the unfamiliar room in fright, but then she remembered where she was, closed her eyes in relief, and snuggled back into her pillow with a smile.

She prayed, *Thank you, Lord*—but then remembered that the Lord wasn't going to be disposed to hear the prayers of a scheming, blackmailing hussy.

I know, Lord, she added sleepily, *and you're right.*

But I'm so thankful, just the same.

Chapter
Thirty-Three

"Get away! Get your paws off me! *Aiieee!*"

Nate paused in mid-cigar puff, tilted his head, and listened, frowning.

"*Ouch!* You dirty old goat, I'll teach you to—*Ow!* Stop it, Jack!"

"No, no, *no!*"

Nate set his cigar down in an ashtray, stood up, and walked to the door of his den. It was well past one in the morning, and he gathered that Molly Clanahan was talking in her sleep from the guest bedroom down the hall.

He opened his door and walked softly toward her bedroom a few paces. Maybe Molly would say something in her sleep that would help the detective. Nate frowned. He disliked eavesdropping on principle, but he was desperate enough now to make an exception.

The muffled voice coming from the guest bedroom was shrill with anguish.

"Lying snake! You should go to jail!"

"I'm *not* a whore, any such thing, and if you lift a hand to me I'll go to ... law ..."

There was a long silence, and then there came a high, trembling cry that made the hairs on the back of Nate's neck stand up, and then the sound of childish weeping.

Heat surged up into Nate's face. Whatever she was dreaming was clearly a nightmare, and her shriek filled him with horror.

"Don't let Jack hit me!" she mumbled and shrieked again.

Nate frowned and set his jaw. He wasn't sure he could trust Molly not to be faking, but she would have to be a very good actress *indeed* to fake the cry he'd just heard.

"I don't have to do that; you can't make me! I won't, I won't, *I won't!*"

Nate pulled his hand over his mouth. At last he couldn't stand it anymore, and he cleared his throat loudly and stomped past her door with as much noise as he could make.

He stopped, tilted his head, and listened again.

Silence.

He walked quietly back to her door and paused, listening. To his relief, there was now only the sound of soft, regular breathing.

Nate walked back to his study thoughtfully and closed the door. He sat down slowly in the leather chair, picked up the smouldering cigar, and blew a contemplative smoke ring toward the ceiling.

He frowned. He could barely credit it—but was it possible that Molly might have been telling the truth when she told him she was desperate?

Not that it would excuse anything that she'd done to him, of course, but if she'd really been talking in her sleep just now, she had clearly been living in misery and fear.

What was the name she'd cried out? *Jack*, that was it.

Her other ramblings—*dirty old goat, I don't have to do that, and*—Nate set his jaw—*I'm not a whore*—suggested that she had been in a house of ill repute, and that Jack had been its pimp.

That she had been unhappy there was evident.

Nate shuddered. That she might have been held there *against her will*, was so horrible a possibility that he refused to allow himself to picture it.

Don't let him hit me, she'd said.

Nate scowled. It would take the lowest gutter blackguard to force a young girl into a life of prostitution. He had heard stories of such things happening in the lawless areas of the American frontier but had never more than half believed them.

What if—what if the stories were true—and Molly had escaped from such a place?

It would explain why she had seized his letter, why she had made up such a ridiculous story, why she'd refused to leave his house, why she kept insisting that she wasn't a bad person.

It would explain why she looked so *angry* when she was accused of being a—

Nate pressed his mouth into a straight line. There were *other* explanations for her behaviour, of course, and they were all more likely to be true.

But he had another possibility, now, to suggest to the detective. A new line of inquiry, based on what he'd just heard.

He frowned again and blew another smoke ring. If Molly had escaped from a house of ill repute, her presence in his house became that much more threatening to his reputation, and Leonie's chances in society. He couldn't think of a more damning scandal if he tried, and if it became known that a fancy house woman was living in his home, their social ruin would be all he feared, and more.

Nate stared up at the ornate plasterwork on the ceiling. Still—if Molly had really been through such a hellish ordeal, then giving her shelter, and some measure of safety until she could resume her life, would only be decent.

It would be the only Christian thing to do, in fact.

Assuming, of course, that it wasn't more of Molly's playacting—like *everything else* he had seen from her so far.

Nate sighed, blew another smoke ring, and watched it float up to the ceiling.

Chapter
Thirty-Four

Nate glanced at his sister over the breakfast table the next morning. Leonie picked a strawberry out of a dish, dipped it in chocolate, and popped it in her mouth. She became conscious of his glance, raised her eyes to his, and dimpled.

Nate returned her glance soberly. "Leonie, you haven't—you haven't said anything to Francie or written anything to our friends back home about Molly—*have* you?"

To his overwhelming relief, Leonie shook her head. "No. I did what you asked," she replied, "though it would be a *monstrous* exciting story!"

"That would be a *fatal* mistake, Leonie," he told her grimly. "I must impress on you again—don't tell anyone about Molly. *Anyone.* And I mean, even the trades people you may see in town or on the rail line. *No one* must know she is here!"

Leonie tilted her head, sighed, and looked at him as if he were a disappointing pupil. Nate squelched an irritated outburst because he knew Leonie was thinking of some nonsense that Mrs Smythe-Thompson had burbled about when she knew no more than *he* knew about tracking Indians through the mountains.

"Promise me, Leonie," he pressed.

"Oh, all right." She shrugged. "Though I wish you would stop harping on the same old string. Nothing awful has happened since Molly came here. From the way you talk, you'd think the roof was about to fall in."

"Leonie—"

The door opened to admit Maria, and Nate fell abruptly silent. He watched the woman as she set a tray of biscuits down on the table, turned, and walked out again.

He wondered if it would be wise to make the servants swear an oath of silence about Molly Clanahan, or if it would have the opposite effect, and incite gossip. The locals in Indian Rock weren't a very pressing threat since his social circle had precious little contact with them, but the number of people who had seen Molly in his house was growing. It included Maria, Jem, and some of the ranch hands, and now, the so-called physician who had tended her injury. The man had called himself a *doctor*, but Nate doubted very much if he'd even *heard* of medical ethics or the sacred obligation to keep patient information private.

More likely, at that very moment he was probably holding forth at the local watering hole about Molly, her accident, and the odd frequency of falling accidents at the Circle T.

Nate drummed his fingers on the tablecloth. Maybe he could *buy* the man's silence. Though even *that* might not keep him from talking.

Nate bit his lip in frustration. His patience was already stretched to the breaking point, but it looked as if it was going to be tested again, while the detective searched for information about his *very* inconvenient guest.

To his surprise, Maria suddenly appeared in the dining room doorway. She was holding a card in her hand.

"You have visitors, Mr Trowbridge," she informed him flatly and handed him the card. To Nate's horror, the inscription read: *Edgar and Clara Chiswick.*

"Good heavens!" he gasped. *"It's the Chiswicks!"*

Leonie's face brightened at once, and she jumped up from her chair. "I wonder if Francie is with them?" she cried and ran out to greet them.

"Leonie, remember what I—" Nate called after her, but she was already gone. Nate rolled his eyes to Maria's face. He couldn't be sure, but it seemed to him that the ghost of amusement flickered across her dark eyes.

"Tell them I'll be right out," he barked, and Maria disappeared.

Nate pulled his hand over his chin, straightened his vest and his tie, rose slowly, and walked out to greet his guests.

He found Edgar, Clara, and the girls sitting in his front salon. His eyes went immediately to Emmaline. She looked as if she belonged in his house, and Nate's face softened as he smiled at her.

"Well, well! What a pleasant surprise!"

Edgar glanced up at him. "We were going to Cheyenne to find some horses for the girls, and we thought we'd drop in for an hour or two."

"We're so glad you did!" Leonie cried and clasped Francie's hand. "I haven't seen you for *weeks*, and we have *so much* catching up to do!" She raised her eyes to his.

"Nate, why don't I show Francie around the house?" She smiled. "This is the first time she's seen it!"

"Well—" Nate stammered.

"What a good idea," Clara agreed. "This is such a beautiful country house, Nate," she told him, and Nate had to tear his attention away from Leonie, as she and Francie flounced upstairs.

"It's been quite a challenge, to bring it up to snuff," he answered absently, still following Leonie with his eyes.

"May we have the grand tour?" Clara asked mischievously, and Edgar threw his hands up in mock despair.

"Women must always see the house!" he lamented, and Nate forced out a tinny laugh.

"I'd be pleased to show you the house," he answered mechanically and prayed that Molly would have the good sense to keep quiet, as they toured the downstairs.

He had no intention whatsoever of taking the Chiswicks anywhere near her room. He prayed that Leonie would also have the discretion to keep Francie on the first floor of the house, but he had very little hope of it.

"Well, ah—can I ring for some refreshments before we begin?" he asked. "I suppose you must be fatigued, after your train trip."

"Oh no, we're fine," Edgar replied jovially. "We dined on the trip down."

"Well then," Nate smiled. "I'd be glad to show you around the house." He extended his arm like a cavalier, and Clara turned to Emmaline and smiled.

"I think that was meant for *you*, my dear." She laughed, and Emmaline cast her eyes down modestly, but rose and took his arm.

Nate squired Emmaline through the salons, the library, the dining room, and all the other grand rooms designed for entertaining.

"You must have a party here, Nate," Clara told him, glancing in admiration at a chandelier in the ballroom. "This house is simply perfect for it."

"Ah!" Nate laughed nervously. "So Leonie tells me, but we've been so busy since we arrived, renovating it, that parties have been the last thing on my mind. You would never believe the state this house was in when we arrived. There was an actual battle here, between the Cheyenne and the U.S. Calvary."

"How exciting!" Emmaline said softly and looked up at him with mischievous eyes.

"Not at all." He smiled but felt a glow of pleasure at her evident admiration. "More like a deuced inconvenience. I had to order almost everything new."

He led his guests out onto the back patio. "We have a small garden here, too," he told Emmaline, "nothing suitable yet, just a little patch. I'll have to have a landscaper up from Denver soon."

Emmaline glanced out over the red roses and clouds of pale blue flax. "I think it's a charming little garden," she told him.

"You're very kind."

Edgar turned to glance back at the house and exclaimed in surprise. "Well, what the—" he laughed and gestured toward the back windows.

"Your house isn't haunted, I trust?" he teased.

Nate smiled uncertainly. "Certainly not. Why do you ask?"

"Well, I just saw a face at that upstairs window." He laughed and to Nate's horror pointed to the guest room window. "But when I looked again—hey presto!—it was gone."

"It must've been Maria," Nate told him in as offhand a tone as he could muster. "She goes upstairs to clean the rooms."

"Oh no," Edgar laughed. "This woman's face was as white as a sheet."

"A mystery!" Clara laughed and looked over at him teasingly. Nate smiled and lowered his eyes.

"Then it must have been another of the servants," he replied and quickly turned the conversation to other topics.

Chapter
Thirty-Five

Molly finished the breakfast tray that Maria had brought up to her and was just about to ring for fresh water and a towel when unfamiliar voices downstairs made her tilt her head and listen intently.

She threw back the covers and slipped out of bed cautiously. She padded to the door and opened it a crack.

There was no one in the upstairs hall, but several new voices wafted up to her from downstairs. A robust, mature male voice; an older woman's pleasant voice; a girl's piping voice, and another, barely audible female voice that made Molly's spine stiffen and hairs on the back of her neck stand up.

A *young woman's* voice.

Molly peeked out in curiosity. What if the girl was Nate's *sweetheart*?

Molly peered through the crack and strained to hear. She was pretty sure that Nate didn't want anybody to know she was there. But she was seized by a strong desire to see what kind of woman Nate Trowbridge liked—because the odds were good that this girl was his intended.

Molly opened the door wider, looked up and down the hall, and crept to the edge of the top landing. She could just see the far end of the downstairs hall and the feet of several visitors. There were the older man's wide black slacks and big, shiny shoes; the lady's blue ruffled dress;

the girl's white pinafore, and the young woman's diaphanous pink gown, and her tiny pink slippers, darting in and out under the hem.

Molly frowned and looked down at the floor. It looked like this girl was a proper lady, all right. Just the sort of woman that a man like Nate would admire, with her soft voice, her small feet, and her pink gown.

But Molly strained to see more. She couldn't help being curious about how this girl looked. Was she dark or fair? Was she pretty?

To judge by her feet, and the width of her gown, she looked as if she was slender.

Molly heard Nate's voice suddenly, as he walked out to greet his visitors. His voice sounded more *scared* than excited to her, but soon he was laughing and talking normally.

The sound of their footsteps on the hall below made her scurry back to the door of her bedroom. She hurried inside but kept the door cracked. To her relief, the voices turned away from the stairway and faded into the distance.

The sound of Leonie's door opening at the end of the hall made her close her own door and dive back into bed, but the sound of girlish giggling trailed harmlessly down the stairs.

Molly set her mouth in disappointment. She wasn't a member of the family, and she had no right to be there, she knew that, but it still felt odd and lonely to be hiding upstairs when there was company in the house.

She drifted to the window of her bedroom and pulled the curtain back just a bit. She could see Nate and his guests in the garden below, and now his young lady was plainly visible. Molly pulled her mouth down.

The girl was a willowy brunette with a delicate face and porcelain skin. Her hair was piled up on her head in an elegant styling, and tiny silver earrings winked when she turned her head.

One white hand was on Nate's arm, and the other held a frilly parasol, to shield her smooth, milky skin from the sun.

Molly was so busy staring at the girl that she didn't notice the old man had seen her until it was too late. She stepped back instantly and let the curtain fall. Her heart was pounding, but she couldn't resist peeking out through the tiny sliver between the window frame and the curtain. She saw the older man point toward the window, and Nate's quick, grim glance toward her. She saw him shrug, say something, and turn away, and then the little party walked on.

Molly faded back from the window and sat down on the bed.

So much had happened since she came out to Colorado, and it had all happened so fast, that she hadn't really had much time to think about who she was, and where she was going. It had been all she could do, just to keep a roof over her head, and food on the table.

But now in Nate Trowbridge's guest bedroom, the full weight of her isolation hit her.

The sight of the smiling young lady on Nate Trowbridge's arm brought it home to her with terrible force. *That* young woman was secure, loved, and surrounded by adoring family and friends.

She, by contrast, was all alone. She had no family, no friends, no home, and no occupation. Her only security was the letter she'd been using to blackmail her host.

Molly reached into the bosom of her dress and pulled the letter out. Now that she could put a face to the words, the letter made much more sense.

My dear girl,

I am keenly aware that the two of us have known each other very briefly, and your maidenly sensibilities must shrink from joining yourself to a man you have only just met. But I hope that you will not allow our imperfect acquaintance to prejudice your answer to the question I am about to ask.

Our last meeting led me to hope that you would look favourably on my request for your hand in marriage. You are a sweet and beautiful young woman, and I would count it an honour beyond my deserving if you would agree to be my wife.

I do not have the gift of a glib tongue, and it is difficult for me to express my feelings. But be assured that should you agree to be my wife, I will do my utmost to make you happy and to make your life as comfortable as is within my power.

I await your answer with a hopeful heart.

Sincerely,

Nate Trowbridge.

Molly's lip trembled. The letter belonged to that girl down in the garden, and not to her.

And in spite of the fact that he hated her, Molly had to admit that Nate Trowbridge was an honourable man and deserved such a woman: a woman with a delicate face, an elegant look, and a perfect, polished way about her.

He was a gentleman, and he deserved a lady.

Molly felt ashamed suddenly, thinking of the young woman's face. She looked like a sweet girl, and she'd been robbed of a *marriage proposal*, the most important thing that could happen in any young woman's life. All because Molly Clanahan had only been thinking of herself and didn't give a rip what happened to anybody else.

It was true that she was all alone and still as desperate as she'd been the night she stole the letter. This big house, and Leonie's childish faith in her, and good food and pretty clothes had made her forget it for awhile, but it was the truth.

But her own desperation still wasn't any excuse to rob someone else of their chance of happiness. It would be hard to give up such a nice setup, and three sure meals a day, and nice clothes and all, but she had a feeling she'd sleep better, and feel better about herself, once she gave the letter back and went on her way.

Anyway, she'd gotten what she came for, even if she wasn't going to get it for as long as she hoped. She'd wanted a place to hole up and hide until Jack McGee went back to Cheyenne, and she was pretty sure that he was gone now.

Time for her to let Nate and little Leonie get on with the lives they were meant to live.

Leonie, in an overflow of sympathy for her injuries, had made her a gift of some money, and she could use it to buy a train ticket out of town. She might be better off not going back to Denver since Jack had seen her there. Maybe she should head out to San Francisco where there were likely to be jobs for women who could do fine embroidery work.

And once she got settled in a new place, she could pay Leonie's money back, a little at a time.

The sound of the guests returning from the garden broke in on her thoughts. Laughter wafted up from downstairs, and the voices nattered on for a little while, and then got louder—probably they were saying farewells—and then they fell quiet.

Molly walked to the door, opened it a crack, and peered out again. She could only just see the downstairs hall. This time, there were only two pairs of shoes in it, standing very close to one another.

The tiny pink slippers, and Nate's shiny black dress shoes.

Molly sighed, closed the door, and pressed her brow against it sadly.

Chapter
Thirty-Six

Molly peeped out into the hall, looked both ways, and slipped out of her room. She hurried silently down the hall to Nate Trowbridge's private den.

She paused outside the door. It was bad to invade her host's private rooms, but she consoled herself with the fact that it would be the last time, and that if he knew why she was doing it, he'd probably open the door for her, himself.

She put her hand on the ornate doorknob and twisted it. The door swung back to reveal a panelled den with a big fireplace, a leather chair, a sofa, and a big desk.

Molly smiled because she'd been counting on that desk. She crossed the room quickly and pulled open the top drawer. Sure enough, there was a packet of writing papers.

She carefully peeled one thick sheet out, palmed a little box filled with pen and ink and other accessories, and hurried back out again. She closed the door behind her and got herself back inside the bedroom, just in case someone decided to come upstairs.

But no one did: and so she had the leisure to settle back in bed, pull her breakfast tray across her lap, and set the paper and writing utensils on it.

She put the end of the pen to her mouth, and after some consideration, wrote:

Dear Mr Trowbridge:

I couldn't help seeing you with your lady friend today and notice how happy the two of you looked together. It made me feel ashamed of the sorry way I've treated you. You deserve your chance at happiness, same as anybody else, and I'm sorry I got in the way.

I didn't have any call to steal your letter, and to hold it over your head, except that I was in a bad way, but that isn't any excuse. Thank you for letting me stay in your house when I needed a place to stay.

Anyway, you and your lady friend make a pretty couple, and I'm sure you'll be very happy. Here's your letter back, and I'm truly sorry for the worry and trouble I've caused you.

Thank you for behaving like a gentleman, even when I didn't act much like a lady. That meant a lot to me. More than you could ever know.

And my hand on the Bible, I won't breathe a word to anybody that I was ever here or that I ever met you. I guess that's the best wedding present I can give you.

Good luck with your proposal. I have a feeling your lady friend will say yes.

Sincerely,

Molly Clanahan.

Molly read the letter through, considered that it said what it needed to, and folded it up inside an envelope. She tucked Nate's letter in with it and sealed it up with a wafer of gum from the little box.

She stared at the envelope for awhile, then sighed and wrote: *To Mr Nate Trowbridge. Personal.*

Then she tucked the envelope under her pillow to be ready for when she decided to leave.

The sound of approaching footsteps made her stuff the little box of pen and ink under her pillow too, and to set the tray down beside her bed. She had no sooner done so than a soft knock rapped at her door.

"Who is it?"

"It's me, Leonie!"

"Come on in."

Leonie came in with a rush and settled down on the edge of her bed with a smile. "Oh, Molly, I wish you could have come down to meet the Chiswicks!" she exclaimed. "Nate is so strict and stuffy; it makes my head hurt!"

"Are the Chi—the Chiswicks your good friends?" Molly asked softly.

"Oh, yes! I stayed with them when I first came over because Nate had to take care of business in London and couldn't come out right away. Francie and I are like sisters! And Nate wants to *marry* Emmaline!"

Leonie caught herself and put a hand over her mouth with an almost comical expression of dismay. "Oh, Molly—I'm sorry, I shouldn't have said that! *Can* you forgive me?"

Molly looked at her affectionately. "I'm not the least bit busted up," she replied warmly. "You couldn't make me mad if you tried, Miss Leonie. I really appreciate all the things you've done for me. I wouldn't have lasted one night here if it wasn't for you."

"I could do no other!" Leonie replied dramatically, and then dimpled. "And it *was* great fun to see Nate *warm* about something at last! He has the most even temperament, he never gets excited! But you changed that."

"I'll just bet," Molly agreed wryly. "I'm really thankful to you, Leonie. I'll always have a warm spot in my heart for you."

"And you'll always have one in *mine*," Leonie replied and hugged her impulsively. "Because Nate will relent at last, and admit he loves you, you'll see! And then we'll be sisters *forever*."

Molly couldn't meet Leonie's innocent eyes, and so only coughed and said: "Well, we'll see. Have your friends gone?"

"Yes, they're going to Cheyenne to buy horses," Leonie replied. "It sounds like great fun."

"So they caught the last run today?" she asked.

"Oh no," Leonie told her absently, "the last run goes up to Cheyenne again, at eight o'clock tonight."

Molly smiled and nodded, and Leonie made a grieved face. "Poor Molly, you're stuck in bed and have to listen to me talk about other people having fun! But you'll be out of bed soon, you'll see."

"Oh, I'm sure of it," Molly agreed.

"You're so brave," Leonie replied and leaned over to kiss her brow. "But it's almost lunchtime. Can I bring you something up on a tray?"

Molly bit her lip. "That would be wonderful," she replied slowly. "I'm *real* hungry today."

Leonie's eyebrows twitched together in distress. "Poor Molly! I'll have Maria make you up a beautiful tray *full* of good things. And after you're finished eating, I'll come back and tell you all the gossip from Denver. They say the chairman of the chamber of commerce has been ruined—involved in some sort of scandal! I asked Mr Chiswick what *kind* of scandal, but he wouldn't tell me. It's all very mysterious."

Molly rolled her eyes to Leonie's but said nothing, and soon Leonie took herself off to fetch a lunch tray.

After she was gone, Molly determined to stay long enough for dinner since it might be the last good meal she'd have in a long time—and to catch the evening train up to Cheyenne, and then the Transcontinental line, west to San Francisco.

She looked up at the ceiling and offered a rueful prayer. *Well, Lord,* she prayed, *I've decided to do the right thing at last. Better late than never, I guess. Thank you for having mercy on me.*

But I will miss this place something terrible when I go.

Chapter
Thirty-Seven

That night, Molly asked for and got a tray heaped up with twice as much food as she needed. Some of it she ate, and some she tied up in a linen napkin and put into her little handbag. She dressed in the plain but elegant blue linen gown that Leonie had forced Maria to make for her.

Molly turned to and fro in front of the mirror. The new dress matched her eyes and fit her like a glove. She thought of her white ball gown with a pang of longing, but she had to travel light, and she most likely wouldn't need any fancy white gowns where *she* was going.

She took the dainty little slippers that matched the blue dress and stuffed them into her handbag as well. She didn't want to ruin them on the long walk to the Indian Rock depot, and so she pulled on her old shoes. After weeks of living in luxury, the cheap black shoes looked twice as ugly and felt even clunkier than they had before.

Molly scanned the bedroom to see if there was anything she'd forgotten. There was nothing, except a farewell to Leonie.

It wouldn't be right to just disappear without a word to Leonie; that might cause hard feelings between her and her brother.

On an impulse, Molly unearthed the writing box, and another sheet of paper, and scribbled out a farewell to her friend.

Dear Leonie,

I just wanted to say thank you for all you've done for me since I came to your home. I really appreciate how you took up for me and believed in me so strong that you even defied your own brother.

But I want you to understand, Leonie, that your brother was right about me. I'm ashamed to say it, after how good you've been to me, but I didn't come here because I was in love. I was in trouble, and I needed help. I saw my chance to get some money out of your brother, and I took it. I knew it was wrong, but I did it anyway. I'm sorry that I didn't deserve the faith you put in me.

I hope this doesn't make you stop believing in true love. I know a sweet and pretty girl like you will find the right fellow one day. And I hope your brother finds happiness with his lady friend. You are a fine, upstanding family, and you deserve to be happy. I truly hope you will be.

I hope you won't think too hardly of me, Leonie, after I am gone. Although I don't deserve it, I hope that you will be good to me one last time, and remember me with kindness. I will always remember you fondly, as a sweet and generous young lady.

Your friend,

Molly.

Molly sniffed, wiped her eyes, and put the letter into an envelope. She addressed it to Leonie, and put it in her bag. Last of all, she reached under her pillow and retrieved the letter to Nate.

She had the money for her train ticket, her shoes, another meal, and her farewell letters. She was ready to go at last—all but for one thing. She reached under her bed and pulled out her pistol. She hiked up her skirts, secured it with a garter, and shook her skirts out again.

She was about to leave this safe, peaceful haven, and return to the real world; and she needed *all* the help she could get.

***

Molly opened the door a crack and looked out into the hall. It was dinnertime downstairs. Nate and Leonie were in the dining room, and Maria was shuttling back and forth to and from the kitchen.

Molly bit her lip. She didn't dare march down the stairs and out through the front hall for fear of being seen. She was too deeply ashamed to face Leonie and Nate, and if Maria or Jem McClary saw her on her feet and walking around so soon after her accident, they'd accuse her—and rightly, too—of being a faker.

Neither prospect appealed to her. But she suddenly remembered the little tunnel she'd discovered in the root cellar and decided to take that hidden way. The route might require a little nerve, but she had plenty of *that*. The main thing was that it would get her out of the house, and clean gone, without anyone seeing her.

She looked down at the letters in her purse. Her first idea had been to slip them under Nate's and Leonie's bedroom doors, but they might come back and find them too soon. On second thought, she'd leave them with the man at the train depot and tell him to deliver them tomorrow.

Molly glided down the stairway as softly as a breath of air. The lower hallway had a door to the service stairway at the far end, and once she was in it, she could get down to the basement level unseen.

She stopped at the foot of the stairs. Nate's voice wafted down the hall from the dining room, as he and Leonie talked and laughed softly. The sound made Molly pause to listen for a long moment. Then she turned into the back hallway, and was gone.

Chapter
Thirty-Eight

The next morning, Nate went down to the dining room to have his cup of coffee and a buttered scone and to read the latest newspaper. It was not yet eight o' clock, and Leonie wasn't down yet, but to his surprise, he had a visitor.

He looked up and was startled to see the grim face of the stable boy staring at him.

"What the—what do you mean by just walking in on me like this?" he sputtered. "I'm in the middle of my breakfast. You can talk to me later."

The boy stared at him, unmoved. "I guess you ain't heard that the redheaded woman lit out."

Nate choked on his coffee. "What's that you say? *Gone*? Are you sure?"

"I saw her go," he replied laconically.

"Well—*good*, then! But when, and how? I never saw Molly come through here last evening."

"That's because she used the tunnel to go from your house to the barn. Likely nobody saw her come out, but me."

Nate stared at him, dumbfounded. "*Tunnel*? See here now," he replied severely, "if this is your idea of a joke—"

The boy shook his head. "Ain't no joke. They's a tunnel runs from your basement, up to the barn," the boy replied. "I hid out in it when the Cheyenne attacked this house. Everybody knows about it."

"Apparently!" Nate replied, with asperity. "But why did you tell Molly Clanahan?"

"I ain't never spoke two words to that woman," the boy replied. "Not even when I saw her go last night. I figured that you *wanted* her to go, and she *was* going. No need for me to go sticking into the thing."

"Well!" Nate replied and leaned back in his chair. He was surprised and yet felt oddly deflated. He wasn't sure *what* to think. Molly had given every sign of planning to stay in his house for *months*. Why would she suddenly change her mind and disappear?

And there was still no sign of his letter. Did Molly's departure mean that she'd decided to do the right thing at last—or that she was preparing to denounce him in Denver?

His mouth twisted. Molly had clearly been faking her leg injury. She was a liar and a blackmailer, and probably mad into the bargain because *nothing* she did made any sense.

"I just thought I'd tell you," the boy drawled.

"Here now—she didn't try to steal one of the horses, did she?"

"Like I'd let her!" the boy cried and drew himself up proudly. "I know what goes on in that barn, mister, night *or* day. She never tried to take a horse, and if she had, I'da mashed her mouth, girl or no girl."

Nate nodded. "Well—good. Thank you, Will."

"Yessir."

"Oh—did you see if she was taking anything with her?"

The boy shrugged. "Just a little hand bag like women folks usually carry. She tiptoed through the barn real quiet-like, and then made off down the drive, out toward the road."

"What time was that?"

"Oh—a little after seven thirty."

Nate's brows rose. "In time for the evening train," he murmured softly. An odd wistful feeling crept over him. He was tempted to feel *sad*, even though that made no sense.

"Thank you for telling me, Will," he murmured, and the boy turned and walked out of the room.

He stood staring at his plate. It was hard to know *how* to feel. For weeks he'd alternated between dread and rage because of that woman, and now she was suddenly gone—without warning and without explanation.

And without any resolution to their dispute, either. Should her sudden departure make him deliriously happy, or was it the ominous prelude to their complete ruin?

The sound of Leonie coming down the stairs made him set down his coffee cup. Leonie would be terribly upset to learn that Molly was gone, and he dreaded having to tell her. But it was impossible to shield Leonie from every bad thing in the world, as much as he might want to.

It was going to be a sharp lesson to Leonie to be more careful about who she trusted. He sighed. Molly's betrayal would hurt her, but if it taught her to be even slightly more sensible, something good might come out of it, in spite of everything.

Or at least, that was what he told himself.

Leonie came rushing into the dining room. "Nate!" she breathed, "Molly isn't in her bedroom! Is she all right? Nothing *bad* happened, did it?"

"Molly's all right, Leonie," he told her soothingly. "Sit down. I'll have Maria bring you a cup of tea."

"But—where is she?" Leonie asked, frowning. "I looked in all the guest rooms. She's not there!"

Nate stared into her eyes sympathetically. "Leonie—Molly's gone," he replied gently. "She left last night. The stable boy just came here to tell me that he saw her go."

Leonie stared at him blankly. "But—that's *impossible!*" she sputtered. "Molly had a broken leg!"

Nate looked at her sadly. "My dear, the fact that she was *able* to leave is proof that Molly's leg wasn't broken at all."

Leonie pursed her lips unhappily. "But she would never just *leave* here, feeling the way that she feels about you! She *loves* you, Nate, and she and I are just like—"

Leonie's lip quivered, and Nate got up and went over and took her in his arms. "There now, Leonie," he told her soothingly, "Molly decided, for reasons of her own, to move on. If that means she's given up her absurd demands, then we can breathe easy again, and go on with our lives."

"Oh, Nate," Leonie whispered, "Molly was so—so in *love* with you. I *know* it; I *saw* it in her eyes."

"Leonie," he replied softly, "you're *always* seeing love. And sometimes you see it when it isn't there. I'm sorry that you were hurt, poppet. But let this be a lesson to you, that you can't trust everyone you meet. We are very wealthy, Leonie. There are people out there who will take advantage of us if they can. For money."

"No, no. I *won't* believe it," Leonie told him. "I can't! Molly is a sweet, beautiful girl, and—and even though I don't understand, I'm sure there's a good reason behind this," Leonie insisted. "You'll see, Nate!"

Nate sighed and kissed her brow. "Very well, Leonie," he murmured. "Have it your way."

Chapter
Thirty-Nine

Shortly after breakfast, Jem McClary came knocking on the dining room door. Nate looked up from the table. He was consoling Leonie, who was slowly ruining his waistcoat with her tears.

Jem looked taken aback. "Oh—I didn't mean to interrupt," he mumbled, glancing down at Leonie's unhappy face. "I guess it's true then. That bob—I mean, Molly Clanahan—has cleared out at last?"

He nodded. "It looks that way, though apparently she took the letter with her. I have no idea what she means to do."

Jem set his jaw. "Well, at least she ain't here anymore, and *that's* something," he muttered.

Leonie raised her head suddenly and flashed out: "I wish you would both stop *rejoicing* that poor Molly is gone! You're *men*, and you can't understand what it is to a woman, to see her true love on the arm of another girl!"

Nate frowned at her. "Surely, Leonie, you can't be suggesting that Molly Clanahan left out of a fit of jealous pique?"

Leonie nodded. "Molly had her womanly pride! You snubbed her for Emmaline, Nate, you know you did!"

Leonie's eyes widened as she warmed to the possibilities of that idea. She sat up and added thrillingly: "I can only imagine what *agonies of torment* she must have gone through, to see you pay such *particular* attention to Emmaline. And under her very nose!"

Jem groaned softly and shook his head, and Nate gave Leonie a quelling glance.

"Leonie, I understand that you were very fond of Molly. I won't quarrel with you about whether she deserved that loyalty. But the fact is that she's gone now, and there's nothing we can do about it."

"That's right," Jem added quickly. "Ain't no use for you to pester yourself about it, Miss Leonie. What's done is done, and we all have to go on." Jem glanced at him wryly over Leonie's head.

"There, dry your eyes now," Nate told her, and pulled a handkerchief out of his pocket. Leonie took it, and blew her nose, but she told him:

"My heart isn't just breaking for Molly, Nate. It's breaking for *you*! Your *callousness* toward your soul mate has caused her to fly. You may never be reunited!"

"I'll just have to solider on, then," Nate replied resolutely, and stood up, brushing crumbs off of his jacket.

"Oh, Mr Trowbridge—the news almost made me forget. You got a telegram. Bob brought it over from town." Jem reached into his vest pocket and pulled out an envelope.

Nate took it and tore it open. To his surprise, the Burlington man in Denver was already sending him a progress report.

Some promising leads stop Will contact you when I have more stop

Nate looked down at his weeping sister and pulled his mouth into a tight line. His worst suspicions were being confirmed. They had been put upon by an adventuress, who was quite possibly also a criminal. What had he been *thinking*, to let that woman stay in his house, so close to his sister? She might have done *anything*.

"Stop crying, Leonie," he told her briskly. "Molly is gone, and that's the end of it. It will do no good to tease me about her now because she's not coming back."

These distressing facts had the opposite effect of the one he wanted, however. Leonie's chin quivered ominously, and she broke out into fresh tears. Nate looked at her face, decided that she was crying for effect now, rather than in true grief, and decided not to encourage further drama. He put the telegram in his pocket.

"I'm going to the library to look over our books. I'll be there if anyone wants me."

He walked out of the dining room and down the hall to the library. He closed the door behind him, settled in at the desk, and gazed out at the garden through the big windows.

It felt deliciously peaceful in the library, with no troublesome intruder in his upstairs bedroom, wearing curvy dresses that couldn't quite hold her, and spying on his guests through the window, and crying out in her sleep.

Now if the Chiswicks returned, he could entertain them comfortably, without having to look over his shoulder.

His mind returned to the telegram. His first instinct had been to tell the detective to suspend his work since Molly had gone, but he had to assume that she still had his letter.

Perhaps it would be wisest to let the detective find what he could on her, in case she ever decided to come back. He was fairly sure that if he could hold a possible jail term over her head, Molly would drop any further attempt to blackmail him.

Still, it was odd, her disappearance. Why would she throw away the comfortable little pillow she'd made for herself in his home, just as soon as she'd won it?

In spite of Molly's protestations of love, and Leonie's ridiculous theories, he had never even considered that he might *really* hold some strange charms for Molly. But his mind returned to Molly's face at the window, and her incredible request that he *marry* her, instead of simply demanding the blackmail money that he'd been perfectly willing to pay.

She had behaved very odd for a blackmailer, that first night. Her eyes had looked *hurt*. Her tone had been *hurt*.

Why shouldn't I have dreams, the same as anybody else?

He wondered, just for an instant, if Leonie of all people had been on the right track. If, as strange as it seemed, that pale face at the window could actually have been—*jealous of Emmaline.*

He rolled a pen between his fingers and allowed himself to wonder what the real truth was about Molly Clanahan.

Not that he was ever likely to know. And that was probably for the best.

Chapter
Forty

After Nate walked out of the dining room, Jem looked down at Leonie's tearful face and rubbed the back of his neck. She looked *awful* torn up. It was a rotten shame that Molly Clanahan had taken advantage of a little innocent girl who didn't know any better than to love everybody.

He crouched down beside her chair and offered her a sweet as if she'd been six years old. "Here," he told her, and opened a little wax paper envelope. "I bought some candy in town. Have some, it's good!"

Leonie looked over at him doubtfully. "What is it?" she sniffed and gave it a tiny glance.

"Why, it's rock candy," he told her and held out a piece. "See that? It's clear as crystal. I bought it off a miner who told me that he's working a vein of it at the bottom of the Rocky Mountains."

A slow smile crept over Leonie's face. "That's *silly*," she scoffed but took a piece of the candy into her hand.

"Be careful," Jem grinned. "It's *rock* candy, after all! Don't break those pretty teeth!"

Leonie shrieked and dropped the candy as if it burned her hand. She looked up into Jem's grinning face and sputtered in sheepish laughter.

"Oh, you're sweet to try to make me laugh, Jem," she said, drying her eyes, "but I'll never have a moment's peace until I know what became of my Molly. She's all alone in the world, Jem! Imagine it!"

"Now, you don't go worrying yourself about that, Leonie," he assured her. "Molly Clanahan can take of *herself.* You don't see your brother crying that she's gone, do you? He knows best. You listen to him."

Leonie shook her head impatiently. "Nate knows as much about *love* as I know about ranching! He's never looked at any girl except Emmaline, and *her* only when he was ready to propose! Nate's a wonderful person, and will make a fine husband one day, but—he puts so little stock in *romance.*"

She raised imploring blue eyes to his face. "Sometimes I wish I could just *give* him the feeling of being in love," she whispered sadly. "I don't want him to go through life with numbers, and clocks, and business papers. He needs someone like Molly to shake him up!"

Jem gave her a sceptical look. "I don't think your brother wants to be shook up *that* bad, Leonie," he replied. "Seems to me that your brother's a sensible fellow and doing just what he should to keep you and this ranch safe. What he thinks about romance, is his business."

"That's just it, Jem. He doesn't think of it at *all!*"

"He looks happy enough to me. Why don't you let him live his life, and you live yours? I'm not being ugly, now, I'm just saying."

Leonie's eyes smiled. "Oh, I could never be angry with you, Jem. *I understand.*"

Jem smiled. "Well, there you go, then," he said softly and pulled one of her ringlets. He would have stood up, but her hand on his arm stopped him.

"Would you like to make me feel better, *truly*, Jem?" she whispered.

Jem's smile faded. "What do you mean ..." he started, but Leonie leaned over suddenly and planted a kiss on his shrinking mouth.

"*Here now!*" he sputtered and leaned back on his heels. He rolled horrified eyes to the door before replying sternly: "Leonie, if your brother walked in and saw that just now, he'd kick me to the moon, and I wouldn't blame him! You can't just haul off and *kiss* me. I could lose my *job*. You understand that, don't you?"

Leonie pled with her eyes. "Don't you *want* me to kiss you, Jem?" she asked forlornly.

"*No*. No, I *don't* want you to *kiss* me," he told her emphatically. "You're too young to think about kissing, anyway. Why don't you get a hobby like other girls? I know—next time I'm in town, I'll buy you a picture puzzle, like a map of Denver, or a painting of Chief Blue Hand. How about that?"

But to his dismay, Leonie's hopeful expression crumpled up into disappointment. She clapped a hand to her mouth and ran out of the dining room in tears.

Jem sat back on his haunches and tilted his hat back on his head. "Well," he muttered to himself, "I never saw such a case of puppy love in all my days." He shook his head and unfolded his tall frame. "I wish she'd get excited about something besides *me*."

He turned toward the door, but to his surprise, Will was standing in it. Jem stared at the boy in dismay.

"How much of that did you just see?" he demanded, hands on hips.

"I ain't going to rat on you if that's what you're skeerd of," the boy replied disdainfully. "It ain't nothing to me if that girl likes you."

"Well, it's something to *me*," Jem told him, in an urgent undertone. "I didn't ask her to do what she did, and I ain't never laid a *hand* on her!"

The boy shrugged. "I don't care either way," he mumbled. "And I won't tell."

Jem relaxed a bit but warned him: "See that you don't. I got *enough* making trouble for me, without having that girl thrown in. Why are you up here, anyway?"

"Clem sent me to the depot, and I picked up the mail," he replied, and tossed a stack of envelopes and a newspaper down on the table.

"Well, now that you've done it, I need three horses this afternoon for the men who are riding line. I'll go with you to get them."

They both turned and walked out, and a few moments after they were gone, Maria emerged from the door on the other side of the room and began to silently collect the breakfast dishes.

She said nothing but gave the doorway they had passed through a short, speculative glance as she worked.

Chapter
Forty-One

The sun had dipped behind the tall pines, and the shadows were lengthening to dusk as Molly reached the train depot. She was just in time for the train's arrival. It was the last departure from Indian Rock that evening, and she was confident that she'd gotten clean away from the Circle T without anyone seeing her.

She paid the sleepy railroad employee in the depot shack, and was gratified to see his look of surprise, and to hear him call her "ma'am." Her fine dress and her new way of styling her hair made people see her as the lady she had always hoped to be.

Not the desperate gutter lily Jack had forced her to become, for one horrible afternoon.

Molly opened her bag and looked down at the two letters. Now that push came to shove, she didn't have the heart to mail them. She would, of course, but maybe it would be better to mail them from a greater distance than the Indian Rock depot, just to be certain they really would be the last word.

It would be painful and embarrassing to be caught in the act of leaving. Molly decided that she would keep the letters until she got on the train, and then mail them from some stop on the way to San Francisco.

She walked back through the cars to third class. The seats in third class were hard wooden benches, not the plush velvet she had enjoyed on her ride down from

Denver; and for once she was the best-dressed woman in the crowd. Molly settled into a seat by the window at the very back of the car. That position allowed her to scan the other travellers. Most of the other passengers looked like working folks on the way to the city. Like her, they were looking for a new job, or a place to start over.

Molly looked down at her own dress. Leonie's parting gift to her was that she had a nice outfit to wear, for when she went to look for work in San Francisco. She would have to send money to repay her when she could.

Molly sighed. She'd stolen a few weeks from Nate Trowbridge's life to live in a palace, and to ensure her own safety. It had been nice while it lasted, but she was back to the *real* world, now.

And that meant she had to stay alert. She had searched every face in the car to make sure Jack's wasn't one of them, and she was going to mind her own business and keep a low profile.

The train whistle moaned a low, lonesome note, and the train began to pull away from the Indian Rock depot. Molly watched forlornly as the depot faded away, and the little town slid past. It hurt her to think she'd never see pretty little Leonie or the handsome swell again. She was going to miss them, though no one in the place but Leonie would miss *her*, it stood to reason.

Still, the darkening countryside rolling past blurred for a little while, and Molly found that she had to rub her eyes more than she liked, in public.

But if she *really* wanted to do right by Nate and Leonie, she had to leave. They'd soon forget her and move on with their rich lives. They'd be too busy enjoying parties and dances and important business to remember her.

But she'd remember *them* for the rest of her life.

Molly rested her head against the window and settled in for a long, solitary journey as the twilight countryside rolling by deepened into night.

***

The train rolled into Cheyenne a little more than an hour and a half later, and Molly gazed out at the station listlessly. It looked almost empty that time of night since there were only a few runs still scheduled. Her switchover, the Transcontinental run, was one of them, and when the train came to a stop, she rose and followed the other passengers out into the station.

The ticket counter was across the way from the boarding platform, and Molly hurried over to buy a ticket to San Francisco. She looked over her shoulder as she waited in line. She was in Jack's town now, and even though she looked very different, she couldn't afford to let her guard down.

When it came time for her to pay for her fare, the man at the ticket window nodded to her deferentially. "Where to, ma'am?"

"San Francisco, third class, ticket for one," she murmured and ignored the eyebrow that he raised. It was somewhat scandalous for a woman to travel long distances alone, and people looked askance at any woman bold enough to do it. Molly raised her chin proudly and took the ticket he gave her without another word. It chafed her that even now, the taint of the Golden Nugget still clung to her skirts.

She couldn't wait to get to San Francisco and turn the page on the most disastrous decision she'd ever made. Maybe she could find a man there the old-fashioned way. But one thing was for sure; she was never going to answer another ad for a mail order bride.

She looked down at her little yellow ticket to San Francisco, with its crowded type, and bold letters. It had been expensive, and it left her only a little pocket money, but she still had the leftover food that she'd wrapped up in her bag, and she walked over to a little bench to eat her dinner as she waited for the train. She unwrapped the biscuits and slices of roast beef and cheese, and made herself a nice little sandwich.

She had chosen the bench because it was under the spreading fronds of a big potted palm, and she was half-hidden under it. She often scanned the passers-by as she waited. Cheyenne was still a bawdy town full of untrustworthy men, quite apart from Jack McGee, and the sooner she was out of it, the better. The little pistol was still loaded and lying snug against her right leg, and its presence comforted her. It was the only friend she had in a strange place, and would be her only travelling companion.

Molly finished her sandwich and wondered sadly if anyone back at the Circle T had noticed that she was gone. It made her remember the letters, and she raised her eyes to the ticket counter, a few dozen yards away. There was a sign by the window reading *Post Office*.

She opened her bag, pulled the letters out, and looked at them with a sigh. Maybe she couldn't bring herself to mail them because once she did, it was *really* the end.

But she thought of Leonie's smiling, innocent face, and of Nate's straight carriage and proud eyes, and bit her lip. Mailing the letters would be hard because mailing them was the right thing to do.

And she had learned that the right thing was almost *always* the hard thing.

Lord, she prayed briefly, *I hope you're looking. I'm going to do what I should, and I hope we'll be on a little better terms now.*

The shriek of a train whistle alerted Molly to the approach of the Transcontinental. She only had a few minutes to get the letters off, and so she brushed the crumbs off her lap, took the letters in her hand, and made her way across the floor to the ticket counter. She was thinking of how she would find the courage to hand them to the man behind the counter.

And had taken her eyes off the other people passing by.

Molly hadn't taken five steps toward the ticket window when a hand clamped her elbow, and a man's voice whispered fiercely in her ear.

"Yell, and I'll cut your heart out."

Something cold and sharp dug into her side, and she rolled terrified eyes to the speaker, but he hustled her across the floor so quickly that she only got a glimpse of a swarthy, powerful man in a bowler hat and a dark jacket. All she could be really sure of was that the man wasn't Jack.

But since he had a knife in her ribs, that was hardly a comfort.

She twisted around and rolled anguished eyes to the ticket counter, but to her dismay, the attendant had pulled the shade down for the night. The sign on the window read *Closed*.

The man wrenched her arm so hard that she shrieked out in pain, and the letters that she'd been holding in her hand fluttered to the floor. The roar of the oncoming engine filled the station, and her shriek was drowned by its din. Most of the other travellers in the station were looking at the train, and those who might have seen her anguished face didn't raise an eyebrow, or make any outcry.

Once she'd been wrestled out onto the darkened street, the man yanked her down the hill and into the first side alley next to the train station. The alley was lit only by one dim window high on the facing building, and the man was only a hulking shadow. Molly stifled a scream as her assailant pulled the knife out of her side and used it to cut the bag off her arm.

He opened the handbag and yanked out her small stash of money. And as he bent over the bag, Molly clenched her teeth, leaned over, and hiked her skirt up to the knee.

Chapter
Forty-Two

Molly's fingers closed over the cold handle of the revolver just as two grimy hands closed on her throat. The man was so close that she could smell onions and tobacco on his breath, and she could feel his coarse laughter vibrate in his chest.

"You don't remember me, but I *shore* remember you," he whispered into her ear. "Nobody in the Golden Nugget was going to forget the little redheaded tart that knocked Jack McGee on his can!"

His fingers tightened around her throat like a strangling rope, and Molly closed her eyes. He was slowly choking her, and lights began to pop off in her head. She had to force herself not to drop the gun and claw at the hands that were cutting off her air.

"Oh, did we hee-haw! And you'd best believe that ol' Jack was mad as a hornet about it, too. I ain't never *seed* a man so red-faced and riled. You done hurt his *pride,* missy. That makes a man *turrible* mean."

He lunged suddenly and crushed his mouth against hers, and she almost gagged as his wet tongue left a trail of sticky slobber in her mouth and across her face. "I figured you'd show up sometime," he mumbled into her neck. "It's hard for a redheaded woman to hide for long. And Jack promised a re-ward to any man who could find you," he breathed.

Molly's eyes widened, and she turned her head away, but he yanked it back and forced her to look at him.

He pushed his body against hers and pinned her to the wall. "Jack was right generous," he said cackling softly, "and I decided to take him up on his bounty. His face is gonna be a sight when I bring you back to the Nugget.

"But I don't reckon ol' Jack will mind if I give myself a little bonus, first."

His hands moved down from her throat. The crushing pressure lifted from her windpipe, and Molly gasped for air. She scowled in revulsion at the touch of the man's grimy hands, but his preoccupation gave her the chance to raise the gun, and she jammed the barrel into his temple as hard as she could.

Her assailant froze.

"*Get off me!*" she snarled. When the man didn't make any move, she cocked the revolver with a loud *click*.

"*I'll blow your brains out!*" she spat.

The man suddenly pushed off her and was swallowed up by the darkness. The instant she was free, Molly slid as far away from him as she could along the alley wall. No sooner had she moved, than the man threw his fist at the spot where her face had been, and hit the brick wall instead. There was the sound of a sharp *crack*, a howl of pain, and a stream of savage obscenities.

The sudden cry made her jump in terror, and her gun went off with a *bang* and a flash.

Molly shrieked, threw the revolver down, hiked up her skirts, and flew for the street as fast as she could run. She almost knocked a drunken cowboy down as she burst out, and she went running back up the hill and into the train station with her hair falling around her shoulders. She vaulted up the station steps, burst through the doors, and stopped dead on the threshold of the deserted boarding platforms. The Transcontinental was sitting there, exhaling steam, and the last passengers were climbing aboard.

Molly looked down at herself. The throat of her dress had been ripped open, her hair was falling down, and her handbag was still lying on the floor of the alley. Her ticket and her money were there, too, but she couldn't, *couldn't* go back there now.

Maybe the no-account was dead—and maybe he *wasn't*.

But the train station was the biggest, most public place within three blocks that she dared to enter. She could only pray that if the man was alive, he wouldn't find her gun and follow her.

She put her hand to her head in despair. *Oh God,* she prayed, *please help me. What can I do now?*

But the sky didn't part, and no angel band came to rescue her. No miracle happened. The last traveller entered the train, and the porter cried, *"All aboaard!"*

Molly watched in despair as the porter hopped up into the train car. The blast of the train's whistle hurt her ears, and with a roar of steam, and thunder that made the platform shake, the train that should have taken her to San Francisco and a new life, left her standing on the Cheyenne platform shaken, penniless and alone.

Molly stood there with her head in her hands, sobbing, as elegant first-class passengers stared at her curiously from their curtained windows—a bedraggled redheaded woman with a tear-stained face and frightened eyes.

Molly watched them as they passed: idle, curious faces sliding by high above her. She wondered wildly if she could somehow climb onto one of the cars as they rolled past, but her beautiful dress, with its elegant sweeping skirts, made that impossible.

She was stuck in Cheyenne. And she hadn't even been back for an *hour* before she'd been set on, robbed, and assaulted.

The thought of going to the law flashed through her mind, but no sooner had it occurred to her, than Jack's smug words replayed themselves in her mind.

The lawmen here are some of my best customers. Remember that.

She turned away from the platform, weeping. The thought came to her that she could go to the water closet in the station and wash that no-account's onion-tasting slobber out of her mouth and off her face. Then she could button up her collar, and smooth her dress, and fix her hair.

But that was as far into the future as her imagination could reach. She had no idea where she could go or what she was going to do after that.

The only thing she was sure of was that she was in Jack's town now, stranded and with a pack of bounty hunting scum searching high and low for her. She was a fox in a town full of dogs, and unless she sharpened her wits and found a way out, they'd tear her apart.

But in spite of the disasters she'd just endured, the disdainful expressions on strangers' faces made Molly pull herself up, square her shoulders, and march across the floor with her head high.

She might not be able to make other people treat her right, and she might not be able to make them respect her, but by George, she was going to respect *herself*.

That self-respect was all she had left, and once it was gone—she really *would* be at the mercy of the world.

Chapter
Forty-Three

Nate Trowbridge sat at his desk in the downstairs library and tapped his pencil against the desk absently. The Burlington man had sent him a telegram hinting at progress with his investigation. And if the man had found evidence that Molly Clanahan had committed some *crime*, then the threat of exposure would force her to return his letter—*if* she ever resumed her threats.

His nightmare would be over at last. He could relax and get on with his life.

He could go ahead and propose to Emmaline with a clear conscience and an untroubled mind.

Even the thought of such a happy outcome flooded him with relief. He hadn't realized, until just then, just how pent-up and distressed that redheaded woman had made him.

It was terrible to live your life looking over your shoulder, constantly dreading some fearful stroke.

It was also terrible to live all jumbled up, not knowing what to expect next from the woman: craft, blackmail, lies, tears, pathos, or even ...

Nate tapped the pencil on the desk again and decided not to let his mind wander down *that* path. The day that he let himself be influenced by Leonie's ridiculous fancies was the day he could be committed as a madman.

Still, he had to admit that Molly Clanahan was probably the bravest and most beautiful woman he'd ever met in his life. He was sure she had quite enough nerve to burgle Buckingham Palace.

It was a pity that she wasn't a woman of integrity. He'd never met any woman quite like her. Which was a mercy, of course, but—

He couldn't stop wondering who the *real* Molly Clanahan was. He'd caught glimpses of another woman when the brazen, nervy façade had slipped and he'd seen her lips tremble, or caught tears in her eyes. Maybe those tears had been a lie, in the same way that her 'broken leg' had been a lie.

But he was inclined to think not.

Molly was an actress. *That* was indisputable. But which Molly was the assumed identity—the earnest young woman who only wanted someone to love, or the brazen adventuress bold enough to risk blackmail?

Or, perhaps—*desperate* enough. Wasn't that what she had told him herself, over and over? He hadn't believed her, then.

Nate stared at his desk with dark, troubled eyes. The thing that bothered him most was—what if the words Molly had cried out in her sleep had been *real* memories of a *real* abduction? In spite of all the wretched things she'd done, that possibility haunted him.

He would have to mention them to the detective when they talked. Nate rapped his pencil against the desk a little harder. The idea of Molly, or any woman, being forced into prostitution by some blackguard made his blood boil. If the detective found that there was any such place in Denver, he would have it closed down summarily, and the proprietor sent to prison.

Nate raised an eyebrow. Although he *had* heard that the locals sometimes dealt with a rotter by introducing him to 'Judge Rope', and in such a case, he would not be disposed to interfere with their wisdom.

Nate came back to himself with a sigh and shook his head. Why was he letting his mind run on that woman? Now that Molly had vanished, it was pointless to tease himself about her anymore. He pulled a hand over his eyes and got back to work.

He opened the book of accounts and began studying the entries, but after twenty minutes, he found that he was quite unable to concentrate, and shut it again.

Speculation was useless. What he needed was to go to Denver, put the thing before the Burlington man, and have him get on it at once. Then he would know how to proceed.

He rapped the pencil against his desk in frustration.

The questions in his mind were driving him mad. They were going to make work next to impossible.

Questions like: How was it possible that Molly had used a *tunnel* in his house before he had even *heard* of it?

"Bah!"

Nate threw the pencil down on his desk in disgust, got up, and left the room.

***

"Nate, you haven't eaten a bite."

Nate looked up from his dinner that evening to see Leonie's sad eyes questioning him.

"Oh, don't mind me. I'm just thinking, that's all."

Her hand crept across the table and clasped his. "About what?"

"I was thinking it might be good for both of us to visit Denver for a few days. You could visit with Francie, and I could—conduct some business."

To his astonishment, Leonie shook her head. "You go on, Nate. I wouldn't have a speck of pleasure in it, not even if I got to visit the Chiswicks."

Nate looked at her listless face and suffered a pang of worry. "Come now, Leonie," he told her gently, "I'm sorry if I wasn't as sympathetic to your feelings as I might have been. No doubt I'm a hulking brute."

He smiled at her and was gratified to see a tiny, answering gleam in her eyes. The edge of her mouth curved up.

"You're not a brute, Nate," she confessed. "You just don't *feel* enough. And when you don't have your *own* feelings, how can you enter into someone else's? I don't blame you."

"Thank you," he replied dryly and shook out his napkin. "But I do wish you'd come with me, Leonie. It's unhealthy to mope about something you can't change. Molly is gone, and we can't change that."

"You *could* change it, Nate—if only you would."

His startled eyes lifted to hers over his coffee cup. "What are you talking about?"

Leonie traced an intricate pattern on the tablecloth with her finger. "You could find Molly if you tried. She can't have gone far. She doesn't have that much money."

Nate stared at her, frowning. "Leonie, if she caught the train, she could be in Chicago by now. And neither you nor I need to worry that Molly will find herself without *money*. She's demonstrated great skill in that area."

"Don't joke about it, Nate. I won't get a wink of sleep tonight, worrying about her."

Nate set down his coffee. "Leonie," he said softly, "Molly left of her own free will. If we brought her back, she'd just leave again. You can't force someone else to stay with you if they don't want to."

Leonie raised her eyes to his, and the look in them was reproachful. "Molly only left because she saw you with Emmaline," she replied. "She *despaired* of you, Nate. She left because she lost *hope*. She left because her heart was broken. Can't you see that?"

He stared at her in silent consternation and chose his words carefully. "Very well, Leonie," he said, in an even voice. "I will go to Denver and talk to a detective about Molly. Would that please you?"

His little sister sat up, eyes bright. "Oh, *would* you, Nate?" she cried. "*Please* do! Maybe we could at least be certain that nothing *bad* has happened to Molly. You can't know the torments I've suffered, imagining all the things that could have gone wrong!"

Nate pinched his mouth into a straight line. Leonie's imagination was getting out of hand, and the next chance he got, he was going to tell Maria to confiscate those deuced romances of hers and *burn* them.

But he only smiled and reassured her: "I'll do it when I go to Denver. Still sure you don't want to come along? I could be persuaded to take you shopping."

Leonie squeezed his hand. "And I know how you *hate* shopping, too, Nate," she said gratefully. "But no, not this time. I'm just not up to it. Maybe later when we've ...

we've *satisfied* ourselves that Molly is all right. I couldn't look at anything until I was sure."

"All right then, Leonie. Another time. But I'm sure that Molly is quite all right. Don't lose sleep teasing yourself over it."

"I wish I could be as sure as you are," Leonie said plaintively and got up from the table.

Nate watched her go with a frown and promised himself that when he got to Denver, he'd go to the detective first thing.

So that—absurd as it was—both he and Leonie could escape the overhanging cloud of their blackmailer's *uncertain well-being*.

Chapter
Forty-Four

Nate arrived at the Burlington office in Denver a little after noon the next day. He opened the door and walked into the neat brick building, and as before, the young man at the desk welcomed him.

"Good morning, Mr Trowbridge," he said briskly. "How can I help you?"

"I'm here to see Detective Jameson," he replied. "I don't have an appointment, but I was in Denver on business and thought I'd drop by. I was hoping he might be able to see me."

"I'll check with him," the man replied and disappeared up the narrow stairs.

Nate glanced around the room while he was gone. There were framed newspaper articles on the wall proclaiming the capture of famous criminals by Burlington agents and several awards for outstanding bravery.

There was also a small glass case just opposite the desk containing several mementos of past cases: a silver duelling gun belonging to the famous desperado Little John Baldwin; a small book filled with the names of nine men marked for murder during a railroad strike, and a small glass vial that the Murdering Madam, Bessie Mae Colson, had used to poison one of the upstairs girls who'd stolen her young lover.

Nate stroked his moustache. That last one reminded him very uncomfortably of Jem's ordeal at the boarding house, and he wondered for the thousandth time if he was losing his mind to humour Leonie's flights of fancy. But then the young man reappeared and motioned to him from the stairs.

"Detective Jameson will see you. Come this way."

Nate followed him up the stair to the office on the second floor. The detective rose to greet him and extended a beefy hand. Nate shook it and took a seat.

"I'm glad to see you," Jameson told him, "I've had good luck with this inquiry, and I have several fresh leads. I was just about to get in touch with you."

"I'm entirely at your disposal," Nate replied. "Tell me what you've learned."

The man frowned. "Well, I'll have to backtrack a bit," he began. "I searched this woman's name and couldn't find any criminal history or current warrants against it. So I began to search in her last place of residence.

"She was living at an O'Malley's Boarding House here in Denver. I talked to the woman who runs the place and several of the people who knew her there. They said she was a seamstress who worked for a custom embroidery shop in town. I checked that out, and it was true. She'd been working there for about a month, and the people there didn't know where she'd worked before. But one of the girls told me that she'd said something about coming out here alone from her home in Kansas.

"Women don't often come this far west unless they're travelling with their families, so a woman travelling alone really narrows it down. Women sometimes come out here alone if they're prostitutes looking for work in a boom town. Places like Cheyenne, and certain parts of Denver, provide a lot of business. Or sometimes, women come out here alone if they're responding to an ad for a mail order bride."

"She did say something about mail order brides, the first night she came to my home," Nate replied.

"Usually a woman who answers an ad like that is desperate in some way," Jameson went on. "The woman's husband left her, or died, and she's out of money. Maybe she's an unmarried girl, and some disaster happened to her family, and she's alone, and has no work, and is about to be homeless. So the offer looks like a way out.

"And so she comes out here, and sometimes the man waiting for her is exactly what he said he was, and everything works out fine.

"But sometimes he *isn't* what he said he was. Sometimes he runs a brothel and is kidnapping girls that he knows likely don't have any relatives to protect them, and that he can advertise as fresh and free of—the health problems that one often finds in brothels."

Nate stared at him. "Then the rumours I heard were true!" he exclaimed. "I could hardly credit it!"

Jameson nodded. "It's a slave trade, pure and simple, Mr Trowbridge, you're right."

Nate glared at him. "Well, what's being *done* about it?" he demanded. "Surely you aren't telling me that such an outrage is *tolerated* here?"

The detective scratched his ear and coughed. "Well, prostitution *per se* isn't illegal here," he replied. "Kidnapping is, if you can prove it, and that's always the biggest legal hurdle. You need witnesses, and the people who can testify, are the least likely to do it."

"The devil you say!" Nate barked. "That's—"

"A shame, yes, Mr Trowbridge," Jameson replied. "A real shame."

Jameson, seeing that he was livid, went on: "Anyway—there are a few main companies that connect men and women interested in mail order marriage. I contacted them for any recent information about a Molly Clanahan, and one of them turned up positive."

He pushed a telegram across the desk, and Nate picked it up and glared at it. It read:

Our records show that a woman by that name answered Ad No. 325, run by a gentleman from Cheyenne, Wyoming stop That's all the information we have stop

"I heard her one night, crying out in her sleep," Nate blurted. "She was begging not to be beaten. She kept talking to someone named *Jack*."

Jameson's eyebrow went up, and Nate flushed and hastened to add: "She was sleeping in my guest bedroom, down the hall from my den. I heard her even from that distance. She was almost *screaming*."

Jameson nodded. "Cheyenne has been a rough place for a long time, and some of the bawdy houses there are real dens. If your Molly Clanahan was kidnapped, I wouldn't be surprised if one of the houses in Cheyenne turned out to be the place she was taken to.

"And if that's the case, Mr Trowbridge, I'm surprised she got away. Most of the time, the pimp threatens to kill the girl if she leaves, because he knows that the longer she stays there, the harder it is to leave. Once the girl becomes known in town, there's not many opportunities for her to ... do other kinds of work. She's trapped there."

"Blackguards!" Nate snarled. "Any man who would do such a thing to an innocent girl should be shot on sight!"

"I agree with you there," Jameson replied soberly. "It's a shameful thing, and it happens more often than you'd think.

"Which brings me back to the present," he said, with a sigh. "The woman who runs the boarding house told me that Molly was a quiet boarder, up until a few days before she left. She says a man showed up one day at the boarding house asking for her. She described him as a big fellow, six feet tall, with red hair and light eyes. She said she noticed a scar on his face.

"He asked to see Molly, and she told him that Molly was at work. She says he refused to leave a name but said to tell Molly that he'd be back. The woman said that when she told Molly about him, the girl went as white as a sheet but denied knowing any such man.

"But she said that Molly started behaving strangely from that point on. Nervous. Jumpy. And that a few days later, when another man came to give her a letter, she got into a cab with him and never came back."

Nate sat ramrod straight in his chair, his mouth pressed into a thin, furious line. He imagined how *he* would react if someone tried to do to *his* sister what that blackguard had done to Molly, and he saw himself strangling the villain with his bare hands.

Everything Molly had done made sense to him now. When his letter had come to her, she'd been so desperate to escape that monster she'd been ready to grab at any straw. In such terrible straits, he couldn't blame her for doing whatever she had to, to get away.

He shook his head. Everything that had baffled him—Molly's refusal to take his money, her demand to be married for a year, her machinations to stay inside his house, even to the point of faking a broken leg—all of them had just been the desperate attempt of a hunted girl to be safe for a little while.

A wave of shame rolled over him. He'd been wrong about Molly Clanahan, *completely* wrong. She was no more an adventuress than Leonie, and he felt heartily ashamed of the things he had said to her in the heat of anger.

Nate pulled a hand across his eyes and then massaged the throbbing spot between them.

"Molly left us two days ago," he said at last. "The man at the Indian Rock train depot told me that she bought a ticket to Cheyenne. Do you have any thoughts about that?"

The detective raised his bushy eyebrows. "Just that I'm surprised. Do you know how much money she had at the time?"

"My sister says she gave Molly close to fifty dollars a day or two before," he replied, and the man grunted.

"If I had to guess, I'd say—based on what we know about her—that she was going there to catch the Transcontinental. Maybe she decided to go back home to Kansas, or further east. It was a nervy thing to do if Cheyenne is where she escaped from. Do you have any idea why she left your house?"

Nate felt his face going warm. "Nothing definite," he replied. "It seemed odd to us. She had worked so hard to stay."

The detective nodded and looked down at his hands. "Well, that's about where it stands now," he said at last. "Now that the woman's gone, what do you want to do? Does she still have your letter?"

Nate made an impatient gesture. "I have no fear of what she'll do with the letter, now. She just used it to find shelter in my house."

"Well, then," the detective replied slowly, "it looks to me as if your problem is solved."

Nate shot him a piercing glance. "It is not!" he exclaimed indignantly. "If you think for an instant that I'm going to fold my hands, while that reptile is still out there, preying on young women, you're much mistaken, my man! The first thing I'm going to do is find Miss Clanahan. And then I'm going to track down that villain Jack, wherever he may be hiding, and thrash him within an inch of his life!"

The detective blinked at him. "Yes, well. There's a few problems with that plan, Mr Trowbridge—"

"I will require you to come with me to Cheyenne," Nate went on, pulling on his gloves, "with at least a dozen Burlington men, and as many more as you can spare."

The detective raised an eyebrow and asked, in a slightly amused tone: "Have you ever, er—been in a *fight*, Mr Trowbridge?" he asked.

Nate gave him an irritated glance. "If you mean, do I engage in drunken brawls in houses of ill repute, *no*, Mr Jameson," he replied briskly, "but I boxed regularly at my club in London, and I can say without vanity that I am accounted to have a blinding right."

The detective scratched his moustache and nodded. "Well, Mr Trowbridge, I can promise you that any man you'll fight in a Cheyenne saloon won't ever have heard of the Marquess of Queensberry rules. He'll be more likely to shoot you, or throw a bottle at your head, than to put up his fists."

"If you're implying that I don't know how to take care of a blackguard," Nate began indignantly, "I can only tell you that I'll prove myself in action. Are you willing to do what I ask, or not? Speak up!"

Jameson gazed at him patiently and then replied: "I have an idea, Mr Trowbridge. It won't require as many men, or as much bloodshed, and it'll be more likely to succeed. But you'll have to follow my advice to the last detail."

Nate glanced at him impatiently. "What is it, then?"

Jameson folded his hands across the desk and leaned over it. "Here's how we can do what you want, and stay *legal.*"

Chapter
Forty-Five

Jack McGee leaned over the bar at the Golden Nugget and swept the room with his light eyes. It was a busy Friday night because cowboys and bullwhackers from a half-dozen outfits had just rolled into town to get drunk and laid.

He looked out across the hazy barroom and smiled to himself. They just kept rolling in like they was on a conveyor belt—greenhorn suckers and horny old goats, sick of cows and dust and other men. All of them *desperate* to give him their money.

And so he likkered 'em up, and sent the girls out to 'em, to get them ready to go upstairs and rent a room.

And if they *didn't* rent one, after a little while, he had the girls put a dash of the Jack McGee Special into their beer and told the bouncers to carry 'em out to the back alley, take their money, and dump 'em there.

Either way, they woke up the next morning face down on the pavement, flat broke and wondering what the fool happened, but it didn't matter, 'cause the next day the drovers and bullwhackers and cowboys had to roll on, and so they never came back to ask nosy questions.

Business wasn't booming like it had been in Cheyenne's wildest days, but it was still all right. He looked out across the crowd and saw one of the sheriff's deputies whispering into a girl's ear. He paid the little squirt almost twenty dollars a month to look the other way, but it was worth it.

Cheyenne was beginning to fill up with them lousy holy rollers, and they was screechin' about *morals*. They were raisin' Cain with the sheriff and were sending letters to the local papers, trying to get places like his *shut down*.

In the old days, he and his boys would've paid 'em a little visit one night, and rid them out of town on a rail; but Cheyenne had changed, and there were too many of 'em now to do what he'd like to do.

A little insurance never hurt.

He looked out across the room and narrowed his eyes. Selma was just sitting in the corner, doin' *nothin*. He was going to have to teach her a lesson if she didn't perk up and get to work. He was getting tired of her whining. There wasn't nothin' more useless than a lazy whore, and it looked like he was going to have to *remind* her.

The new girl, a skinny little blonde, was about to get a lesson too. He had told her to *smile*, but her eyes was all red and puffy and ugly, and instead of acting like she was havin' a good time, like he *told* her, she looked like she was going to be sick.

Nobody liked a lapful of pale, sniveling little *Mamma's* girl.

He sent her a look that said she was a hair away from a broken jaw, and she caught his look, sobbed, and straightened up.

That's more like it, he thought grimly, and swept the room again. The sight of a bowler hat in the mob made him frown. It looked like Atlee was back. He was one of the men who'd gone out looking for that redheaded wench, and maybe he had news.

241

Though it looked like Atlee hadn't had any better luck than the rest of 'em since he hadn't brought no *redhead*.

Jack fumed to himself. Why it was *so hard* to find a woman with a head of hair as red as infernal fire, he didn't know. He had found her in Denver easy enough and would've dragged her right back, too, if it hadn't been for all them people around. There had been too many *witnesses,* that time.

She'd gotten away once, but she wasn't going to get away a second time. A hundred dollar bounty was going to see to *that*.

Or at least, you'd think so, but so far, the men who'd taken him up on the offer hadn't put much time into the search. Seemed to him that a hundred dollars would be enough reason for a man to make an *effort*, but then, the men who came to the Golden Nugget weren't exactly the sharpest knives in the drawer. He couldn't complain about their puny brains since they was making him rich; but even so.

He pushed off from the bar and swam through the crowd until he was standing at Atlee's elbow. Atlee lifted his face from Louella's neck and blanched.

"Jack!"

He clamped an arm around Atlee's shoulder and pulled him out of Louella's embrace. "I'm glad to see you, Atlee," he told him. "Why don't I buy you a beer."

Atlee was watching him out of the corner of his eye. "Thanks, Jack."

They shouldered up to the bar, and he put up two fingers. The bartender drew two beers and slid them over.

Atlee picked one up and took a long pull. He seemed to be a little nervous.

"Have you had any luck looking for that redhead, Atlee?" Jack asked. "My offer still stands. One hundred dollars, American."

Atlee hunched over his beer, threw him a quick look over his shoulder.

"Are you just payin' a re-ward for the *girl*, or will you pay for *tips* about her, too?"

Jack stared into Atlee's small, dark eyes. "Why?"

"I think I saw her," he said at last, in a low voice. "But I'm not sure."

Jack narrowed his eyes. "You saw her?" he repeated. "Here, in *Cheyenne*?"

Atlee shrugged. "It was dark, and she had her face turned away. I couldn't be sure."

"*Where* did you see her?" Jack asked evenly and looked up at the ceiling.

"Over to the train station," Atlee mumbled. "But I don't think she took the train."

Jack's glance drifted down from Atlee's face, and he frowned. "What's that long mark on your neck, Atlee?" he grumbled. "It looks like a graze wound. Have a close call?"

Atlee turned up his collar and looked away. "It's nothing."

"*Hmm*. Well, Atlee—so, the redhead was near the train station but didn't go in?"

"That's—that's right."

"And this happened when?"

"Two nights ago."

Jack raised his eyebrows. "*Two* nights ago! Well, well, well." He sucked his teeth with a loud, sharp *smack.*

"Tell you what," he said at last, "you follow me to my office, and I'll give you your reward for that information."

Atlee's tiny eyes searched his face. His expression was a painful mixture of fear and greed. Jack smiled and left the bar, certain that Atlee would follow. His kind always grabbed for shiny things, and got burned or buzzed, depending on what the shiny thing turned out to be.

He walked through the velvet draperies that separated the public saloon from the business end of the Nugget. He turned into his office and waited.

A minute later, Atlee entered, his head tilted cautiously to one side. Jack let his wary guest get a pace or two inside the room and then burst from behind the door.

He slammed the smaller man up against the wall and clamped both hands around his neck.

"You *lied* to me," he hissed, and tightened his fingers. Atlee's eyes seemed to double in size, and he rolled them to Jack's face in terror. He tried to shake his head.

"I know you *did*," Jack nodded. "You saw her, all right. You had her in your hands, just like I have you now, because you grab first and think later." He tightened his grip, and the veins in Atlee's neck jumped out.

"And somehow, *somehow*, Atlee, she ain't here with you. If you were a smarter man, I'd say she ain't here because you *kilt* her, but you're not a smarter man. My money says she had a gun, and that you didn't think of that until it was too late. I think that's why you have a fresh graze on your neck. *She got away*. And that's why you're here trying to grift me for information that's *two days old*, instead of handing her over."

Atlee croaked: "*No. Swear—*"

"Now she knows there's a reward on her, and she's probably a thousand miles away because you think with your crotch, instead of your tiny little brain."

"*No*," Atlee wheezed, and rolled up his eyes. "*Stole. Her. Bag.*"

Jack tilted his head. "What's that?"

Atlee's lips were turning a bit blue, and he slackened his grip just enough to allow him to croak: "*Stole. Her. Money.*"

"She doesn't have any money?"

Atlee closed his eyes and shook his head as well as he could.

Jack abruptly released him, and Atlee slid down the wall and collapsed into a gasping heap on the floor.

"Get out," Jack threw over his shoulder, and Atlee scrambled up to his knees, and then to his feet and away.

Chapter
Forty-Six

Jack stood at the window of his bedroom, a tumbler of whisky in hand, and looked down on Witcher Street. The sky was just turning light, and everyone had cleared out of the Nugget except the men who'd rented rooms, and in about thirty minutes he was going to have them turned out, too.

The place would calm down, and the girls would go to sleep, and the bouncers would mop the spilled beer and tobacco juice off the floor, and sweep up the little pieces of silk and feathers and sequins that had been torn off the girls' dresses, and wipe down the tables and chairs.

He made a mental note to have a tuner come out to look at the piano because last night a drunken cowboy had put another man's head into the works, and now it didn't sound right.

He took a sip of whisky.

It was pretty quiet, except for what sounded like sniveling, coming from the girls' rooms. Probably that new girl. He was gonna have to *learn* her, but it could wait until later.

He looked down at the empty street without seeing it. He was thinking about the early days when Cheyenne was a *real* frontier town, and the only women in it, whores who'd followed the cowboys and miners. Those had been the great days, a time when *anything* went. Cheyenne had been as dangerous as any place in the world, with girls hanging out of the windows, yelling at passers-by, and a killing every night—sometimes more than one.

Some of those killings had been his, and he'd never lost a minute of sleep over 'em because there'd been no law to make him pay, and no one else with the guts to face him.

He'd been the king of Cheyenne, there for awhile. He'd made himself a name for running the wildest whorehouse that side of the Rockies, and famous men came to his door: gunslingers, and desperados, and buffalo hunters, and even generals and judges and politicians.

Because there wasn't a man on earth who didn't have a low, mean side he hid from the world. And they all came to *him* when they wanted to indulge it.

He glanced at a big leather case sitting on a table near the window. His *own* low, mean side, some might say, was lower and meaner than most. He had a whole set of toys that he hadn't played with in quite some time, but that he hadn't forgotten.

He took another sip of whisky.

Yes, he'd been the king around here when Cheyenne was wild. Before the law men and the politicians and the do-gooders and the wagon trains full of snot-nosed families and the stinkin' holy rollers had ruined it.

Now they lobbied the sheriff and the mayor against him and wrote letters to the newspaper with words like *filthy* and *degenerate* and *lawless*.

There had been a time when any man who'd breathed those words to him would've been dead before he hit the floor. But now, his power had ebbed so low that he had to stay *quiet*, and *pay bribes*, and watch the river of money that had once flowed to his door dry up a little more every day.

He'd sunk to the point that when a brand new girl broke a bottle of wine over his head and knocked him to the floor, the whole saloon had just sat there and laughed.

He had dragged himself up off the floor and stomped off to his office, but there had been a day when he could've killed them *all* for that and paid no penalty beyond that day's custom.

He couldn't kill them all for shaming him, now, as much as he might want to.

But he could kill that little redheaded witch, all right. Cheyenne wasn't so civilized or pious yet, that it concerned itself with the well-being of its whores. She would be just another floozy who'd reaped what she'd sown, and the *proper* folks would nod their heads and say that she'd gotten *just* what she deserved.

A generous payment to that squirt deputy would guarantee that no one in the sheriff's office would get curious about what happened, but everyone who'd been in the Nugget that day, and every girl and bouncer and bartender in his place, would understand that Jack McGee was still a man to be feared.

Jack's eyes narrowed. He was going to make such an example of Molly Clanahan that no one would ever dare to cross him again. His revenge would be just as spectacular, and just as shameful, as what she did to him.

His eyes returned to the leather case. He set down the tumbler of whisky and slowly opened the lid. Three shallow shelves slid out to present a glittering array of surgical knives. He lifted one to the light and turned it over, relishing the way the light slid over its keen, curved edge.

There were all kinds of instruments in the case. Small, delicate knives for the most intricate surgical work; regular scalpels, probes, needles, small saws, and other devices he didn't know the use of, or at least the *intended* use of.

He'd gotten it from a young doctor who craved laudanum so bad that he'd been willing to swap his whole surgical set for a single bottle. And he'd been glad to make the trade.

Jack smiled, remembering Ola. She'd been the first girl he'd introduced to his little toys—oh, ten years ago now. It didn't seem like that long to him, though.

He remembered it as if it were yesterday.

It had been his first time out with the tools, and he'd been a little ham-handed; but he'd gotten a real charge out of them. He'd never felt more powerful in his life, more in control.

He guessed there was no more important man in the world than the one who held your life in his hands. And Ola had known it, too. He lingered over the look in her eyes. He'd never seen more pure terror in his life.

Yes, sir, that was *power*.

Then there had been Sarah, a few years later. She'd put up a bit of a fight, but that only added to the zest of the thing. He'd almost been found out that time, too, when he forgot to clean up proper after, and that had its own, strange thrill.

The sense of having gotten away with something *big*. Of fooling the world.

Then there was the Piute woman, but that one didn't properly count since he'd done it while travelling, and without most of his kit. Without the full range of possibilities. It had been kind of funny, though, because it turned out she'd been a chief's daughter, and the Piutes raided a wagon train on account of it and kilt a wagon master and twelve settlers in re-venge.

That had tided him over for a few years.

Jack ran his thumb along the edge of the scalpel and watched as a thin red line jumped out on his skin. He didn't like to play with his toys too often. He liked to space things out for years at a time. That kept things safer for him, kept folks in town nice and sleepy.

And it gave his appetite a chance to build up. He liked to wait until his appetite was keen. Almost *unbearable*.

That was when it was most satisfying to indulge his own low, dark side.

It had been three long years since the last time, and now he was keen to play with his toys again. He'd decided that this time it was going to be that little redheaded witch, and he was going to dream up something really *special* for her.

And what was more, this time he wasn't going to hide it. He was going to do the thing right here, in his own bedroom, and he wasn't going to stuff anything in her mouth.

No, he was going to leave her tongue in, so everyone in the place could hear her scream. That would make a real big impression on the girls, so the next time he told them to do something, they'd *jump*.

The others, too.

Everybody who'd seen him lying on the floor downstairs.

It would show them *all* what happened to anyone who crossed him. He might be going through a dry spell right now, but he was still Jack McGee, the king of Cheyenne, a man sought out by both the famous and the infamous, the owner of the *wildest* whorehouse this side of the Rockies.

He turned and placed the scalpel carefully into its designated slot and pushed the drawer closed. The little velvet trays retracted into the case, and he locked it up with a *snap*.

Chapter
Forty-Seven

Molly spent a miserable night shivering in the women's lounge at the train station. She had to walk into a supply closet to hide from the security guard when he made his rounds, but to her relief, he only gave the room a cursory glance before moving on.

She crept out, curled up on the velvet settee and tried to rest, though she knew she'd *never* be able to sleep.

Her mind was too busy trying to think of what to do *now*. She had no money, no way to protect herself, not even anything to eat. She didn't know a soul in Cheyenne, or at least, nobody *decent*, and she was ashamed to go back to the Circle T, where they were no doubt celebrating to be rid of her at last.

A faint *pop pop pop* outside reminded her that it was Saturday night, and even inside the lounge, she could hear the dim report of wild revelry in the street outside.

Molly hugged herself and buried her face into the velvet cushions. The sound of gunshots and raucous laughter reminded her just how vulnerable she was. At six o'clock the next morning, the Cheyenne station would open up to the world. *Anyone* could come walking in.

Jack could come walking in.

She wondered if Jack knew she was back in Cheyenne. If that man who attacked her had—had *survived*, he might go back and tell Jack she was in town.

Molly closed her eyes. The *alternative* possibility—that she might really have *killed* the snake—was so terrible that she couldn't think about it, not now, not when she needed her wits clear and *sharp*.

The first thing she had to do was get away from the train station.

She wracked her brain, wondering where to go, and as she did the sound of bells wafted faintly into the room. They were just loud enough to be heard over the shouting and tinny music on the street outside, and Molly opened her eyes. Those sounded like *church* bells, marking off the hours. She hadn't known that there *were* any churches in Cheyenne.

And tomorrow was *Sunday*.

Molly sat up. If she went to one of the church services tomorrow, told the minister her story afterwards, and begged for help—maybe they'd let her stay with them for a night or two until she could find some way out of town. Or maybe they'd know of someone who could give her a little needlework, so she could earn money for a ticket out.

At any rate, *church* was the last place on earth Jack McGee and his bounty hunters would ever go and was probably the best hiding place the town could offer.

Molly glanced down at her gown and thanked God that at least her dress looked respectable and that it hadn't been torn by that monster.

She could tell the minister that she'd been set on by a madman, and that he stole her purse, and her money, and that she was without friends in Cheyenne. She wasn't sure, but she *hoped* at least that such a story would move them to help her somehow.

At least, that was her best chance. She closed her eyes and prayed:

Oh, God, please help me. I don't have anyone left but you!

And although she was still overwrought, she finally fell asleep on the settee and slept deeply for a few hours.

***

The sound of a train whistle woke her the next morning. It was followed by a loud cry:

"Transcontinental to San Francisco, boarding on Platform Two in fifteen minutes!"

Molly sat bolt upright and looked around her wildly. She was actually fumbling for her handbag before she remembered that she didn't *have* a handbag any more, or any ticket for the train.

She sighed, pulled her palm across her brow wearily, rose, and went to the little laver in the lounge to wash her face and hands. It felt early, but she couldn't afford to oversleep. She had to find that church building in time for the morning service if she was going to get help.

She opened the lounge door and peeked outside warily. The train was sitting on the track, but the station still looked relatively empty. She glanced at the station clock, and to her relief, it was just a little past eight. Church usually started at nine, so she had some time.

She swept the station again with her eyes. There was no one there that looked like Jack McGee, but that was no comfort. Any one of the men she saw could be one of his hirelings sent there to find her.

Her stomach rumbled loudly, and she licked her lips. She'd slaked her thirst at the water cooler in the lounge, but her stomach felt like an empty bag. She hadn't had anything to eat in almost 24 hours, but she was just going to have to be patient.

She slipped outside, into the lobby, and was about to walk out when she remembered the letters she had dropped on the floor. She turned and searched the broad station floor, but to her dismay, there was nothing there. The letters must have blown down onto the track or been thrown away by one of the station employees.

Two *more* precious things that she'd lost—and she devoutly hoped, the *last* ones.

***

Molly hesitated at the station entrance for a long time. She scanned the street a half-dozen times before she dared to reveal herself. It frightened her to bolt from her hiding place, but it was no longer any protection to her, and early morning was the safest time for her to emerge.

Jack and most of his friends were probably hung over and dead to the world.

She could just see the top of a church spire a few blocks west, and she hurried across the big thoroughfare and moved quickly down a side street. Cheyenne looked sleepy and half-empty on a Sunday morning, but the scent of someone cooking breakfast tickled Molly's nose as she walked along. It smelled like sausage and biscuits, and she moved on as quickly as she could because the delicious aroma made her stomach complain.

Molly crossed two more blocks of shuttered mercantiles, banks, and cafes before she found the church. It was a one-storey clapboard building with a little bell tower. It was painted a stark white, and was a one-room building facing onto the street. A sign in the front yard read, *First United Church of Cheyenne.*

There were already a few buggies pulled up to the entrance, and Molly's heart rose to see men and women climbing out and entering the building. It reminded her so sharply of her childhood that quick tears sprang to her eyes.

She was back among *home folk* again, back with *plain decent people*. She picked up her skirts and crossed the street almost at a run.

When she gained the other side, she followed the trickle of church folk walking in and sat down on a bench at the back of the church. She looked around and noticed that the people were dressed respectably, but not at all fine. They were small merchants, ranchers, people with farms.

People she *understood*.

Molly closed her eyes and slumped back against the pew in relief. The fear that they might not help her just shriveled up and blew away. She might not have met them before, but she *knew* them. They were the same type of folks as her own family and their neighbors back in Kansas. They were going to help her.

They'd probably do more than they *should*.

A plump middle-aged woman moved down the pew and sat down beside her. She smiled up into Molly's face and said: "You're new here. I just wanted to say good morning, and welcome to our church."

Molly blinked back tears and smiled back at her weakly. "*Good morning.*"

Chapter
Forty-Eight

To Molly's intense relief, she'd had the good fortune to arrive at the church on a Sunday when they were having a picnic on the grounds. After worship, her new friend, Dolly Culver and her husband Tom introduced her to the Reverend Luther P. Allen, a portly, balding man with round wire glasses and a solemn face. Molly was invited to sit down at a table with the Culvers, and Reverend Allen and his wife.

She spent the first thirty minutes eating everything she was offered—fried chicken, biscuits, mashed potatoes and gravy, glazed carrots, green beans cooked with bacon drippings—and then second and even third helpings, and the rest of the time telling her story.

It was a heavily edited version of the truth, and crafted to be as appealing to home folks as possible, and to Molly's relief, it seemed to make a big impression on her audience.

"It's terrible that a young woman can't even feel safe in a public place!" Mrs Culver exclaimed in alarm. "To be dragged away bodily—from the train station, mind you! —and robbed of all your money—my dear, it's just the mercy of God the wicked creature didn't kill you!"

Molly shuddered. "Yes, ma'am. It is."

Mrs Culver turned to her husband as he lifted a forkful of pie to his lips. "Tom, we're going to have to petition the city to clean up these streets. It's a scandal when respectable women can't even go out in public!"

The Reverend nodded. "I've written the paper again and again, but these politicians are useless. I wouldn't be surprised if they were being paid off. *Graft and greed*—that should be the city's motto because it's the truth!"

He turned to Molly and added: "Miss Clanahan, Mrs Allen and I will be happy to have you as a guest in our house until you can find some way to get back to your own home. But first, I'm going to escort you down to the sheriff's office and file an assault report. These city streets are a scandal!"

Molly stared at him in blank dismay. She'd never *dreamed* that these people would want to file a report with the law!

She remembered her revolver going off in that dark alley and shuddered. No, the sheriff's office was the last place on earth she wanted to go!

"Oh, *please*," she stammered, "I've had such a trying time, and I'm *so* tired. And if I had to relive that—that *awful* memory, I'm sure I—I'd *faint* dead away!"

Mrs Culver gave her a look of overflowing sympathy and slid a motherly arm around her shoulders. "There, now, don't trouble yourself my dear," she soothed. "I'm sure that the report can wait awhile. *Can't* it, reverend?" she asked and gave the minister a look of heavy significance.

The pastor cleared his throat and replied: "Yes, of course. But remember, Miss Clanahan—the sooner we file the report, the better the chances that polecat will be caught. You don't want to give him a chance to escape, do you?"

Molly lowered her eyes to the tablecloth and murmured: "No, of course not."

***

They all stayed in the little backlot of the church, eating and talking, well into the afternoon. They were all clearly visible from the little side street running down beside the church, and now and again Molly scanned it. She felt like a fish in a barrel, sitting out there in plain view, but she never saw anyone walk by in all the time they stayed there.

And she couldn't imagine that even Jack McGee would dare to kidnap her out there in front of so many people.

After the picnic was over, Mrs Culver gave her a hug and said: "I'll ask around and see if any of my friends have some needlework that you can do. I expect they will. I'll let you know."

"Thank you, Mrs Culver," Molly murmured and meant it from the bottom of her soul.

Mrs Allen appeared and smiled at her. "We live just right next door, Molly. I'll fix up the guest room for you."

Molly said farewell to her new friends and followed the Allens to a trim white clapboard house on the little side street. It wasn't a big house, or an especially hidden one, but when the door closed behind them, Molly felt a rush of relief that was hard to describe. It was just one door, between her and the world, but it felt *mighty good* to be on the inside of that door.

Her hostess showed her to a small guest room with one little single bed covered in a quilt, a nightstand with a pitcher and washbowl, and a chifferobe. It looked a little like her own bedroom back home, and Molly sat down on the bed gratefully.

"If you need anything, just let me know," Mrs Allen told her. "We turn in early, and we get up around six. Breakfast is at seven."

"Thank you for letting me stay here," Molly told her. "I don't know what I would've done."

"Oh, sweetie, we're glad to do it," the older woman assured her. "We'll make sure you get home all right."

She closed the door behind her, and Molly undressed, hung up her gown, and collapsed on the little bed gratefully. She hadn't had much rest the night before, and soon she was deeply asleep. She slept dreamlessly all that night and woke the next morning refreshed.

The scent of frying bacon made her eyelids flutter open. Her first impulse was to stretch and yawn, and the second, to throw off the covers because Mrs Allen was making breakfast alone.

Since she was staying free at the Allen's house, Molly figured that the least she could do was help with the cooking. She washed and dressed quickly, and found Mrs Allen in the kitchen, hard at work over a small cast-iron stove.

"Can I help you with anything?" Molly asked with a guilty pang. It was already almost seven.

"You can set the table for me," Mrs Allen answered, nodding toward platters full of biscuits and ham; so Molly took the platters and set them out on the dining room table next door.

The reverend was already seated at the table and was making small clucking noises of disapproval as he read the paper. He took off his glasses and used them to point at the headline.

"Another murder—and in broad daylight, too!" he exclaimed to the room at large. "Those gambling dens stink to high heaven. Why they're still tolerated, I can't guess! If Cheyenne wants to be known as a respectable place for new business, and for decent people to come and live, it's going to have to sweep out the trash!"

He fixed his glasses back on his nose as Molly set a platter of biscuits down on the table. "A Mr Tompkins from Crested Butte was found face down in the alley behind the Golden Nugget saloon," he read aloud. "He had been dead for several hours and is thought to be a victim of laudanum poisoning."

Molly dropped the platter of ham, and it fell on the table with a clatter.

"Oh—oh, I'm sorry," she mumbled and hurried to set the platter straight. But the reverend still had his head in the newspaper.

"The *Cheyenne Bugle* has repeatedly called on the city fathers to investigate the saloons and gambling houses in response to multiple accusations of poisoning and fraud," he read on, "but as of this edition, they conduct their sordid business unchallenged, and the tally of dead bodies continues to rise."

Molly put a hand to her head. A strange, swimmy feeling washed over her suddenly, and the dining room went grey. She swayed and grabbed a chair back to keep from reeling over.

Mrs Allen, who was just entering the room, cried out sharply: "Molly, are you all right? Luther, catch her!"

The reverend looked up just in time to see Molly slide down onto the table and from the table to the floor. He threw down the paper and pushed the chair back.

"What the—why, she's *fainted*!" he exclaimed.

Mrs Allen was already on the floor beside Molly, patting her hand. "You should know better than to read evil news to a girl who's just been set on!" she scolded. "Of course she fainted, poor thing! Luther, go and get me some cool water, and a cloth."

The reverend leaned over to look at Molly's pale face, and then took himself off to the kitchen to retrieve the cloth. When he returned, he handed it to his wife and opined: "Well, it's as plain as print that she ain't going to be up to going to the sheriff's office. But no one should get away with such a brazen crime! I'm going down to the sheriff's office myself, and I'm going to get someone to come here and record her story. She'll be more comfortable that way."

"You do that," his wife nodded. "But first, help me to carry her over to the couch. We should be able to do it."

Her husband grunted and moved over to take his guest by the arms, and together they carried Molly through the dining room, into the front room, and onto the couch.

The reverend wiped his brow with his handkerchief. "Well! That's that, then," he sighed. "I'm going down to the sheriff's office right now and get this thing taken care of."

"Aren't you going to have your breakfast?" his wife asked in mild surprise.

"Not this morning. I'm going to take care of this matter first," he told her, "because I won't be satisfied until I *do* something."

Chapter
Forty-Nine

Molly woke up to the sound of someone patting her hand and the sensation of something cold and wet dripping down her cheek. She opened her eyes. She was lying on the sofa in a small parlour, and it took a few seconds for her memory to catch up with her recent movements.

She turned her head. Mrs Allen was sitting at her elbow and patting her hand.

"What happened?" she mumbled.

"Why, you fainted, my dear," she replied softly. "I scolded Luther for reading those awful newspaper articles in front of you. He should have known better!"

Molly closed her eyes. The swimmy feeling threatened to return, for a dizzy moment, but to her relief, it gradually passed.

"Do you think you could take a little something?"

Molly nodded, and Mrs Allen pressed a cup of hot tea into her hand. Molly raised it to her lips and sighed.

"Poor thing, you've had the most *awful* time in Cheyenne, haven't you?" her hostess commiserated. Molly rolled her eyes to Mrs Allen's and nodded mutely.

"Well, we're going to see to it that you get *justice*," Mrs Allen continued. "Luther went to the sheriff's office, and he got one of the deputies to come back with him. They're waiting in the parlor, and you can tell him what happened without having to go anywhere."

Molly sat bolt upright. "What?"

Mrs Allen put a hand on her arm. "Don't move so *suddenly*, my dear! You might have another spell."

The older woman gave her a reassuring pat. "I'll go tell them you're feeling better now."

She rose with a rustle of skirts, and to Molly's dismay, she soon returned with her husband and a young deputy. Molly moved instantly to a sitting position because there was a look in the young man's eye that she'd seen before and didn't like.

"Miss Molly Clanahan, this is Deputy Sheriff Winters."

Molly nodded warily, but the deputy only looked over at the reverend and drawled: "Well, this is the gal, then?"

"Yes, this is the young lady. She says she was set on near the train station by a man with a knife."

"That's a serious charge, all right, Reverent," the deputy replied. "I thought you meant that they had an argument or something like that."

The reverend frowned. "Why, I told you *plainly*—"

"If she wants to make a charge of violent *assault*, I'm afraid she's going to have to come down to the sheriff's office to fill out a formal complaint," he drawled and scratched his chin.

"But I brought you here specifically because she wasn't feeling *well* enough for that," the reverend replied indignantly, and the young man shrugged.

"I wish I could help you Reverent, I really do, but I ain't in charge of such things," he replied. "We have to follow procedure, every time. The sheriff would have my job if I didn't do like the law requires."

"It's all right," Molly broke in. "I'm thankful for what you've done for me, Reverend Allen, but I—I really don't feel up to moving now," she went on in a weak voice. "I'll come down to the sheriff's office and fill out the complaint some other time."

"But—"

The deputy shook his head. "Oh, I'm afraid you're going to have to come down with me now," the young man told her. "If you accuse another person of a serious crime, you have to come down and fill out a report, same day."

"That's nonsense!" the reverend barked, and Molly stared at the young man in suspicion and dismay.

"Oh, it's an old law in this city, Reverent, though not many people know of it. The gal has to come down with me."

"You act like *she's* the one done something wrong!" Mrs Allen exclaimed indignantly.

"Yes, I'm as sorry as I can be, but that's the way of it," he replied. His eyes moved to Molly's face.

Molly returned his stare and felt her blood going cold. Something wasn't right, and she had a good idea of *what*, and *why*. She didn't believe a word that was coming from his lying mouth.

But something else bothered her, something worse. He looked faintly familiar. She could swear she'd seen him someplace before. She just couldn't remember *where*.

And she was afraid that somewhere was the *Golden Nugget*.

He walked up in front of her and looked down into her face. "Come on."

"I'm not going!" she blurted, and turned pleading eyes to the minister's face. "I don't feel well enough. I'll faint on the way!"

"Leave her alone!" Mrs Allen cried as the young man took her arm. "You don't have the right to take a guest out of our house!"

"I'm just upholding the law, ma'am," the young man replied and yanked her up to her feet so suddenly that she almost fell onto his chest. "And I'm bound to warn you that if you try to hinder me, you'll be prosecuted for interfering with a law officer."

"Why, I *never*—" Mrs Allen gasped, and her husband drew himself up in indignation.

"You may be sure that the sheriff's office will hear from me!" he cried, as the deputy dragged her out of the house by her arm. "*And* my lawyer!"

But Molly looked back over her shoulder at their unhappy faces and wondered miserably if she'd *live* long enough to know if the reverend made good his threat.

Chapter
Fifty

Molly stumbled along the dusty street with the deputy's hand clamped painfully on her arm. Little lights were popping off in her head, and the street greyed out twice before her vision returned.

She tried to shake him off once, and the young deputy jerked her arm so savagely that she almost fell. "If you yell out, it'll go bad with you later," he replied, in a cheerful, pleasant tone that made her skin crawl.

"Where are you taking me," she gasped and struggled to regain her balance, "you lying rattlesnake?"

"Where do you *think* I'm takin' you?"

She rolled her eyes to his, and to her horror, he winked and grinned.

Fury boiled up in Molly's heart and surged up into her limbs. She yanked her arm violently out of the man's grip, whirled and flew. The sudden movement made the sky turn over, but she pushed herself to the limits of her strength.

The street in front of her seemed to heave up and down as she ran. A middle-aged woman was walking down the sidewalk toward her, but her own body was already weakening, slipping out of control, and she couldn't avoid a collision. She plowed straight into the shrieking matron and fell with her onto the ground in a tangle of arms and legs.

The woman's sputtered objections and her own panting was all she heard for a few moments, but then the deputy's bland, apologetic voice arrived.

"Let me help you up, ma'am," he was saying. "I'm terrible sorry. I'm taking this woman down to the jail." His voice fell to a conspiratorial whisper.

"She's a little intoxicated."

Molly opened her eyes and cried: "He's lying! I'm not drunk; I'm being kidnapped! Call the—"

But a sudden blow to her temple landed her on the ground. The world flashed white and then faded altogether.

***

Molly woke to the sound of her own groans. A crushing pain in her temple made her feel almost sick to her stomach. She sat there with her eyes closed, unmoving, as the pain pulsed in time to her heartbeat ... *thump ... thump ... thump.*

Low voices mumbled in the background, but at that moment, her whole world was the darkness and the throbbing pain. Molly let the voices mumble for a long while and only tried to ride out the fiery pulse.

After a long time, the pain receded just enough to allow one other sense to intrude on her burdened mind.

Sound.

The mumbling in the background gradually resolved itself into a bland, smooth voice, and a rough, hard voice. For a long time, they were as unintelligible as the grunts of pigs or the cries of birds. But slowly Molly began to pick out words from the running stream of sounds.

"That's a hundred dollars cash, Abel. I like a lawman who understands business."

Molly's brows contracted, and the resulting surge of pain almost made her cry out. *That* was a voice she dreaded, even though her muddled senses couldn't identify it. It filled her with the urge to flee, to crawl under something and hide.

"There's going to be a bit of a ruckus up in here in the next few days, Abel, and maybe some complaints. I'll pay twice what you just got, for makin' sure nobody from your office comes around asking questions about it."

The deputy's voice held the dawn of surprise. "Why—you're going to *kill* her, ain't you, Jack? Now, I don't know about *that*. I thought you was just going to learn her a lesson. I ain't sure I can cover for you if you kill the girl *outright*. The whole town just saw her with *me*. How do I explain if she turns up dead a day later?"

Molly frowned, and her eyes fluttered open and quickly closed again. The sudden rush of light into her brain made her head feel like it was going to explode.

There was a long silence, broken when the deputy stuttered out again. He sounded a bit frightened.

"Now, Jack, too many people saw her *with* me. I drug her out of a preacher's house, and he was threatenin' me with a *lawyer*. Him and his wife is two witnesses that saw me take her away. Three, if you count a woman that saw us on the street, and maybe more I didn't see.

"If the preacher and his lawyer come down to the jail and ask to *see* her, and she ain't *there*—what am I supposed to tell 'em?"

"You said she passed out," the rough voice answered. "Tell 'em she got sick in jail and died."

"*Mmm*, I don't know," the first voice replied uncertainly. "If it warn't for the preacher promising to call a lawyer down on me, I might take the chance, but it's powerful risky. I ain't *never* stuck my neck out so far. I like doing business with you, Jack, but now you're asking somethin' that could land *me* up in jail if I got caught."

"Some folks would say that it's *powerful risky*, to say *no* to Jack McGee," the rough voice answered softly. "Or do you want me to do to you what I'm going to do to her?"

There was a brief silence, and then the sound of a chair clattering to the floor, and a violent scuffling. Molly could feel the heavy *thuds* where she sat, and heard the sound of grunting, and something shattering on the floor, and then a high, fading shriek, a horrible gargling sound, and finally—silence.

Panic rolled up from the lowest well in Molly's heart and surged up through her chest and into her eyes. She opened them very slightly and very slowly.

She was seated in a chair facing a wall. It looked like she was in a man's bedroom because there was a big bed with a carved mahogany headboard and velvet quilts on her left, and a big window on her right. There were oil paintings on the wall in front of her; one of a nude woman, and the other of a landscape.

She let her gaze move past the bed toward the door. To Molly's dismay, she saw the young deputy lying full length on the floor. His eyes were starting out of his head and fixed on the ceiling, and his mouth gaped open horribly.

A man was standing over him, a tall man with red hair and light eyes. Molly's eyes widened in recognition.

It was Jack.

As she watched, Jack bent down, grabbed the deputy by the ankles, and dragged him across the floor and into the doorway of a small bathroom on the far left of the room. There came the sound of a grunt, then several heavy *thumps*.

There was silence for a few moments, and then, to Molly's horror, the sound of a half-dozen heavy *cracks,* one after another.

Chapter
Fifty-One

Molly closed her eyes and slumped in despair. The thing she feared most had happened. She was upstairs at the Golden Nugget, locked in Jack's bedroom, as hopelessly trapped as a fly in a spider's web.

Jack had just murdered the deputy and was about to murder *her*. It was only a matter of time because she couldn't save herself, and there was no one else left to save her. The preacher and his wife didn't know where she was, the law was corrupt, and Leonie and—and *Nate* were far away.

The memory of how safe and happy she'd been with Nate and Leonie made Molly's lip quiver because she was never going to see them again. Her heart began to race, and another wave of faintness threatened her, but she bit her tongue and *forced* herself to stay conscious.

She had to keep her wits about her if she was going to have any chance at *all*.

Molly looked down. She was seated upright in a simple wooden chair. Her wrists were bound behind the chair back, and her ankles were tied together with rope.

She tested the ropes, but she knew before she confirmed it: she couldn't move.

There was a small table directly in front of her, with a long, flat leather case lying on it. Molly frowned at it. She didn't know what it was, but it had a sinister look.

Anything that Jack McGee displayed so prominently must be evil *somehow*.

Her eyes moved to the windows. The light pouring through them made her head hurt, but she could see that it was now close to noon. People were walking past on the street outside. If she could only catch their attention somehow—but for now, Jack was busy in the bathroom doing his horrible work. The last thing she wanted was to draw his attention to her.

To her dismay, the sound of a knock at the bedroom door eventually drew Jack out of the bathroom.

"What is it?" he shouted, and a man's voice answered: "I got the stuff you wanted."

"Leave it outside the door and go back downstairs. Don't come up again, and don't let anybody else come up."

A grunt from the other side of the door signaled the man's compliance. There was a soft scraping sound outside the door, and then the sound of receding footsteps. Jack turned, and Molly quickly closed her eyes and pretended to be unconscious, but she was seized by the fear that her shivering heart would be visible through her clothes.

She could hear Jack open the door and then pull something heavy across the floor. When the sound had moved past, she opened her eyes just a sliver and rolled them in the direction of the sound. To her horror, Jack had slung a heavy coil of rope over one arm and was pulling a big trunk into the bathroom.

Molly closed her eyes to shut out that terrible sight, but she couldn't shut out the sounds: the *thud, thud, thud, scrape, thud*; then the sound of the trunk lock clicking shut, and the sound of rope being wound around the trunk, being pulled taut, being tied and knotted securely.

She heard Jack straighten, and sigh, and then she heard the sound of water, sloshing around in the bathtub and swirling down the drain with a loud gurgle.

Then the sound of Jack's heavy footsteps walking out across the wooden floor of the bedroom. Three steps, and then ... nothing. Molly went blank and quiet. Her heart was pounding, and she hardly dared to breathe.

There came the sound of footsteps again ... *one, two, three*. The sound stopped in front of her, and there was a sound like movement.

Then the touch of Jack's hand on her jaw.

"You can open your eyes," he mocked. "You ain't a good actress. I know you've been awake for a *long* time."

Molly unwillingly opened her eyes and gasped at how close he was. He was squatting down on the floor in front of her, excitement shining in his eerie pale eyes. His fingers on her jaw were still wet, and dozens of little red specks dotted his face.

Jack grinned in triumph. "Naw, missy—I don't mind that you know about Abel. I'm not worried that you'll blab. You and old Abel are going the same road."

She expected him to strike her, but to her surprise, he straightened and wiped his hands on a towel. He threw one leg over the end of the bed and nodded toward the little leather case lying on the table.

"The difference between you and Abel, is that Abel died quick and easy, and you—you, little girl, you're going to die hard. *Real* hard. I'm going to take my sweet time.

"You're going to learn what it means to raise your hand to Jack McGee. I'm going to make an example of you that no one will *ever* forget."

He leaned over and opened the little leather case. To Molly's horror, it displayed three shelves full of small, razor-sharp medical knives. Jack picked up a small scalpel and twirled it easily between his fingers.

"I've been playing with these for ten years," he told her with a smile. "They're beautiful for carving. They make the cleanest, prettiest cuts. They slide across a woman's skin just as smooth as silk and make any kind of mark you like. Thin and shallow, say"—his hand flashed out and drew a red line across the top of her hand— "or wide and *deep*."

His hand shot out again, and the glittering knife froze just short of Molly's left eye. Jack smiled at the fear on her face and pulled it back, wiped it clean of her blood, and placed it carefully in the case.

"Thought I'd give you a little taste of what's coming," he mocked. "Just a tiny little taste. You'd be surprised how many tools there are in that case and what they can do. And you're going to learn every last one of them. Yes, sir, we're going to take our time."

Molly flinched. The sting of the knife in her skin was as sharp as the tooth of a baby snake. But she was too preoccupied by the look on Jack's face to mind the pain. Crazy was radiating from his face like waves of heat. A sick excitement was building in his eyes, something he was barely holding back, and terror slithered up her spine like a little desert adder.

"I'm afraid old Abel isn't going to keep very long, what with the heat, so I'm going out now to see him to his final resting place," he told her. "And when I come back, I'm going to concentrate on *you*. With any luck, you'll still be alive this time next week.

"You'll just *wish* you'd died the first day."

His eyes raked her over, head to toe, and Molly couldn't repress a shudder of revulsion. To her overwhelming relief, he passed her by, walked back to the bathroom, and slowly pulled the trunk across the floor, and out into the hall.

He closed the door behind him, and the sound of dragging slowly faded into silence.

The tears that Molly had been holding back sprang to her eyes, but she refused to cry.

Instead, she watched in amazement as, a little while later, Jack McGee drove Deputy Sheriff Abel Winter out of Cheyenne—right down the centre of Main Street, and in broad daylight. The sheriff was standing at the front door of his office, and she saw Jack throw up a hand in greeting, and the sheriff nod, as the wagon rumbled past.

Chapter
Fifty-Two

"You're gonna *have* to wear it."

Nate glanced at the detective in irritation. Under ordinary circumstances, he'd rather endure a thrashing than appear in public wearing a perishing *bowler hat.*

He took the object in his hand and inspected it in disgust. It was a torn, *dirty* bowler hat.

"You're a swell, and there *ain't* no swells in a Cheyenne saloon," the detective told him briskly. "It's a den of *cutthroats*, and if you walk in all duded up, we're done before we begin."

Jameson gave Nate's gleaming, precisely-barbered hair a sceptical glance. "I wish we could cover your hair with a sock cap," he muttered. "We need to look shaggy, and dirty and smell as if we ain't had a bath in weeks. *That's* who goes to the saloons. Trail-riding cowboys and miners, just into town." He sighed. "Be sure to mess your hair up real good, and don't take off that hat."

His glance moved to Nate's hands. "Your nails, too—you need to rough 'em up. I've got a spittoon down in the lower lobby. You need to stick your hands into it, and rub 'em around. Get the brown colour under your nails and then tear 'em ragged."

Nate stared at him in speechless revulsion, and Jameson added: "If you're *serious*, Mr Trowbridge, you best do as I ask. This ain't going to *work* if they can tell who we are as soon as we walk *in*."

Nate pulled his mouth down in disgust. "Very well," he muttered.

"You'll need different clothes, too," Jameson sighed, glancing at Nate's crisp suit and spotless shoes. "*Work* clothes and *work* shoes. I'll have my secretary scrounge some up."

Jameson pulled a hand across his jaw. "And your *accent*. It won't do. You're going to have to keep your mouth *shut*. One word from you, and it's all over. Just let me do the talking."

Nate stared at him indignantly. "I trust there's something I *can* do?" he asked, with asperity.

"Yes." Jameson nodded grimly. "If things go wrong, you can fight your way to daylight.

"'Cause you'll *have* to."

Nate pinched his lips into a straight line but bit back the sharp retort he would have *liked* to utter. It was dangerous to ignore your guide when embarking on a hunting expedition, and Jameson was his guide to the jungle they were about to enter.

Jameson sat on the edge of his desk and poured out a tumbler of whisky. He offered it, and Nate shook his head.

"I'm not being sociable," Jameson drawled. "This is a *test*. I want to see if you can take bad liquor. You need to be able to swallow rotgut with a straight face because everybody in a saloon is there because they *like* rotgut. If you choke, you'll stick out."

Nate took the tumbler doubtfully, sighed, and threw it back. It burned his mouth, his throat and his stomach like liquid fire, all the way down.

"Wha—what *is* that?" he gasped and coughed convulsively. "Tastes like—*kerosene*!"

"Okay," Jameson sighed. "I'll try to get you up to the second floor before there's any drinking done. If you get into a tight spot, just *pretend* to sip the stuff."

Jameson walked back to his desk and pulled out a revolver. As he was loading it, he asked: "Do you know how to use a gun?"

Nate stared at him in disgust. "Of course I do. I was raised on an estate with a thousand acre-park. I've been hunting since I was first able to hold a rifle."

"Good. How are you with handguns?"

"I can hit my mark at two hundred paces."

"Then we'll each take two pistols. I'll have my men waiting around the place, and they'll have shotguns and rifles, just in case we need backup."

Nate's brows twitched together. "I thought you said this would be legal," he objected, and Jameson shrugged.

"It will be if it goes as *planned*," he amended and grinned. "If it goes off the rails, why then, Mr Trowbridge, the *legality* of it will be the *last* of your worries."

Nate gave him a dark look. "I intend to take that scoundrel down, whoever he is, by whatever means present themselves," he replied shortly.

"I think we have a good idea of who *Jack* is," Jameson told him. "There's only one saloon in Cheyenne run by a man name of Jack—the Golden Nugget. It's a real den, too—there used to be murders every weekend, just about, and there are still a fair amount. He's probably bribing someone to keep it open. That's usually the way the dens stay in business ... until the town gets enough families and businessmen to push 'em out, or at least tone 'em down."

"So we can't trust the authorities?" Nate frowned.

Jameson sucked his teeth soundlessly and shook his head. "I don't know. Somebody there in town is probably on the take, or the Golden Nugget would've been closed down long ago. If you had to choose between closing the place down and getting Miss Clanahan out safe—you want to get her out, ain't that right?"

Nate looked out the window. "Yes."

"No guarantees, Mr Trowbridge," the detective replied softly. "But I think the odds are good of that much, at least.

"We'll see," he sighed and stuck the revolver into his coat pocket.

***

It took the Burlington man some time to gather the things they needed for their expedition: scruffy clothing and shoes, two dusty, ill-kempt ponies, and a wagon for the armed men who would be coming with them. It was almost ten when they set out, and it would be almost noon when they arrived in Cheyenne.

"Now, remember, Mr Trowbridge," Jameson warned as they set out, "no matter how riled you get, *don't lose control*. You're going to a lot of trouble and risk here, and you don't want to throw it all away. You'll endanger yourself, and all my men, if you don't hold your temper."

Nate nodded but bit his lip and fumed as the ponies and wagon jogged down the road toward Cheyenne. He had promised Jameson, but if they found Molly back in that den, he couldn't answer for what he'd do.

Fury boiled in him again, as her whimpered words echoed in his mind.

"Stop it Jack!"

"No, no, *no!*"

"Don't let Jack hit me!"

"I won't, I won't, *I won't!*"

Nate set his jaw grimly. If he got his hands on that blackguard, he was going to *throttle* him, promise or no promise.

He noticed Jameson's eyes on him and made an effort to clear his expression, but ten minutes later, he was fuming again.

Chapter
Fifty-Three

They arrived in Cheyenne about half past noon. Nate was relieved to see that the traffic on the streets was heavy enough to make the arrival of a wagon full of men unremarkable, but the town itself was one of the ugliest he'd ever seen.

It was a collection of ramshackle clapboard buildings, all just dropped down onto the flat prairie floor like they'd fallen out of the sky. There wasn't a single green thing in sight—no tree, no bush, not even a blade of grass. Cheyenne was brown and dusty and full of people moving from one place to another. It reminded Nate of an anthill.

And—just as Jameson had said—it was full of dusty, dirty men. They were rolling past on the street, dozens at a time, and Nate turned away as the breeze wafted his way. The scent of old sweat, beer, and tobacco juice almost knocked him down as they passed.

Jameson nodded at something ahead of them. "There's the Golden Nugget," he said quietly. "Once we're inside, just follow my lead."

Nate followed his glance. The Golden Nugget was just another ugly clapboard building on the street. The only difference from all the other ugly clapboard buildings was its large, brightly-painted sign, and the din issuing from its swinging doors.

Nate raised his eyes. There was a big picture window on the second floor of the saloon, and he thought he saw a man standing in it, for just an instant.

They rode ahead, and the wagon full of men pulled to the opposite side of the street because there was already a wagon parked on the street in front of the Golden Nugget.

They dismounted and left the ponies at the hitching post. Nate hung back and followed Jameson as he elbowed through the swinging door and stepped into the saloon.

The smell that struck him when he stepped inside was indescribable. Nate almost gagged at the potent cocktail of stale beer, rancid, oily hair, body odour, and old tobacco juice. He noticed an old man scratching his beard as they passed and was horrified to see fleas jumping in his matted hair.

Jameson sat down at a table, and Nate sat down beside him. They had no sooner done so, than a middle-aged woman wearing a thin silk dress came over to greet them. The sound of raucous laughter, and singing, and an out-of-tune piano made it hard to hear any but loud words; so she bellowed.

"Welcome to the Golden Nugget. What would you gents like today?" she asked loudly and with a wink.

"Two whiskies. And one redhead," Jameson told her, matter-of-factly.

The woman looked nonplussed. "Redhead? Well, um—we ain't got no redhead today," she mumbled. "Are you set on one? We got three pretty blonde girls, who'd be glad to make your acquaintance."

"Oh, well, that's too bad," Jameson mumbled and stroked his chin. "We really *were* kind of set on a redhead. Hey

Boone—let's go to the bar across the street and ask again. I bet *they* got a redhead firecracker, all right!"

Nate, seeing that it was his cue, nodded and pushed the chair back.

"Oh, don't be in such a hurry!" The woman laughed nervously. "I'm sure we can—*er*—work *something* out! Let me get you your whiskies!"

She hurried off to the bar, and Nate scanned the room. There was no sign of Molly anywhere in it, which was a relief, but also no sign of his quarry. Jameson had told him that Jack McGee was a tall redheaded man with a scar across his chin, and Nate searched the room grimly.

His hand was curled around the pistol in his coat pocket. He'd no more hesitate to shoot Jack McGee than he'd hesitate to shoot a mad dog slavering in the street.

Nate became conscious of Jameson's eyes on him. Jameson cleared his throat, and Nate relaxed his expression slightly and pulled his hand over his face.

The woman came bustling back and set down two whiskies in front of them. "I can bring you a bottle, too, gents, if you're thirsty," she told them. "And when you're ready, we rustled up a redhead for you. She's upstairs now, and if you'd like to rent the room, it's two dollars.

"*Each.*"

She winked at them again, and when a drunken miner came listing past and pulled her away with him, they were left to stare at the drinks.

Nate picked his up and lifted it to the light. The glass was smeared with what looked like lipstick and greasy fingerprints.

Jameson cleared his throat again, and Nate lifted the glass dutifully to his lips and pretended to take a sip. He glanced at Jameson over the rim, and the detective put his hand out briefly—five minutes. Nate nodded.

Someone on the other side of the room began to sing and soon was joined by what seemed like half the room. The noise made it hard to hear other sounds, but Nate frowned and tilted his head toward the staircase in the back that led to the second floor.

It sounded like a woman *screaming*. Perhaps not uncommon, in such a place, but the sound was unmistakably *agony*.

Nate rolled his eyes to Jameson. The detective was staring at the table, and he had stopped drinking.

The sound came again, only barely audible over the din. Nate clenched his hands on the tabletop and glared at Jameson's face. To his relief, the detective rose slowly, stretched, and swam through the crowd to find the woman who had brought their drinks.

"We're ready for the room," he mouthed and pushed four dollars into her hand.

She nodded, smiled, and pressed a key into his outstretched palm. Jameson closed his fingers over it and made his leisurely way to the back of the saloon, through a doorway covered with a velvet curtain, and up the narrow, rickety stairs to the right.

The room they had rented was the third to the left, and Jameson opened it with the key. When they stepped inside, to Nate's shock, a thin blonde girl was lying in the big bed with a ridiculous red wig clapped over her head.

She looked terrified, and she reminded Nate so strongly of Leonie that he could barely contain his fury toward the man who committed this—*outrage* against a helpless child.

"It's all right. We're not going to hurt you," he reassured her.

Jameson nodded toward her. "We rented the room for an hour," he told her. "No one will bother you."

A spark of hope glinted in her eyes. "Are you the law?" she quavered. "*Oh, please, get me out of here!*" she sobbed.

"Get dressed," Jameson told her, "and we'll take you with us when we go."

The girl's face flushed red, and Nate added, kindly: "You can get out of bed. We'll turn our backs."

He turned away from her, toward the door, but he'd no sooner done so, than the sound of a shivering scream rang out in the hall outside.

The blood drained from Nate's face. "That's *Molly!*" he cried, "I recognize her voice!"

"Trowbridge!" Jameson barked, but Nate was already gone.

Jameson ran after his client and just caught sight of him as he disappeared up a second flight of stairs at the end of the hall.

Jameson cursed savagely, shot a glance back over his shoulder, and followed at a run. It was too late for strategy, too late for the *legal* way now.

Nate Trowbridge had lost his self-control, and they were *all* going to have to fight their way to daylight.

Chapter
Fifty-Four

Nate followed the sound of Molly's screams up a flight of narrow stairs. He tried the door at the top and found it locked.

Jameson arrived behind him. "Together," he panted, and the two of them pulled back and kicked the door open with a thunderous *bang*.

It swung back sharply, and they had a split-second to register a tall redheaded man inside as he raised his hand. They dived, Nate to the right, and Jameson to the left as bullets spattered the wall behind them.

Jameson scrambled up and grabbed at the man's gun hand. He pulled the man down to the floor, and the two of them fought for the gun. Nate kicked the gun out of the redheaded man's hand, and it went spinning. He leaned down, took it in his hand, and turned to point it at the villain's heart.

But to his shock, when he turned around, he found Jameson lying on the floor, unconscious, and McGee was standing behind Molly with a knife jabbed to her temple.

"You wanna see me kill her?" he said grinning. "I was only a *little* way into it, and it's a shame to hurry such a pleasure, but when I come to think of it, *this* might be more fun, after all."

Nate looked up and saw Molly for the first time. She was bound hand and foot, tied to a chair. To his horror, both her hands were cut to ribbons and covered with blood. A thin line across her scalp was oozing blood, and pulsing red rivulets coursed down her face. Her eyes were dull, glazed in hopeless misery.

Rage flashed from Nate's heart to his hand. He lifted the gun and pulled the trigger instantly to send Jack McGee to everlasting fire. There was a *bang* and a flash, but to his amazement, Jack McGee didn't fall down dead.

Instead, the next instant Nate found himself pinned against the wall, fighting like a madman for the gun. The big man had a grip like iron, and Nate strained to keep him from prizing the gun out of his hands.

Jack's breath was hot on his face, and the big man laughed as they struggled.

"I'm going to kill *her*, and I'm going to make *you* watch," Jack breathed. Nate ground his teeth and poured all his strength into the struggle, but McGee's inexorable grip was bending his hand, forcing him to slowly loosen his hold on the gun.

Molly suddenly screamed, and with a surge of adrenalin, Nate broke out of McGee's grip, *but he'd lost the gun.* As soon as he knew it, he landed three lightning-fast right hooks: one to McGee's jaw, one into his stomach, and a third into his shoulder. There was a loud *crack*, and McGee grunted and cursed as he tried to lift his arm—and failed.

Nate grabbed the gun, only to go flying when McGee smashed his good fist into his jaw. He crashed headlong onto the floor, rolled, and jumped up again.

He found himself facing McGee across the bed, *with* the gun. He lifted it and pulled the trigger again. There was a *bang*, and McGee went spinning face down onto the floor.

Nate crawled over the mattress cautiously, but when he leaned down to check McGee, the big man surged up suddenly and grabbed his throat with his good hand. That massive hand clamped down on his windpipe and slowly tightened. Nate dropped the gun and clawed at the vise that was suffocating him. Nate could feel his windpipe cracking. Just a little more pressure, and McGee would break it.

Nate braced his feet against the floor, lowered his head, and with a violent push, rammed Jack McGee with all his strength. The big man was thrown across the room and into the picture window, and Nate watched as Jack McGee exploded through the glass with a splintering *crash* and plunged to the street below.

Nate pulled himself up, panting, and dragged himself over to the window. There was an empty wagon tied up outside the saloon, and McGee's big body was splayed grotesquely across it. His head was tucked oddly under his shoulders, and he was utterly still.

Nate leaned back against the wall and closed his eyes for a moment; then he turned and knelt down beside Molly's chair.

She was crying, and Nate felt a tear trickle down his own cheek as he cut the ropes that held her. "Are you badly hurt?"

To his overwhelming relief, Molly shook her head. "He cut me all right, but not too bad, yet. He was toying with me like a cat with a mouse. He told me—well, *never mind* what he told me. It doesn't matter now."

"I'll get some water and bandages," Nate promised, and on an impulse, took Molly's face in his hands, and kissed her brow.

She looked up at his face. "I can't believe you're here," she murmured. "Why did you come? I did nothing but wrong to you. *Nothing* but wrong," She started to weep again.

Nate stared into her eyes sadly. "You never did any wrong to me," he whispered. "It was I who did wrong to you." He kissed her cheek; then went to crouch down beside Jameson.

He found the detective barely conscious and dizzy and sick from a heavy blow to the head. "I'll call a doctor," Nate told him, but Jameson clasped his arm.

"Go get that girl," he said hoarsely. "People will be coming up here from everywhere. Get the women out of here, and then you can take me to a doctor."

Nate stared down at him with respect. "Good man," he murmured, and went to fetch the little blonde girl.

When he opened the door to her room, he found her dressed in a thin silk slip, but ready to leave. Her expression—a painful mixture of hope and fear—made his heart twist in his chest.

"You don't have to be afraid anymore," he assured her. "Jack McGee is dead."

She closed her eyes and staggered back against the bed so suddenly that he was afraid she might fall. "Praise the Lord!" she said, in a small voice. "I know I'm not supposed to be glad when a man dies; but he wasn't a man, he was a devil, and the world's better off without him!"

"Quite right," Nate agreed briskly. "He's gone to perdition, where he'll get everything he's earned. I won't give him another thought, and I hope you don't either." He shouldered out of his jacket and put it around her shoulders.

The girl stared at him in wonder. "Who are you, mister?"

Nate stared at her. "Why do you ask?"

The girl nodded and bit her lip. "I want to remember your name. I'm going back home, and I'll never tell another soul that I was ever here. But I want to know the name of the man who got me out of hell."

Nate looked down at the floor and shook his head slightly. "Thank God, if you must thank someone," he said at last. "Things could easily have gone worse than they did, but they didn't."

He extended his arm to her, and she took it with a smile.

"We can both be thankful for that."

Chapter
Fifty-Five

Leonie sighed and toyed with a piece of French toast on her breakfast plate. "Why doesn't Nate ever take me *with* him when he goes to Denver?" she asked the room at large.

Maria set down a plate of bacon but didn't hazard an opinion. She had a newspaper tucked under one arm and gave it to Leonie.

"Here's your mail," she said.

Leonie glanced at it listlessly. "No letters," she murmured in a voice of gentle melancholy. "No invitations, no parties. I'm going to *die* of boredom, Maria. They'll carve it on my tombstone—*Here lies Leonie Trowbridge. She was just plain bored—to—death.*"

Maria gave her a dry glance. "I don't think so, *senorita*," she replied and walked out of the room.

Leonie turned her attention back to her French toast and ate a few apathetic bites before opening the paper and scanning it idly. She lifted her coffee cup to her lips, but the blaring headline of the *Denver Bugle* made her lower it incredulously. She grabbed the paper up in both hands and read:

MURDER ON THE STREETS OF CHEYENNE. SALOON OWNER FALLS TO HIS DEATH AFTER BEING SHOT TWICE.

Cheyenne—Jack McGee, the infamous owner of the Golden Nugget, fell to his death last Friday through the second-storey window of his own saloon. He had been shot twice by men who said that they came there to rescue a woman. The men said McGee had kidnapped her and was holding her in his saloon against her will.

A Mr Nate Trowbridge of Indian Rock, Colorado, and Detective Lucius Jameson of the Burlington Detective Agency in Denver entered the saloon on Friday afternoon and were seen there briefly before going upstairs. Several minutes later, customers say they heard sounds of an altercation and gunshots before McGee fell from the upstairs window.

Trowbridge claimed to have shot McGee in self-defence and said that McGee was in the act of torturing the young woman when they arrived.

Leonie clapped a hand to her mouth. *"Oh!"* she shrieked.

The woman in question, a Miss Molly Clanahan of Bolingbroke, Kansas, said that she was lured to Cheyenne when McGee made her a deceitful offer of mail order marriage. She said he claimed to be a respectable businessman, but that when she arrived, McGee attempted to force her into a life of prostitution at his saloon. She said she ran away from the Golden Nugget, but that McGee found her again and brought her back forcibly.

Leonie's mouth crumpled up. *"Oh, poor Molly!"* she cried.

Jem found her sobbing over the newspaper when he walked in, a few minutes later. He took one look at her face and pushed his hat back on his head in astonishment.

"What're *you* squallin' about?" he asked, hands on hips. "It can't be *that* bad, whatever it is."

"Oh, Jem!" she sobbed, and shook her head, "it's horrible, *horrible!*"

She pushed the newspaper toward him, and he took it and read it in growing disbelief.

"What the—well I'll be—" he muttered and scratched his head. "You could just knock me down with a—"

He read aloud: "Miss Clanahan said that she saw McGee murder Cheyenne Deputy Sheriff Abel Winters that same day and said that McGee put the deputy's body into a trunk and drove it out of town in a wagon. She also claimed that McGee told her that he'd murdered three women over the last ten years."

He shook his head and continued: "Miss Clanahan stated that Winters was also taking bribe money from McGee. The mayor of Cheyenne, and the city council have promised a thorough investigation into her claim.

"Trowbridge, Jameson, and Miss Clanahan have entered sworn testimony about the incident. Trowbridge will stand trial for the killing in Cheyenne, but neither man is being held in custody."

He looked up into Leonie's tearful face in astonishment. "Well, I never!" he gasped. "I would never-a thought your brother had that much *grit!*"

He stopped abruptly, gave Leonie a quick glance, and coughed before adding: "And it never crossed my mind that Mr Trowbridge had feelings for that bob—*er*—I mean, Miss Clanahan. But he busted into a saloon and turned the place upside down. *Shot* a man, even! I'll say one thing for your brother—he *sure* plays his cards close to his vest!"

"Oh, but Jem," Leonie cried, "Nate's going to be tried for *murder!* I don't see how that's possible when that horrible man had kidnapped poor Molly, and even—oh, I can't bear to think of it!"

Jem gave her a troubled look and tucked the newspaper under his arm. "You'd best lay down and rest, Miss Leonie," he told her. "It won't do no good for you to fume and fret. It says they ain't holding Mr Trowbridge, so at least he ain't in jail."

"Oh, isn't it *just like* Nate to do all of this without a word to me!" Leonie complained. She turned pleading eyes to Jem's face. "Jem—you don't think a jury will *convict* Nate—do you?"

Jem considered. "Well, *I* wouldn't. Seems plain as day that the man he kilt was pure rattlesnake. I can't speak for nobody in Cheyenne, but if it was *me*, I'd be more like to shake his hand than send him to jail."

"Oh, I hope the jurors will see it that way!" Leonie replied fervently. "When do you think Nate and the other man will be tried?"

Jem returned to the newspaper and scanned the article with a frown.

"It says here that they're up for trial in a week."

Leonie jumped up from the table and yanked the bell. "Maria!" she cried, "Come and help me pack! I'm taking the train to Cheyenne!"

"Here now!" Jem retorted in alarm, "You can't just up and go to Cheyenne all alone! It ain't proper for a young girl like you to travel alone. It ain't safe!"

"I'm going to Cheyenne, to be with Nate and my *poor* Molly," she replied tremulously, "and *no one* is going to stop me!"

When Maria appeared in the doorway, Leonie told her, "Maria, drop what you're doing and come upstairs with me. I'm going to pack for a trip to Cheyenne, and I'm leaving on today's train."

"Yes, miss."

Jem called after her: "Well if you're going, I'm going to have to go, too!"

But Leonie was already gone, leaving him to grumble under his breath before he returned to the newspaper article with a frown and a sigh.

Chapter
Fifty-Six

Leonie settled into the plush seat of the first-class train compartment and clasped her gloved hands unhappily.

"How long will it take us to get to Cheyenne?" she asked in a querulous voice.

Jem glanced at her from the opposite seat. "For the third time, Leonie, it'll take *two hours*. You need to calm down now. You don't wanna work yourself into one of them fretty things that females get, like hysterics."

Leonie's sunny face clouded over. "I've never had the vapors in my life!" she replied tartly. "Even though it's *fashionable*, and many *very* refined ladies get them all the time."

Jem gave her an uneasy glance. "Yes, well, you don't want to die away on me here in the train, or in the street, once we get to Cheyenne," he replied. "I ain't had any experience doctorin' high-strung females, and I don't know that anybody in Cheyenne has, either. All them refined ladies live somewhere else."

Leonie glanced out the window impatiently. "Oh, *why* aren't we moving yet?" she fretted.

Jem shook his head, settled back into his seat, and pulled his hat down over his eyes. Leonie watched him in irritation.

"*How* can you go to sleep at a time like this?" she demanded. "Poor Nate is being tried for *murder*, and

Molly has been through *torment*, and you just fold your hands like nothing's wrong!"

"Ain't nothin' I can do about any of that right now," Jem replied from under the hat. "Ain't nothin' *you* can do, either, so you may as well just settle down. Why don't you read one of them books you like?"

Leonie shook her head impatiently. "I couldn't *think* of reading a book at a time like this! Honestly, Jem—you have no sensibility at all!"

There came a knock at the cabin door, and a porter appeared in it. "Would either of you like some reading material during your trip?" he asked quietly. "We have a selection of popular books, magazines, and newspapers."

"Do you have the Cheyenne newspaper?" Leonie asked anxiously.

"Yes, miss."

"I'll take it," Leonie told him, and the man searched through his cart and gave her the morning edition before withdrawing.

Leonie unfolded the paper and instantly uttered a scream that jerked Jem bolt upright. "What in thunder!" he complained, "Don't screech like that! It's too tight in here to yell. You'll bust my head open!"

Leonie shook her head in dismay. "Look, look at this, Jem!" she cried, and he took the newspaper, frowning.

GOLDEN NUGGET KILLER TO STAND TRIAL FOR MURDER OF SALOON OWNER. CRIME OF PASSION OVER FEMME FATALE.

Jem whistled soundlessly. "*Law*," he murmured. "They're makin' Mr Trowbridge out to be a—" He glanced quickly at Leonie and let the rest of his thought fade into silence.

Cheyenne—Confessed killer Nate Trowbridge will stand trial next week before a Cheyenne jury for the murder of Jack McGee, late owner of the Golden Nugget saloon. Trowbridge has admitted to shooting McGee twice and throwing him out of a second-storey window. Trowbridge claimed that his motive for the attack was McGee's treatment of Molly Clanahan, a woman who formerly worked at the Golden Nugget.

Lucius Jameson, a Denver detective and a confederate in the attack, stated that he and Trowbridge came to the saloon with the intention of taking Miss Clanahan away, but that when they found her in McGee's bedroom, a fight quickly ensued.

The Golden Nugget, a well-known fancy house and saloon, has been the scene of several deaths over the last ten years, and many complaints of poisoning and robbery have been lodged against it by its customers.

Leonie turned to him in dismay. "They're twisting it all around!" she cried. "Nate would never attack anyone who wasn't a *criminal*, and Molly didn't *work* at the Golden Nugget, she was *kidnapped* and dragged there! They make it sound like Nate was just *jealous* of that awful man, but it's no such thing. That Jack person was the real killer. Nate's a *hero*, and he saved Molly's life!"

Jem grunted. "Sounds like somebody's trying to make a plain story into a fancy one," he mumbled. His eyes moved down the page grimly.

Clanahan's claim of being kidnapped by McGee has yet to be verified by the other women who worked at the Golden Nugget. Several have told the paper that they don't remember her, though many eyewitnesses have stated that they once saw Clanahan break a bottle over McGee's head.

"Oh, Jem, it sounds *terrible*," Leonie moaned. "And Nate has always been so careful about his name and his reputation! This scandal is going to kill him!"

Jem glanced at her sympathetically. "Leonie, your brother knew what could happen before he went down there. He got himself a de-tective, and probably a bunch of hired men to back him up, and he went down to Cheyenne to *get that woman,* or bust."

Jem gave Leonie a rueful look. "If he'd-a cared all that much about his *reputation*, he wouldn't have done it. Who woulda thought, that you with your hearts and flowers and *la-te-da* romances, was right all along?" He grinned.

Leonie lifted tear-stained eyes to his face. "What do you mean?"

Jem shook his head. "You could knock me down with a feather, after what she done to him, but that woman musta *got* to him, after all. Your brother would never-a done what he did if he hadn't been *head over ears in love.*"

Leonie stared at him. Her pink mouth dropped open to form a perfect O, and her blue eyes widened as the light of victory streamed in.

Chapter
Fifty-Seven

Nate sank down into a chair opposite the sofa where Molly was sitting. He had settled her in the finest hotel Cheyenne could offer and had provided for a doctor and new clothes. She was neat and prim in a little brown dress, and her hair was swept up on the top of her head. She was composed, though her pale skin, the thin red mark that followed her hairline, and her heavily bandaged hands bore witness to her ordeal.

But she was alive and otherwise whole, and the doctor had predicted that with time, she would regain the full use of her hands.

"I don't know what to say, Mr Trowbridge," she murmured and lifted stricken eyes to his face. "I can't begin to thank you for all you've done—"

Nate sighed and searched her face. "You don't have to thank me. Or to feel guilty," he assured her gently. "But I wish I had known the truth about you, Molly. If I had, I would've opened my home willingly and invited you to stay with us for as long as you liked."

Molly nodded and bit her lip. "I sure didn't tell you the truth, did I?" she replied softly. "I told you anything *but* the truth."

Nate tried to meet her eyes. "Why did you leave us so suddenly?" he asked quietly. "Leonie was devastated. And I—I was upset, too."

At that, Molly looked up into his face in surprise. "You *were*?"

Nate smiled. "Yes, I was. Though I didn't admit it, right away. Why did you leave?"

Molly looked down again. "I saw you with that lady you wrote the letter to," she replied, in a small voice. "I felt so *low*, to think that I'd come between the two of you and stole that girl's marriage proposal. She was so pretty, and the two of you looked like you belonged together. You deserved to be happy. So I decided to give it up and do right, like you asked me to, that time."

Nate nodded. "I see."

"I wrote out a letter to you, and to Leonie, to say goodbye," she went on, "and I meant to mail them from the train station here in town. But I was waylaid by a man, and he made me drop them."

Nate looked up sharply. "What?"

"A man came up behind me in the train station and stuck a knife in my ribs," she told him. "Jack had put out a bounty on me, and this man was trying to collect. He meant to take me to the Golden Nugget, but first he dragged me off to an alley next to the train station, and stole my bag. I meant to go on to San Francisco, and I'd bought the ticket, but he stole my ticket and all my money, and so I got stuck here."

"Did he *hurt you?*" Nate demanded, and she shook her head.

"We kind of wrestled," she said softly and looked away. "I might have shot him, I don't know. I had a gun, and it popped off. Anyway, I—I got away."

Nate stared at her in speechless amazement and pressed his lips into a straight line. "I'll put the detective agency onto it. Do you think you'd recognize the—the *man* if you saw him again?"

Molly shook her head. "Oh no, *please*. I just want this whole nightmare to be *over*.

"I met a nice couple here in town, a preacher and his wife, and she said she could find some sewing work for me, to help me earn the price of a ticket back to Kansas. I mean to look her up again and take her up on that if she's still willing. Although, after all this thing with Jack got splashed over the papers, she might—she might not be willing."

Nate looked down at his hands. "I was really rather hoping that after this trial nonsense is over, you'd come back to stay with us for awhile, Molly. Leonie has been moping about the house ever since you left. And she's right. It doesn't feel the same since you left."

Molly looked up at him with gratitude in her eyes. "It's so nice of you to say so," she murmured. "And after all I've done to wreck your life!" She shook her head and tears sparkled in her eyes.

Nate reached out and took her face in his hands. He made her look at him and said earnestly: "You haven't wrecked my life, Molly. I want you to stop saying that. I want you to stop thinking it."

She raised her eyes to his with a frown. "How can you say that?" she objected. "At least that *Jem* fellow knows what I am—I drugged him and lied to him! I lied to you, too. I came between you and the girl you love. I even lied to that sweet little sister of yours, after she stuck up for me, and believed in me."

"Leonie was the only one who saw what you really are," Nate whispered. "*One* good heart knows *another*."

Molly gave him a pained look. "The plain fact is, Mr Trowbridge—"

"*Nate.*"

"Nate," she murmured, looking down. "I'm praying that jury decides the right way. But if they don't, you could be—" she tried to finish her thought, failed, and continued, "—all for getting tangled up with me. If that happens, I don't know *what* I'll do. But I know this—it would've been better for you if you'd never *met* me." Her lips quivered, and she pressed a bandaged hand to her mouth.

"Molly," Nate replied softly, "haven't you wondered why I came down to the Golden Nugget after you?"

"My hand on the Bible, Mr Trowbridge, I can't imagine," Molly blurted and placed a hand across her eyes. "Though the Lord only knows how glad I am that you *did*. It's just like you to do something so generous. You've been nothing but good to me, in spite of how I treated you."

She shook her head. "But I've brought nothing but disaster to *you*. I'd take it all back if only I could. But I can't!"

She put her hands over her face and dissolved into tears. "If you come out of this thing all right," she wept, "I want you to go back to Denver and propose to that girl and forget you ever knew any Molly Clanahan. You're a good man, Nate Trowbridge, and I want you to get the life you *deserve*."

She jumped up from the sofa and retreated to an adjoining room. The door clicked shut behind her, and

Nate stared at it sadly for a moment or two. Then he stood up, placed a small envelope carefully on the table, and left her room with a sigh.

Chapter
Fifty-Eight

Nate returned to his suite of rooms down the hall and closed the world out when he closed the door behind him. He had taken more than his usual care in dressing that morning, but now he shrugged out of his coat and vest, and changed into a comfortable smoking jacket.

He planned to stay quiet in his hotel suite until the day of the trial.

He had settled with himself not to read the local newspaper or to discuss the trial with anyone in town. Speculation was useless in any case, and he wanted to use the time he had to take care of the business still left outstanding in his estate.

Nate sat down at a writing desk overlooking the street, retrieved a sheet of paper, and dipped a pen in the inkwell. He wrote:

I, Nate Trowbridge, being of sound mind and memory, declare this to be my last will and testament.

I commend my soul to God, and in the event of my death, I direct my body to be decently interred at the discretion of my executors.

Firstly, I will and bequeath my half of the Circle T Ranch in Indian Rock Colorado, with all its houses, lands, livestock, and assets, to Miss Molly Clanahan of Bolingbroke, Kansas, to be used by her at her own discretion for as long as she lives.

Secondly, I will and bequeath my house in London, and my share in my family's estate in Devonshire, England, to my sister Leonie Trowbridge of Indian Rock, Colorado, for as long as she lives, and to her heirs forever.

I nominate and appoint Mr Jem McClary Of Indian Rock, Colorado, and Mr Lucius Jameson, of Denver, Colorado, executors of this my last will and testament. In witness thereof, I have set my hand and seal this twenty-fourth day of August, the year of our Lord One thousand eight hundred and seventy-eight.

Nate leaned back, read the document, and then re-read it. Having satisfied himself that it was clear and correct, he folded it up and put it in an envelope, to be called for later.

He had arranged for a local attorney and three associates to arrive at his lodgings later that day. They would stand witness as he signed his will, and then he'd be satisfied that he had responsibly disposed of his worldly possessions and provided for his family.

Nate looked out the window of his rooms without really seeing the street.

He might not ever have the joy of making Molly Clanahan his wife. But he could see to it that Molly would never again be destitute or without protection in the world.

He smiled, thinking of how delighted Leonie would be to know that *he'd fallen in love with Molly Clanahan*, and as completely as any character in her ridiculous books—even if he didn't wear it on his sleeve.

Molly had streaked into his life like a comet, just as he'd been about to marry a beautiful but tepid girl who'd never once made him *feel*.

But Molly had instantly summoned his most vivid passions: *rage* at her impudence, *fear* at her threats; then, as he began to see her more clearly, *compassion* for her plight, and a profound respect for her courage.

And all the time—yes, from the first time he saw her—she ignited in him the desire of a man for a beautiful woman. Molly's luxurious hair, red as the sunset, and her lovely blue eyes had haunted his waking hours.

And the rest of the voluptuous Molly Clanahan had inspired dreams that he would never admit to anyone unless it was to her. He smiled again, remembering his dumbfounded amazement when he saw her standing at the top of his stairs in that dazzling white satin gown.

She had been a vision—the most beautiful woman he'd ever seen in his life.

He closed his eyes, remembering the way one fiery tendril of her hair had curled over her smooth white shoulders; the way she had made that white gown blossom out like a sail in the wind, or like a fresh, full-blown rose.

He remembered how horrified and guilty he'd felt when she'd been so badly injured on those stairs.

He looked down at the table. That was when he'd first started to admit that he cared for Molly. It had been hard to deny when the thought of her being injured had hurt as well as frightened him.

He hadn't understood those feelings at the time, and he'd employed harsh words and a frowning face to keep Molly from seeing them. No sane man would fall in love with an adventuress. It was madness.

But then, Leonie had always assured him that every true lover was always a *little* mad and that every woman looked for that little tinge of madness, as a sign of her lover's devotion.

Nate looked down at his hands sadly. He had been sure that Molly would understand that he loved her when he came to Cheyenne to rescue her from that monster. When he threw away all thought of his reputation, all connections with his past life, and jumped feet-first into a scandal the likes of which neither Cheyenne nor Denver had ever seen.

Perhaps she *did* understand. Perhaps her guilt hadn't been the real reason that she'd refused to let him make love to her. Perhaps it had been her gentle way of saying *no* to a man to whom she felt indebted.

He didn't know what was in her heart. He had no choice but to wait and pray that she would come to love him, as he had come to love her.

Nate bowed his head and sighed.

Oh Lord, he prayed, *I once asked you to lead me to the wife that you had chosen. At the time I was sure that Emmaline was that one. And when Molly came into my life, it seemed to me that everything had gone awry.*

But now I see your hand in all of this.

It was you, wasn't it, who led Jem to the wrong house. It was you who brought Molly right to my door.

It was you who made Leonie love Molly and believe in her so fiercely.

It was you who kept Molly safe when I wasn't there to protect her; and it was you who gave me the strength to defend her life.

Lord, you have brought us this far, Molly and me. If Molly is your answer to my prayer, please make a way for us.

But in any case, I commit my life into your hands and rest in your will.

Amen.

Chapter
Fifty-Nine

Molly came out of the bedroom in her hotel suite and peeked out into the plain little anteroom where Nate Trowbridge had just been sitting.

He had gone, and the room was empty.

She drifted out into the room, sat down on the sofa again, hugged herself, and smiled.

Nate Trowbridge had been within a heartbeat of *kissing* her, just then. He had wanted to take her in his arms; she *knew* it. And even though she hadn't let him do that, she allowed herself to be glad that he'd *wanted* to, just for a little while.

It would've been selfish of her to think only of her own pleasure, and to let Nate Trowbridge say and do things in the heat of a crisis, that he'd regret later.

She couldn't let herself dream about Nate Trowbridge. He was a fine English gentleman with all the money and education in the world. And she was just a scruffy Kansas farm girl who'd fallen into bad company. Nate was going to marry that society girl who *belonged* in his world, not some wild Irish harum-scarum who'd gotten herself into one mess after another.

No, she wasn't going to be selfish. But at least Nate had given her a memory to cherish. She'd be more than human not to remember how he'd come charging into that hellish place to save her from Jack McGee. She'd have to be made of stone not to relish the light that had been shining in his eyes just now, to linger over the gentleness in his voice.

Even if it was only for a little while, Nate Trowbridge had *loved* her, and she was going to treasure that like a jewel and keep it locked safe in her heart for the rest of her life.

When times got hard, or if she ever felt lonely, she was going to open her heart, and let that secret treasure fill her with joy.

She glanced at the chair where Nate had been sitting, and to her surprise, there was an envelope on the table nearby. She leaned over and took it in her bandaged hand. Her name had been written on the envelope in a strong, flowing hand.

Molly felt tears prick her eyelids. She couldn't read any letter from Nate, not *now*, not when his life hung in doubt. She would save it for after the trial and pray that all went as well for Nate, as he deserved.

She tucked the little envelope carefully into her handbag and placed the bag safely inside a drawer.

The sound of many approaching footsteps and the rumble of carts in the hallway outside didn't intrude on her worried thoughts until Leonie's urgent voice cried to her through the door.

"Molly, it's Leonie! *Let me in*!"

Molly smiled, rose instantly and flung the door wide. She opened her arms, and Leonie rushed into them with a swirl of satin and the scent of rose water. "My poor Molly, if only you'd *told* us!" Leonie sobbed. "We read all about what happened in the newspapers!"

Leonie stepped back and searched Molly with her eyes. "Oh Molly, your poor hands! When I think of what that monster did to you, I'm *glad* that Nate shot him! I could've shot him myself!" Leonie declared angrily. "Are you going to be all right?"

Molly nodded and smiled. "I'll be fine now, Leonie. You needn't have any worries about me."

Leonie's big blue eyes looked puzzled. "Of course I was worried!" she objected. "But it *does* do my heart good to see you looking so well!"

She sat down on the sofa and pulled Molly down beside her. "I brought you a trunk full of things from home," she confided, "because you've been stuck here with nothing except what *Nate* could think of. Men have no idea how to shop, and I knew you'd be lost."

"Thank you, Leonie, but—"

"We'll have to give each other strength," Leonie added with a troubled look. "I've been out of my mind with worry ever since I heard about Nate—quite by accident! I had to read about it in the *newspaper*, if you can believe that. Nate never tells me anything!"

Molly looked down at her in sympathy. "He was trying to keep you from worrying, Leonie."

Leonie gave her an exasperated look. "Oh, as if it would feel *better* to be surprised! I get so put out!"

A man appeared in the doorway and coughed. Leonie looked up at him and said: "Yes, you can bring the trunks in. Take them to the bedroom and unlock them, please."

"Yes, miss."

Molly watched in amazement as the man pushed a hand truck through the doorway. It was loaded down with three large trunks.

"Really, Leonie, I have everything I need," she objected, as the man dragged the cart into the bedroom, but Leonie waved her words away.

"I have three gowns and matching boots for you, hats—oh, you *have* to see the green one, Molly, it was *made* for you!—some cunning little kidskin gloves, a few parasols, and a special outfit for the trial. I think we should *both* wear white flowers in our hair," Leonie told her earnestly, "and I'm going to prevail on Nate to wear a white rose in his lapel to signify his *innocence* to the jury."

Molly gazed down at her indulgently. "Any man that needs white flowers to tell him that your brother is innocent, shouldn't be sitting on a jury at all," she replied. "Have you seen Nate yet?"

"No. I was on my way, but I had to come and see you first!" Leonie answered, and Molly nodded.

"I'm *just fine*. Nate needs you right now, and I want you to go and talk to him."

Leonie hugged her and smiled into her face. "I'll be back, and we can get all caught up."

"You and I can get caught up after the trial," Molly told her gently. "Until then, I want you to spend time with your brother."

"Yes, I'm going to see him now," Leonie sighed. "Do you—do you think he'll be acquitted, Molly?"

The smile died out of Molly's eyes. "I don't know, honey. You and I just need to pray hard that they'll see the truth, and—and do what's right. You go on, now. I'll talk to you later."

Leonie smiled and retreated, and when the door had closed behind her, Molly turned to her own bedroom.

It was past time for her to take her own advice. She closed the door and sank down beside the bed to pray like she'd never prayed before in her life.

Chapter
Sixty

Molly took her breakfast at seven o' clock the next morning. She had spent a sleepless night stretched out in desperate prayer. A little after dawn, she gave up trying to rest and ordered a breakfast tray brought up to her room.

The owner of the hotel had brought it to her door. He was a round, balding man with a bowler hat, a bow tie, and a nervous tic. He told her, apologetically, that it would probably be better if she and her party didn't go out on the street.

She had asked him *why not?* though she already knew the answer. The sounds in the street outside had threatened to destroy her concentration all night long.

Whoops, gun shots. Shouts, curses. And once, very clearly, a nasty chant:

Judge Rope! Judge Rope!
Find a tree, yank him up
To the sky!
Hang him high!

The din had died down just at sunrise, as the crowd in the street had taken themselves away to sleep off a drunken night, but to Molly's alarm, there were signs that a new demonstration was cranking up outside.

To her amazement, there was a sound like *singing*.

"What's going on?" Molly asked her host as he set out her breakfast tray. The man nodded toward the window.

"This McGee killin' has stirred folks up," he told her, shaking his head. "The streets were full last night, and they're full agin this mornin.' Just about the whole town has turned out, one side or another, to have their say about it."

"Why would anyone be *stirred up* that Jack McGee is dead?" Molly asked the man indignantly. "Anyone who *knew* him would dance on his grave!"

"Well, ma'am, it ain't the *man* that got kilt, so much as it is what ol' Jack *stood* for. Jack was one of the first ones to come to Cheyenne, back when it really *was* wild. They's still a bunch of the old timers that wants the saloons and gambling halls in Cheyenne to stay like they was, in the old days. And they's a new crowd that wants all that pushed out, to make room for banks, and businesses, and churches. The *proper* folks, you might say.

"They've been fightin' each other for years, and this killin' done brought the whole thing to a head," he worried aloud. "The wild bunch wants your friend to be strung up for killin' a man they all knew, and the proper folk want your friend de-clared innocent. The rowdy ones was out all last night, whoopin' and hollerin.' Now the re-spectible folks has come out to answer 'em."

The sound of robust voices wafted up to the room from the street below, and it was clear that the marchers were singing a *hymn*.

Mine eyes have seen the glory of the coming of the Lord; He is trampling out the vintage where the grapes of wrath are stored;

He has loosed the fateful lightning of his terrible swift sword:
His truth is marching on.

Glory, glory! Hallelujah!

Glory, glory! Hallelujah!

Glory, glory! Hallelujah!

His   truth   is   marching   on.

He has sounded forth the trumpet that shall never call retreat;
He is sifting out the hearts of men before his judgment seat.
Oh, be swift, my soul, to answer him; be jubilant, my feet!
Our God is marching on.

Molly frowned and went to the window. She pulled back the curtain, and to her amazement, the street was filled with hundreds of protesters. They were waving brooms and carried signs that read:

SWEEP OUT THE TRASH.

CLEAN UP THIS WICKED TOWN.

A STRANGER HAD TO DO THE JOB.

SAFETY FOR THE WOMEN OF CHEYENNE.

"I wouldn't step foot outside the door of this hotel if I was you," the man told her sorrowfully. "Looks like most of the nighttime crowd is gone, but you never know who might still be hangin' around to pop a shot off. Feelins is runnin' mighty high in this town right now."

"Where's the *law*, then?" Molly asked indignantly.

The man rolled his eyes to hers. "Mostly downstairs, ma'am, standin' guard," he drawled. "They was a bunch here last night that tried to bust our doors down. They wanted to drag your friend away to meet Judge Rope."

"*What?*" Molly rolled terrified eyes to his face.

The man nodded. "Yep, I'm afraid so. They woulda lynched that English fella if they'da been able to get their hands on him."

"Why—then they should take Mr Trowbridge to a safer place, where they can *protect* him!" Molly sputtered.

"I think that's the plan, ma'am. But they wanted to wait until the rowdies had gone home to sleep it off. I expect they'll be up to take him away after breakfast."

He tipped his hat to her respectfully, and added: "I'd just lay kinda low if I was you, ma'am. A word to the wise."

The door closed after him with a soft *click*. Molly stood staring after him, and in the silence, the awful reality of that close call settled down over her.

Nate could've been *murdered* last night, killed before he'd even had a trial.

She could've *lost* him before she even knew what had *happened*.

She stared out through the window. The people marching on the street below were still singing:

Glory, glory! Hallelujah!
Glory, glory! Hallelujah!
Glory, glory! Hallelujah!
His truth is marching on.

Molly stood there, stock-still. The law was coming to take Nate away—might already have taken him away. It was her last chance to see him alone, to give him something that might give him strength.

Something he could *keep*.

She turned from the window, picked up her skirts, and rushed out of the room. The sound of heavy boots echoed on the stairs down the hall, but she still had a moment to act.

She reached Nate's door and burst inside. Her eyes swept the room. Nate was seated at a chair near the window, and he lifted startled eyes to her face. There were other men standing around him, distinguished-looking men, but Molly ignored them all.

She took five steps across the room, her eyes on Nate's face. He rose to meet her, and without a word she threw herself on his chest, twined her arms around him, and kissed him like it was the end of the world.

"Why, the idea," one of the men grumbled, but Nate's arms closed around her, and she kissed him so hard that her lips hurt; then kissed him again.

An instant later, the door opened again, and the sheriff and two deputies filled up the opening.

"Mr Nate Trowbridge, I'm Sheriff Milton. My deputies and I are here to take you into custody," a tall man announced. "You're going to await trial in the Cheyenne Jail for your own protection."

Molly rested her brow against Nate's and closed her eyes, and he put his hands over hers and returned them gently to her side.

"I'm ready," Nate told them, and he stepped around her and walked away. Molly watched in dread as the sheriff put his hands on Nate's straight shoulder; and Nate walked out without a backward look or the faintest hesitation.

Molly crumpled into the chair that he had vacated and bowed her head in tears, but one of the men put a hand on her shoulder.

"There, there, my dear," he said kindly, "he's on the right side of the law, and he has the best lawyers in Cheyenne."

Molly nodded. "I'm glad he has good lawyers," she whispered.

"But what he needs is a good *jury*."

Chapter
Sixty-One

"Leonie? Are you in there?"

Molly rapped on the door of Leonie's hotel suite, and to her relief, Leonie opened the door. Her eyes looked red, and Molly put her arms around her before stepping inside and closing the door behind her.

"The sheriff just came to take Nate down to the jail," Molly told her and forestalled Leonie's objection by adding, "it's the safest place that he can be right now. It's for the best."

"But why can't he stay here?" Leonie cried. "Nate will be miserable in that horrid jail! And he hasn't been convicted of any crime!"

"I know, but—the hotel manager told me this morning that there are some wicked people here who are angry with Nate. I can't imagine why, but he said they're *really* fighting about some local quarrel about who gets to run Cheyenne: the people who run gambling dens or the people who want Cheyenne to be a decent place."

Molly led Leonie to a velvet settee and sank down beside her. "He told me another thing, too. He said that none of us should peep outside this hotel until the trial. It may not be safe for *us*, either. And I want you to *promise* me that you won't go outside the hotel until the trial."

Leonie's blue eyes closed in grief. "Oh, Molly, what a horrible nightmare!" she quavered. "I wish none of this had *ever* happened!"

"So do I," Molly murmured and took Leonie into her arms. "But I met a man just now who said that Nate has the *best* lawyers in town. I'm sure everything will be all right."

There came a rap on the door, and Molly released Leonie to go and answer it. To her surprise, Jem McClary stood outside, hat in hand. They stared at one another for an awkward moment; then Molly shut the door behind her and drew him aside.

"I know what you think of me, Jem McClary," she told him dryly, "but I hope you'll listen to me now for Nate's sake.

"I'm going out," she told him, "and I want you to make sure Leonie doesn't follow me. It isn't safe."

He had listened in silence up to that point, but at that, he put his hands on his hips and tilted his head to one side.

"Like I wouldn't! I know Leonie's just the same as a little child and don't have no sense. You ain't got to spell it out for me," he told her indignantly. "And it ain't exactly news to me that a mob tried to tear the doors off this hotel last night," he added. "I was on the inside of them doors with a Colt revolver in my left hand and a sawed-off in my right."

Molly raised an eyebrow. "*Well*. Thank you."

"Oh, I didn't do it for *your* sake, Molly Clanahan," he told her tartly. "I reckon you could be throwed off the roof of this hotel and still land on your feet like a cat and go scamperin' away! I ain't worried about *you!*

"I did it because I owe it to Mr Trowbridge. He pays me to protect his spread and his family; so I do. I don't need any troublemakin' *woman* to tell me my job."

Molly drew herself up and was about to respond in kind when the door opened, and Leonie's anxious face peered out.

"Is everything all right?" she asked in a tiny voice.

They both turned to her, smiling with all their teeth. "Why, of course," she murmured; and Jem added, "Ain't nothin' wrong, Leonie, you just stay inside and rest."

But once the door closed behind her, they faced off again.

"I don't care *what* rattles around in that big head of yours, cowboy," Molly told him grimly, "as long as you keep Leonie *inside this hotel.*"

She gathered her skirts to go back inside, but Jem's hand on her arm made her throw him a fiery glance.

"Be careful what you say to her," he growled. "I ain't as forgivin' as Mr Trowbridge, *or* as naïve about women, and if I catch you puttin' the wrong ideas in her head, or lettin' that saloon rub off your skirts onto hers, I'll—"

"*Oh!*" Molly screamed, jerked her arm out of his, swept inside Leonie's apartments and slammed the door on Jem with a *bang.*

She stopped just inside and put her head in her hands, but Leonie's small voice made her look up.

"Is everything all right, Molly?"

Molly drew herself up and forced a smile. "Just fine, honey. Don't worry about a thing."

***

When Molly walked out of the suite a few minutes later, she left Leonie lying on her bed with a cool compress on her head, and a soothing cup of tea at her elbow.

Jem was propping up the wall a good distance down the hall, and after raking him with a furious glance, Molly turned downstairs in the other direction.

There was no one at the front desk, and Molly slipped outside unseen. To her relief, there were still marchers on the street, and she picked up her skirts to run after them.

The marchers had erected a small platform at the end of the main street, nearest the courthouse, and a few people were seated there. The crowd had gathered around to hear them speak, and Molly swam urgently through the press.

A balding man with glasses stepped up to the podium and was preparing to address the crowd, but soon the people in the crowd began to murmur:

"That's *her*, isn't it—the redheaded woman?"

"It's Molly Clanahan!"

"Look at her hands! It *is* her!"

Soon there was near-chaos, and by the time Molly had gained the foot of the platform, the people were chanting:

"Let her talk! Let her talk! Let her talk!"

Molly looked up at the platform, and to her astonishment, the man standing there was none other than the Reverend Luther P. Allen.

"Why—here is the young lady now!" he exclaimed and turned to the crowd. "Let's give Miss Clanahan a rousing Cheyenne welcome!"

327

The people in the crowd clapped and cheered, and the reverend extended his hand to her. When she reached the top of the platform, he leaned over and said, "We're so glad to see you again, my dear!"

Molly smiled at him and looked around. The platform was surrounded by town folk on every side, and the crowd waved their brooms and placards at the sight of her. The sight of such a big crowd, all with their eyes on her, threatened to freeze her where she stood, but the thought of Nate made her bite her lip and stand up straight and tall.

"Thank you for coming out," she told them, and people in the back shouted:

"Louder! We can't hear you!"

She licked her lips and cried: "*Thank you for coming out today*. I surely appreciate it."

She looked around again and plucked up her courage. "I want to tell you folks a story. It's about a farm girl whose family died and left her all alone and penniless in the world.

"She came out to Cheyenne from her home in Kansas," she began. "She was a mail order bride, or at least she *thought* she was. She'd been getting letters from a business owner here in Cheyenne who said his wife had died, and who said he wanted to marry again.

"You'll laugh when you hear his name. That man was *Jack McGee!*"

There was angry muttering in the crowd, and Molly was encouraged to go on: "*I am that farm girl*. Jack McGee wrote me lots of pretty letters. He told me he owned a nice little store and promised he was an upright man. He said that if I came out to Cheyenne, he'd marry me that *very* day.

"So I came out here, believing every word. I was an ignorant little girl who hadn't never seen a big town, and didn't know nothin' about men like Jack.

"But I had no sooner got off the train here in Cheyenne than Jack McGee showed me who he *really* was. He dragged me down to that filthy den, the Golden Nugget, and told me to put on a flimsy dress and go out and serve liquor to drunken men. I was raised in a godly home, and I told him I *wouldn't*, and I tried to get away. But Jack McGee knocked me down with his fist and told me that if I didn't do like he said, he'd kill me!"

The angry muttering swelled up into a dull rumble. A woman in the crowd cried out: "You poor girl! Them snakes should be hung!"

Molly added: "I had been *kidnapped*, and I knew that if I didn't get away quick, Jack would force me into a life of shame and degradation. So I defied him. I ran away!"

She paused to look out across the crowd. Hundreds of eyes were riveted to her face. Some of the women were crying.

"The man you're trying for *murder* helped me get back on my feet again. Nate Trowbridge is all the things that Jack McGee *wasn't*. Mr Trowbridge is a gentleman, the soul of honour and respectability. He and his sister helped me get back my self-respect, after having been disrespected so badly.

"But Jack McGee didn't give up and let me go. He came looking for me and dragged me back to the Golden Nugget against my will. When he killed your deputy sheriff right before my eyes, and then said he'd kill me *too*, I gave up hope. Jack was a powerful man in this town, and no one seemed to care what he was doing to girls who didn't have any father or brother to protect them.

"But Mr Trowbridge came down from Denver, looking for me, and he and another man found Jack McGee in the very act of murdering me," she cried, lifting her bandaged hands. "And if Nate Trowbridge hadn't fought him just like a tiger, Jack would've killed me, sure!

"I stand here today because of God's mercy, and Nate Trowbridge's courage!"

By this time, the crowd was fully engrossed in her story, and voices in the crowd cried out:

"God bless you, Molly!"

"Nate Trowbridge is a hero!"

"We're behind him, Molly!"

Molly looked out at their faces with a grieved expression. "Last night," she cried, "a gang of drunken no-accounts tried to bust into our hotel. They wanted to drag Mr Trowbridge out of his bed, hustle him out of town in secret, and lynch him, like the cowards they are!"

There was a collective murmur of shock and outrage, and Molly went on: "They were a bunch of saloon owners and gambling hall sharps! They're the only ones crying for Jack McGee—because Jack protected them, and made them rich, and now his protection is gone, and his money's dried up!

"They're the ones that want Cheyenne to stay a lawless, godless place. A place where no girl or woman is safe. A place where decent people can be shot down in the street. A place where an innocent man can be lynched in the middle of the night!"

"They're the only ones who aren't thanking God for Nate Trowbridge. He rid Cheyenne of a murdering brute! I saw it all, and I testify that Nate Trowbridge killed Jack McGee in *self-defence*!"

The crowd erupted into a cacophony of shouting, and some of the brooms and the placards were thrown into the air. And in the ensuing chaos, Molly didn't notice three masked men riding down the street on the outskirts of the crowd until they spurred their mounts to a gallop and waved their arms and whooped at the top of their lungs. When they'd pulled almost even to the platform where she stood, they all raised revolvers, and one of them screamed:

"This is for Jack!"

Molly stared at them as they flashed past. It was strange, like time had slowed down. She had time to notice the slouch hats pulled low over their eyes; the gaudy bandannas tied around their faces; the flared nostrils of their heaving mounts; the long dust jackets flapping in the wind. She was dimly aware of a half-dozen loud *pops*; the screams of the crowd; Mr Allen whirling to push her down onto the floor of the podium, and wood splintering all around them.

Chapter
Sixty-Two

The door to the cell area creaked open, and Nate lifted his head wearily. He had spent the last twelve hours lying on the hardest cot he'd ever endured, and if that hadn't been enough, the snores of the drunken hobo next door had set the seal on his sleepless night.

The sheriff seemed to be in discussion with an unseen visitor. Nate couldn't quite make out what they were saying, but he did hear snatches of conversation:

"Don't tell him about it. There's nothing he can do."

The mumbled words faded back into incoherence until he heard:

"Shame ... told her, but she didn't listen."

There came a loud jangling of keys, and the sheriff turned up the lamp and walked up to his cell door.

"You have a visitor, Mr Trowbridge."

Nate sat up and watched as the sheriff unlocked his cell, and Jem McClary walked in. The sheriff closed the cell door and grumbled:

"Just call me when you're ready."

They both watched him as he walked out, and after the door closed behind him, Nate looked up with a hungry light in his eyes.

"Well, Jem, how is Leonie doing?"

Jem took his hat off and leaned against the cell bars. "She's doing tolerable, Mr Trowbridge," he nodded. "She ain't happy, of course, but she's holding up. She wanted to come down here with me, but I figured you'd rather she didn't."

"Thank you, Jem. It *would* upset her to see me here. She's better off where she is." He raised his eyes to Jem's face.

"How—how is Molly?"

Jem looked away. "Well, now, Mister Trowbridge, maybe I ain't the best one to ask. Miss Clanahan and me, we ain't exactly friends."

Nate held Jem with his eyes. "I overheard you talking to the sheriff just now," he said softly. "What are you keeping from me? Is it about Molly?"

Jem's blue eyes widened in innocence. "Me? Keep something from you, Mister Trowbridge?"

Nate nodded. "You're a terrible liar, Jem. If something's happened to Molly, I demand to know."

Jem scratched his jaw. "Well sir, now that you mention it, there happened to be a big march through town, of the church folk mostly, supporting you, and she joined it. And they recognized her and asked her to make a little speech. Went over real big, I hear. I just thought you might not approve of Miss Clanahan putting herself forward like that. You bein' such a private person, yourself."

Nate frowned and was silent.

"Is that all?" he said at last.

Jem shrugged. "Unless there's somethin' I don't know about."

Nate glanced at his foreman again but decided not to press him. If something serious *had* happened to Molly while he was trapped inside this jail cell, it was just as well he didn't know.

He'd go *mad*.

"I'd consider it a favour, Jem," he said slowly, "if you'd look out for Molly as well as Leonie, during my trial."

Jem looked dour. "I'll do my best, Mr Trowbridge, but that woman is the most bullheaded, troublous female I've ever seen. The only way I could be sure she wasn't in a mess would be to bring her down here and lock *her* up, *too.*"

Nate smiled and nodded. "Thank you, Jem. That puts my mind at rest."

"I'll do it, but I don't think it's strictly necessary, Mr Trowbridge. You'll be a free man soon enough. You're favoured to win your trial. Last I checked, the betting in town is that you'll be de-clared innocent. Not by much of a margin, I'll admit, but a win is a win."

Nate gave him a wry look. "That's comforting."

"People are riled up about this thing," Jem told him, with a rueful shake of his head. "I never seen a town so split in two. Half of 'em on *this* side, and the other half on *that.*"

Nate said nothing and frowned at the floor. By all accounts his trial was fast becoming a proxy fight between two entrenched camps in town.

His jury might easily vote based on their political leanings, instead of on the facts of the case.

Anything could happen.

He looked up into Jem's face. "Jem, I made out my will yesterday. I named you my executor."

Jem stood up straight in surprise, and a solemn look settled over his face. "Why, I'd take that as a great honour, Mr Trowbridge," he replied slowly. "I'd be proud to do that for you.

"Not that I think there'll be the *need*."

"Let's hope not," Nate replied with a faint smile. "But when you go back to the hotel, I wish you'd take a message to Leonie for me. Tell her that I'm fine, and that I'm looking forward to my trial, because I know I'm going to be acquitted.

"And I'd like you to send a message to Molly for me, as well."

Jem made a face, but nodded.

"I'd like you to tell her that I'd like to talk to her after the trial."

"Whatever you say, Mr Trowbridge."

There was the sound of the door opening again, and the sheriff appeared in the opening.

"Mr Trowbridge, you have another visitor."

Jem rolled his eyes to his employer's and stuck out his hand. Nate shook it and clapped him on the shoulder. "Thank you, Jem."

"I'll talk to you later, Mr Trowbridge."

Jem walked out, and the sheriff held the door open for the next visitor to come in.

To Nate's amazement, it was Emmaline Chiswick. He stood up.

"Emmaline! What are you doing here?"

Emmaline kept her eyes on the floor as the sheriff pulled up a chair for her. He placed it in front of Nate's cell, and she sat down silently.

"Miss, you just call out to me if you need anything. I'll just be on the other side of that door."

Emmaline nodded mutely, and they both sat in silence until he withdrew. Then Emmaline trained her beautiful blue eyes on his face.

"I know it isn't very ladylike for me to come down here in this bold way," she murmured in her soft voice, "but I *had* to come. Momma and Poppa don't know. They think I'm staying with friends here in town."

"You shouldn't deceive them, Emmaline," Nate replied gently. "And you *cannot* be seen with me! I'm on trial for killing a man. You can't be connected to me in any way. Your *reputation* is at stake. Go home, my dear."

"I can't!" she whispered and let her gaze fall to her lap. "I—I suppose I've already broken all the rules, so one more won't make any great difference. Since I've been so bold as to come here, I may as well open my heart to you.

"Nate, when—when we last met, at your home, I hoped that your warm manner, and your *particular* attention, meant that I had found a place in your heart. I can't believe that your heart could change so much, and in so short a time!

"And I can scarcely credit the terrible things we read in the papers about you! It's so unlike the dear Nate Trowbridge that I know."

She looked up at him with tears gleaming in her eyes. "Was I mistaken, Nate?" she asked, in a trembling voice.

"Oh, if you tell me that you still have feelings for me, I will stand by you. I will ask for nothing more!"

Nate looked down at his hands. A wave of shame crawled up from his feet to the roots of his hair, but he mustered his strength and met her eyes.

"Emmaline," he said softly, "you were *not* mistaken that I admired you very much, and that I came to Denver with the intention of asking you to marry me. I thought—and still think of you—as a modest and beautiful girl who will make your future husband very happy.

"But—all my plans soon went awry, my dear. I met another woman, at the same time that I was visiting you and your family. She wrecked my life utterly. She was alone, and desperate, and she meddled with my plans outrageously. She made me furious.

"But she also made me feel other emotions I never dreamed possible. She was like no one else I'd ever met. She was clever and infuriating and touching and sad and brave and beautiful. She made me *come alive.*"

He reached out through the bars and took her hand. "Emmaline, I can't explain it any better, than to say that I just *fell in love* with her. To this hour, it makes no sense, and I certainly didn't plan it. It just—happened."

He squeezed her hand gently. "But the last thing I would ever want to do is hurt you."

Emmaline tilted her head, and her lip trembled. "Then were the newspaper stories true?" she quavered. "You went into a *saloon*, with a *detective*, and—and *shot* a man, and threw him out of a window?"

"Yes, Emmaline," he replied sadly. "I did. To defend the woman I love from a brute who would have murdered her."

Emmaline shook her head and pressed a handkerchief to her mouth. "Oh, Nate," she sobbed, "you're such a good, upright man! I hate to see this low woman and this unnatural affection ruin you! Your name has been splashed all over the papers in connection with a common saloon girl, and her evil name has stained your good one. I pray, not beyond hope!

"This vulgar Irish woman, whoever she is, has hypnotized you. Come back to London with me," she pled, "and her spell will be broken. In a few weeks, you'll marvel to think you could even have *looked* at her. You'll remember who and what you are!"

Nate looked down, and gently released Emmaline's hand. "I'm sorry, my dear," he replied quietly. "I cannot be to you now, what I have been in the past, and if I have hurt you, I beg your forgiveness.

"I'm afraid that the best and most loving gift I can give you now is to remove myself from your life. It's true that my reputation has been blackened. But yours is still bright. Go home, Emmaline. Find an adoring young man, and live a long and happy life."

Emmaline rose and turned for the door sobbing into her handkerchief. Nate watched in pity as the door swung closed behind her, then closed his eyes, and leaned back against the wall.

Chapter

Sixty-Three

Molly opened her eyes slightly. The light hurt her, and she closed them again.

She slowly became aware that she was lying in bed, that her chest hurt, and that it was painful to breathe. A gentle hand put a cool compress on her brow and then pressed a cold spoon to her lips.

"Try to take a sip," the voice urged. It was a woman's voice, and it reminded her somehow of her mother.

Molly opened her lips just enough to let some cool liquid trickle down her throat. It felt good.

A second voice tickled at her ear. It sounded young.

"Molly, can you hear me?"

She licked her lips but made no other reply.

"Oh, I can't stand it," the second voice cried softly. "Why can't the doctor *help* her?"

"The doctor has done as much as he can," the older woman's voice replied softly. "Now she's in the hands of God."

There came the sound of soft weeping, and a man's voice mumbled from farther away.

"I went down to that jail house and lied like a rug," it said, in a rueful tone. "He's gonna skin me when he finds out the truth."

"You did right," the older woman's voice replied. "He doesn't need any more worries right now."

"I guess," the man's voice sighed. "Leonie, you need to come out of here and give her a chance to rest. The doctor said that was important."

"Very well," Leonie said in a small voice. "But I want to be called if there's *any* change!"

"We'll call you," the man's voice promised in an exasperated tone. There was the sound of a door closing softly, and then silence.

The spoon nudged her lips again, and she let the liquid trickle down her throat.

Molly slipped back into her dreams. She was under the big oak tree near her family's house, rocking back and forth in the rope swing her father had made for her. The big oak tree was the only tree to be seen for miles and was almost the only thing that broke up the golden acres of wheat that rolled right to the horizon.

She sighed, and the dream shifted. The landscape changed colour. Now the flat Kansas countryside was brown and barren. Flecks of snow drifted down on the wind, and it was bitter cold.

She pulled her shawl around her shoulders and ran back to the house.

"Pa?"

She opened the door of their little clapboard house, but there was no one inside. She searched from room to room.

"Terry? Joe?"

There was still no answer.

She sat down at the kitchen table and wondered where they'd gone. Soon she began to get hungry, and she searched in the cupboards for something to eat, but every canister and drawer was empty.

When she turned, the man from the bank was standing just outside the front door. He nailed something to the wall, then turned and left.

She walked out onto the porch to see what he'd done. There was a big sign on the wall that read: BANK FORECLOSURE.

The dream churned in her mind, and blackness settled over her. Now she was back at the Circle T, and Leonie was holding a silly hat with a big curling feather.

"Let's see how this looks on you," she smiled and set it down over her head.

Nate appeared in the doorway, and she stood up and twirled flirtatiously for him. "How do you like it?" She laughed.

He smiled and shook his head. She pulled the hat off and was about to put on another one when Jack McGee appeared suddenly in the doorway behind Nate and blocked out all the light. His weird eyes were glowing with unholy fire.

"I warned you what'd happen if you don't do like you're *told*!"

Jack pulled out a knife and abruptly slashed Nate's throat. She screamed as Nate slid to the floor, and Jack stalked into the room and yanked her up by one arm.

"You mind your mouth," he growled. "I could *kill* you, and nobody in Cheyenne would know or care. Just one less whore at The Golden Nugget, that's all. You're coming back with me."

No, no, no, she mouthed.

"What was that, dear?" the voice said softly.

She turned her head. "I won't go," she murmured.

"Don't worry, honey. You're not going anywhere. You must have been having a bad dream," the voice told her, and the compress on her brow was removed, to make way for a new one. It was cool and soothing.

She opened her eyes again. There was an older woman sitting at her bedside. She looked familiar, but Molly couldn't remember her name, or who she was.

"Where am I?" she asked weakly.

"You're in your hotel room," the woman replied with a smile. "You had a real high fever. We've been waiting for you to come back to us."

Molly looked around and frowned. She was in a spacious bedroom with big windows and pretty furniture, but none of it looked familiar.

"I still don't know ..." she began, and her voice trailed off.

The older woman smiled. "You're in Cheyenne, Wyoming, and it's Monday the thirty-first of August."

Molly closed her eyes again, and her memory came flooding back. The first thought that came to her, with a rush of relief, was:

Jack is dead.

Followed quickly by: *Nate's on trial for killing him.*

Followed by:

I've been shot.

Her brows twitched together. It had happened just as she'd finished her speech to the marchers that day. Three masked men had come galloping down the street and shot her.

"What's wrong with me?" she asked faintly. "It hurts to breathe."

"The doctor had to remove a bullet from your shoulder," Mrs Allen replied. "He did a good job, but you got a little infection. You got pleurisy, and a fever."

Mrs Allen pressed a cool spoon to her lips, and Molly let the liquid trickle down her throat.

"Was anybody else hurt?"

"No, honey—thank the Lord. You just lie there and rest."

Molly opened her eyes again. "You said today was the thirty-first?"

"That's right."

She struggled to sit up. "Nate's *trial* is today!"

Mrs Allen clucked at her in dismay. "Lie back down! You'll pull your wound open!"

Molly looked down at herself. Her hair had been braided and pulled to one side, and her left shoulder was bandaged and wrapped securely with a strip of gauze.

"I'm so cold," she shivered.

Mrs Allen nodded. "You're still running a temperature," she replied.

Molly leaned back into her pillow and closed her eyes as the older woman pulled the blanket up around her neck. "Has the trial started yet?"

"Oh, yes. It's been going on since this morning."

"*Oh*, I *wish* I could be there! You will tell me the verdict, as soon as you hear, won't you?"

"Of course."

Molly bit her lip. "Mrs Allen, my bag is in the chest of drawers. Can you get it for me, please?"

"Why sure, honey."

When Mrs Allen returned and gave her the little satin purse, Molly opened it with trembling fingers. The envelope Nate had left her was still tucked safely inside.

"May I have a few minutes alone? I'd like to read this letter in private," she told the older woman.

Mrs Allen smiled. "Of course. I'll check back in on you in a few minutes."

Chapter
Sixty-Four

The older woman left the room in a rustle of skirts. Molly looked down at her own name, neatly written across the envelope in swirling letters.

She opened the packet with trembling fingers.

Dear Molly,

I am writing this letter because I don't know what my future holds, and I wanted to give you something you could hold in your hands.

Something of me that you could keep.

I'm also writing this because I'm not certain, even now, that you understand my feelings toward you. So I am going to write them down, so I can forever remove your doubt.

I love you.

I do not write those words lightly. I think you know me well enough by now, to understand that when I say this, I am committing my whole heart and future to you.

I am asking you to marry me.

Molly put her hand to her mouth and blinked back tears.

If I should prevail in my trial, I hope you will come back with me to the Circle T, so we can be married there.

If I should not prevail, then I hope you will remember me fondly, and remain in touch with Leonie, who also loves you very much.

You haven't allowed yourself to love me, Molly, because you feel guilty for what you did to me. Whatever tiny harm you might have done, I forgive a thousand times.

I think you also believe that you're bad for me. But that was never true, even when we were strangers and at cross purposes.

You kept me from marrying a woman I did not know and—I see now—did not love. Now I know what it is to love truly, and I am really living for the first time in my life.

Do you think that I only let you stay at the house because I wanted the letter? That was true at first, but my reasons quickly changed. I let you stay because I was falling in love with the brave and beautiful woman I glimpsed behind the flimsy mask.

You wore a brazen face, to hide from me that you were frightened and all too human.

But I, too, was wearing a mask, Molly. I pretended to be angry when I had long since ceased to be, to hide from you that I was falling deeply in love.

You stir me, you give me strength, and looking at you now fills me with such feelings of love and joy, that no words could do them justice.

My darling, Jem's mistake wasn't a mistake at all. I believe it was God's providence to bring me to the woman he had chosen to be my wife.

But none of these feelings of mine mean anything unless you share them, dearest Molly.

Do I have your heart? If I do, beloved, then throw away your fears and come to me.

If I do not have your heart, then I will part from you with sorrow but will love you to the end of my days.

I will not speak to you again until after the trial. If things go well with me, yours is the first face I long to see.

If things go otherwise, then consider this my fond farewell.

With all my heart,

Nate.

Molly crumpled the letter up in her fingers, bowed her head, and wept. Mrs Allen found her that way when she returned.

"Why, child!" she gasped, "What's the matter? You don't need to tease yourself about anything right now. Lie down and rest, and put it out of your mind, whatever it is!"

But Molly shook her head. It would be impossible to explain to Mrs Allen the cruel irony that her heart might break once from joy, and again from grief, on the same day.

"I'm going down to the courthouse," she said at last and threw off the blanket.

"You can't do that!" Mrs Allen gasped and feebly attempted to block her way. "You have an infection; you have fever! Your wound is still fresh. You could tear it!"

"I'm going to dress and go down to the courthouse if it kills me," Molly said weakly. "You can help me or hinder me, but you can't stop me."

"I can call the doctor, and I will!" the older woman replied tartly. "But he'll only tell you the same, you foolish girl!"

Molly rose weakly and tottered across the room to the chifforobe. She pulled out a grey dress, trimmed in black, and threw it down over the bed. Mrs Allen watched her in frowning silence and finally sputtered:

"Oh, sit down—I suppose I'll have to help you! But only to keep you from undoing all the doctor's good work, and my own! This is madness!"

But Molly slowly unbraided her hair, brushed it out, and swept it up on her head as Mrs Allen helped her into her underthings, and her petticoat.

"Whatever you do, don't lift your arms, or pull on anything," she warned, "and the *instant* the trial is over, you must come back directly and get back in bed! It won't help your young man to win his trial, only to find himself with a dead sweetheart!"

"I'll be careful," Molly promised and slipped her stockinged feet into the slippers the older woman set out for her.

"I *know* you will because I'm going with you to make sure," Mrs Allen replied, and Molly smiled.

"You and the reverend have been so kind to me. I can't thank you like I should," Molly told her gratefully.

Mrs Allen sighed and stared at her. "I just hope we won't have to carry you back here on a stretcher," she murmured, and shook her head.

***

By the time they arrived at the courthouse, it was packed, and onlookers spilled out onto the street and the wooden sidewalks. Mrs Allen turned to Molly and said:

"There, you see? We'll never get a seat inside, and you can't stand up for hours on end. Let's turn around and go *back*."

But someone in the crowd cried: "Look there! It's Molly Clanahan!"

Molly soon found herself at the centre of a crowd of people.

"Why, weren't you shot by them no-goods, Molly? What you doin' out of bed?"

"I'll swan, ain't nothin' holds her back!"

"That's the style, Molly Clanahan! *Yey-eee*!"

A few people cheered and threw their hats into the air, and the people stood aside as she walked slowly to the entrance. With Mrs Allen at her side, she climbed the courthouse steps.

Inside, it was standing room only, but there as outside, the astonished onlookers made way for her.

"You've become something of a celebrity, my dear," Mrs Allen whispered in an awed tone as they walked, and Molly rolled anxious eyes to the courtroom doors.

A young man standing just outside them looked back over his shoulder, goggled, grinned, and opened the door for her.

Chapter
Sixty-Five

Molly stood on the threshold and swept the courtroom with her eyes. The seats were packed, and people were standing all along the walls. She looked for Nate and couldn't find him for the press of people. She couldn't even pick Leonie out of the crowd, though her elaborate hat should have made that an easy task.

A few people along the back walls caught sight of her standing there and grinned. Molly lifted her chin defiantly as a loud murmur rolled through the courtroom from the back wall, all the way down to the foot of the Right Honourable Lester P. Calhoun's bench. He leaned over it and drawled:

"Order! Young woman, find a seat and take it please, so these proceedings can continue."

Everyone turned to look at her, and Molly glanced around uncertainly, but she heard a shriek from the front that could be no one but Leonie and assumed that her young friend was only restrained from coming down the centre aisle by force.

At last, Jem rose from a seat down the front and sauntered out. He nodded toward the front left as he passed, so Molly smiled at Mrs Allen and left her to make her way down to the front as quickly as she could. She sat down carefully beside Leonie.

Molly put out her hands to keep Leonie from hugging her, and Leonie pressed a chastened hand to her mouth. "Oh! Yes, of course, poor Molly!"

But Molly's glance jumped beyond her to where Nate was sitting, half-turned in his chair. Their eyes met, and Molly could see worry staring out of her lover's startled gaze. Not worry for himself, of that she was sure.

Nate's attorney leaned over and whispered in his ear, and he turned away. Molly watched him anxiously, then asked Leonie:

"What's happening?"

Leonie whispered: "They've finished the testimony, and the arguments, and the jury's been out for over an hour. Oh, Molly, I don't know if I can stand it much longer, and I can't *imagine* what it's like for poor—"

She broke off in mid-sentence because a door to one side of the room opened suddenly, and a row of solemn men came filing out. Molly anxiously appraised each man's face and expression as they emerged, but all of them were looking down at the floor.

When they had all arrived, they sat down in their chairs, and the foreman stood up.

Leonie's hand reached out, and Molly took it and squeezed it.

The judge turned to the foreman and asked: "Gentlemen of the jury, have you reached your decision?"

The foreman faced him, and Molly noticed anxiously that the man refused to look at Nate or anyone else.

"We have, your honour."

"What is your verdict?"

Molly rolled her eyes to Nate. He was sitting ramrod-straight and motionless as he waited.

"We find the defendant—*not guilty*, your honour."

The last two words were drowned out because the rest of the courtroom erupted into cheers and bedlam. Molly slumped back against the bench, and for an instant, the whole room went grey. She heard Leonie's voice at her shoulder saying, "Oh, Molly, you look so pale! You shouldn't have come. We have to get you back to the hotel now. You're still unwell!"

But Molly opened her eyes, summoned her strength, and stood up. Nate was surrounded by his attorneys, and other well wishers, but he shouldered away from them and swam through the crowd to her side.

"Don't, Molly!" Leonie cried, but Molly smiled, threw both her arms around Nate's neck, and this time got a kiss every bit as fiery as the one she gave.

And to her surprise and delight, Nate Trowbridge laughed, hoisted her up in his arms, and carried her out of the courtroom in full view of all the world.

Epilogue

A month later, Molly drifted out onto Nate's bedroom balcony. It overlooked the garden, which was now sleepy with the deep fragrance of late summer and the cool breath of evening. The moon was a white sliver floating in a blue sky, and the first faint crispness of autumn was in the air.

She sat down in a reclining chair and leaned back into the cushions. The chair had been warmed by the sun all day and still felt good against her skin. She closed her eyes and let that warmth soak in.

Nate was already stretched out in the other chair. He reached for her hand and clasped it.

"We could still go to New York, or London, if you feel up to it," he murmured. "We can have our honeymoon anywhere you like."

Molly squeezed his hand and stretched languidly. "I think I'd like to stay in one place and just *rest* for awhile," she replied softly. "And I can't think of any place on earth I'd like better than here," she told him. "The days I've spent here have been the happiest of my life."

Nate leaned over in the darkness and kissed her, and Molly raised a hand to his cheek and leaned into him.

"That's enough," he said, after awhile, but with less than conviction. "That's—*Molly*—remember what the *doctor* said."

"*Mmm-mm. You're* the doctor for me, Nate Trowbridge." She laughed, and the sound of her giggling and his reluctant laughter filled the darkness.

"Come on now, Molly—Molly, I *mean* it," he said at last and in a more serious tone of voice.

There came the sound of sharp scuffling, a trill of feminine laughter, and a muffled profanity.

"That was—"

"Not fair. No," Molly admitted primly and settled back into her chair. Nate adjusted his wounded dignity and returned to his own chair.

"You're going to have a relapse if you don't settle down," he told her, but Molly reached for him again.

"How can I *settle down* on my own honeymoon?" she demanded. "That doesn't even make sense. And I'll tell you something that doctor doesn't know. *You do me more good than all the pills in his bag.*"

She giggled again, and soon Nate was laughing with her. He kissed her again, long and slowly. He murmured:

"It frightens me to think I might never have met you." He wound a tendril of her hair around his finger. "That I might have married Emmaline Chiswick, and this minute be buried in my library, reading the newspaper, instead of making love to a woman I adore.

"Now I wonder how on earth I ever lived that way," he said softly.

Molly smiled up into his face. "I love you with all my heart, Nate Trowbridge," she told him. "And I have since the first day I knocked you down on the sidewalk.

"But you talk way too much for a man on his honeymoon. Kiss me, or I'll throw you over for a man who *will*."

Nate sighed in exasperation, but obeyed; and soon the sound of their laughter filled the darkness, and floated up to the smiling stars.

THE END?

Can't get enough of Molly and Nate? Then don't miss the extended epilogue, "**The Wedding Day**" to find out:

What did Molly wear on her wedding day?
Did Denver's high-class approve this marriage?
Did Nate have second thoughts for Molly?

Click this link or enter it in your browser for the answers:

https://chloecarley.com/cchssb-extended/

Made in the USA
Middletown, DE
03 October 2018